4

THE
KILLING ZONE

A VIKING NOVEL OF MYSTERY AND SUSPENSE

THE
KILLING

ZONE

A GABE WAGER MYSTERY

REX BURNS

VIKING

VIKING

Published by the Penguin Group
Viking Penguin Inc., 40 West 23rd Street,
New York, New York 10010, U.S.A.
Penguin Books Ltd, 27 Wrights Lane, London W8 5TZ, England
Penguin Books Australia Ltd, Ringwood,
Victoria, Australia
Penguin Books Canada Limited, 2801 John Street,
Markham, Ontario, Canada L3R 1B4
Penguin Books (N.Z.) Ltd, 182–190 Wairau Road,
Auckland 10, New Zealand

Penguin Books Ltd, Registered Offices:
Harmondsworth, Middlesex, England

First published in 1988 by Viking Penguin Inc.
Published simultaneously in Canada

LIBRARY OF CONGRESS CATALOGING IN PUBLICATION DATA
Burns, Rex.
The killing zone.
I. Title.
PS3552.U7325K55 1988   813'.54   87-40446
ISBN 0-670-81955-7

Printed in the United States of America by
Arcata Graphics, Fairfield, Pennsylvania
Set in Gael

To Drew Burns

CHAPTER 1

Thursday, 12 June, 1640 Hours

Jo was drowning. Wager knew it even as he fought to reach her outstretched hand and felt himself pushed and tumbled by the river's violent and careless tumult. Behind her, a crest of foaming water plunged upstream into the glassy slickness of the suckhole's current, drawing the raft's debris: a splintered oar, a plastic jug, a shred of canvas, and Jo. She stared at him, her eyes wide with terror and unvoiced plea; and Wager, the current twisting his legs against themselves as he tried to kick, saw the wavering lip of the crest dip toward her even as he lunged for her hand. Then she was gone, a glimmer of orange life vest in the white foam, a flash of grasping hand, a final wide-eyed stare into the center of his screaming soul before blackness closed out the scene.

Detective Gabriel Wager stared at the Homicide office's wall and blinked. The vision of Josephine Fabrizio's death thinned to reveal the equally familiar paint, the scattered notices and calendars, the news photo of William Devine under the headline OFFICER SLAYS SUSPECT and the scrawled note, "Look Out Hoods, Devine's Back on the

Street." He took a deep breath and held his gaze on the torn news clipping. Nine months since Jo had drowned and the nightmare memory still haunted him, bringing the same knotted anger and self-disgust that had drenched him as had the river. That feeling wouldn't go away, and he didn't want it to: He had earned it when unthinkingly he led her into the danger that claimed her. And God damn his eyes, he would take what he deserved.

Vaguely, he heard the steady pulse of telephones jingle in the office and saw the moving shades of men as they weaved between the desks. Somewhere at the edge of consciousness he heard Stubbs's voice and noted a quick alertness in the man's words. But his mind—his feelings—still lingered on the image that had risen in his imagination with even more intensity than the event itself. Then, he had struggled to stay afloat, and the shock of what was happening was cushioned by the effort to prevent it. Now, he knew it had not been prevented. Even if the stab of memory didn't come as often as it used to, it remained as sharp. Instead of welling up only in those tossing sleepless hours between each midnight and dawn, it had begun to attack him randomly during the waking times. Summoned by some vague odor or phrase, by a half-familiar voice or even by the initials on a license plate, it came inevitably like a wave of nausea. He had learned to let it wash through him at its own pace, bowing to the justice of it and giving it the freedom to conquer the moment. Then it would ebb; and, trying to hide the involuntary shudder at what he had seen of himself, Wager would hunch tighter over his work and use that as a barrier against the emotional debris from the last assault and the threat of the next.

The memory tugged at him; the work anchored him. With an effort he held the two in a kind of equilibrium that allowed him to cling to a bit of self-respect for the job he did as a homicide detective. He did good work. He made certain that he did good work. And he even began to welcome the summonses that came pinched and nasal through the small speaker of the portable radio: "Any homicide detective . . . any homicide detective."

"Wager— Wager!" Lester Stubbs, the new man, leaned

down in front of Wager's eyes and called his name, his breath a puff of perfume across Wager's face. "We got a call, man, this fucking late! Can you believe it? Fifteen minutes before the end of the tour, I get my first meat call!"

"Where to?"

"East side. Twenty-fifth Avenue. Fifteen goddamn minutes!"

"You'll get comp time for it, Stubbs."

"Yeah. Compensatory time instead of overtime pay. Big fucking deal."

It was better than nothing, but Wager would have done it for that; a call this late kept him that much longer away from his silent and accusing apartment. "Let's go, Stubbs. You wanted to be a detective—now you can earn the rank."

They ran without lights or siren through downtown and its afternoon traffic that filled the summer streets with a hot flow of automobiles and buses. A sudden snarl of brakes and signal lights, trying to pinch into fewer lanes, told them they were getting near, and Wager lit the flashers and thumped the siren to cut through the knots of traffic. At the curb, a line of police vehicles, their glinting roof lights almost invisible in the sun's glare, marked the weedy and deserted lot where the body had been found. Across the street on the boxy porches of a line of row houses, a crowd of black faces peered toward the excitement. It was a familiar neighborhood, a familiar scene, and a familiar reason for Wager to be there. Stubbs looked around at the gazing faces. "God, any more jigs and we'd have to get the riot squad out."

Wager led Stubbs under a yellow tape that said DENVER POLICE DO NOT CROSS LINE, and in Spanish, LA POLICIA DE DENVER NO CRUCES LA LINEA. The overgrown corner was one of those forgotten plots sprinkled around every city. It was the kind of place bums ferreted into for cardboard refuge, and neighborhood kids prowled through, seeking adventure. Sandy trails tunneled beneath the growth with that vague ominousness of leading to places where people did things they didn't want others to see. This time what someone had not wanted seen was a corpse.

Blue-clad figures of the uniformed division finished

stretching the tape around the rear of the crime scene, looping it over the branches of scrawny shrubs and hackberry; Wager told Stubbs to step where he did and to be careful to avoid the already marked paths of freshly crushed grass that led to the center of the cordon. Then he circled toward a lumpy darkness almost as high as the knee-deep weeds.

Stubbs looked down at the dark bulges humming with flies. "Jesus. Do you ever get used to this?"

Wager, too, stared. What you got was interested. It wasn't something you got used to, exactly, but after a while what you saw wasn't a person but a problem: How did the victim die? How long ago? How did he get here? What evidence might tell who did it? Wager started to tell that to Stubbs, but the man had turned to lean against a stunted tree and vomit.

What was left of the victim's face bent back over his shoulder toward the sky: a black male in his mid-to-late thirties, medium build, nattily dressed in a three-piece gray suit. As Wager gazed the features under the wilting Afro seemed to fill in around the sun-dried, erupted pulp that had been the left eye and forehead; and as the glint of a fly suddenly buzzed away from the flesh Wager knew the face: "Councilman Green!"

Horace Green, city councilman from the predominantly black northeast corner of Denver. On the television a lot lately, as part of a coalition to end bussing while maintaining equal quality in the city's schools. Also one of the loudest opponents of the mayor's plan to redevelop the northern quadrant of the core city into another tourist center with its combination of specialty shops, restaurants, and hotels. It was a nice idea that would bring far greater revenue to the city than the existing blocks of run-down housing like that across the street. But Councilman Green had worried publicly about the tenants who would be pushed out of that housing. He had complained openly about the family neighborhoods that would be lost to more commerce. He had warned in the press against turning another area of Denver into a twelve-hour city. He had worried so loudly, in fact, that he'd been accused of starting his campaign for mayor in the upcoming elections. An accusation he answered only with a smile. Now he wasn't running for anything.

Stubbs spit a little something from his teeth and shoved a stick of gum into his mouth. "I think we better give Lieutenant Wolfard a call."

"Yeah." Wager began filling out a Crime Scene Information sheet. "Give him a chance to crap his pants."

Wolfard, too, was new to Homicide. The department had been restructured from four divisions to five in an effort to put more manpower on the streets. But the real effect was to create more supervisory positions, which was all right because a large number of recent promotions had given the department more administrators than there were openings. "People," the argument went, "who had served the department long and well deserved to be rewarded." Wolfard had never served in the detective division at all, but, with Chief Doyle on leave, there had been a temporary slot for one of the shiny new gold shields. Now he was supposed to tell Wager how to run a homicide investigation.

Stubbs was on the radio, talking to the duty watch, when a sweating Walt Adamo brought his forensics team into the protected area. Walt had finally made Plain Clothes by way of Burglary and Assault, then shifted over to the Police Lab because the pace was slower and promotions just as quick. The little rivalry between him and Wager—begun when Wager made detective grade and Adamo did not—had resurfaced in the more-or-less polite competition between forensics and the detectives. The lab people thought a case was theirs because they were responsible for the scientific collection of evidence at a crime scene. Wager, like other homicide dicks, knew a case was his because a law had been violated and it was his duty to locate and apprehend the criminal.

"We're ready to work, Gabe. What's the story?"

Wager gave a last look around the snarl of leathery shrubs and stunted trees before telling Adamo what the responding officer had reported. "We came in this way," he finished up, pointing to the faint line of broken grass that caught the sunlight like a crooked seam. "McFadden and the kid who found the body came in that way." Another vague line marked that approach to the corpse.

"That's probably how the goddamned victim got there, too," said a disgusted Adamo.

It was the most likely path from the pitted and tilted slabs of neglected sidewalk, and Wager could already hear the topic of the next in-service lecture on crime-scene preservation by responding officers: how to approach the site without destroying evidence, by avoiding the most likely avenues. "We just got the tape strung and took a look at the body." He showed Adamo a brown envelope. "We took his wallet for identification."

"Touch anything else?"

The inevitable forensics question. "What's to touch?"

"Whatever there is, some cop will find it." He finished jotting items on the sheet pinned to his clipboard. "McFadden, the responding officer; the kid who found him; you; Stubbs. Anybody else enter the crime scene?"

"Not since we've been here."

"Definite homicide?"

"One round to the back of the head."

"That's definite." Adamo nodded to the forensics photographer, a short, heavy-set man Wager did not know. He ducked under the tape to start making his record before the other lab specialists worked the scene. "Got a name for the victim?"

"City Councilman Horace Green."

"Jesus H. Christ!" Walt leaned again to peer at the exploded features that had clenched and dried in the sun. "It sure as hell is. Any suspects? Witnesses?"

"Nothing yet."

"Oh boy. We do this one by the book." Adamo looked around the weedy lot. "Hell of a public place to kill somebody."

The body, humped on its shoulder and hip, could almost be seen from the sidewalk. In fact, the kid who found it noticed it from about ten yards away, just this side of the walk, and thought at first it was only another drunk passed out. "Well, he was a public man."

Wager turned to the uniformed officers who had now

finished stringing the yellow tape and stood doing nothing while they stared at the body and the busy photographer. "How about moving those people along on the sidewalk. And make sure nobody gets down here—especially reporters."

Adamo nodded. "It won't take them long—and when they find out who it is . . ." The man stared at Wager for a long minute. "You know, Gabe—this is a riot waiting to happen."

That would depend on who killed him, and why, and how the reporters handled the story. But it was a thought that crossed any cop's mind. "Yeah."

The photographer, a lone figure, bent in awkward positions while his strobe made tiny flashes in the mottled light. He shot and then paused to note the position, time, and angle of each picture before aiming again. Wager gazed with that half-detached and dreamy feeling and tried to see in his mind the victim and the killer as they stopped at the curb. Probably late last night—there where that patrol car sat. Then they walked into the snagging bushes and weeds. Two people? More? Green could have been killed here or somewhere else and dumped here. Pathology would tell them about that. The flicker of light from steady traffic going by. Someone must have seen the car parked at the curb. The killer had been willing to chance that—had been in such a hurry or had been too frightened and nervous to find a less public spot. Had perhaps chanced the noise of a weapon this close to houses. Maybe someone noticed two or more figures getting out of the car, plunging into the tangled black of the empty lot. Maybe someone had heard the shot. Or seen two or more go in, and then one less come out and drive away. Seen something, at least, from the corner of his eye as he flashed past the unlit block. The problem was, of course, to find that someone.

On the other side of the tape, Stubbs was finishing his interview with the kid who had found the victim. Eleven, maybe twelve, he had a sprout of sun-bleached hair and a face that, beneath the summer tan, looked a bit pale and pinched at the corners of his mouth. His Levi's, like his T-shirt with its faded message, were streaked with a few

days' dirt. The message stenciled across his thin chest said
SAVE THE EARTH FOR THE CHILDREN.

Stubbs patted the boy's shoulder in friendly dismissal.

"Can I stay and watch?"

"You really want to?"

"Yeah." He nodded. "I can always leave if I want,
can't I?"

"Stand over there out of the way. And don't go inside the
tape."

He came over to Wager, nodding hello to Adamo and his
crew, who waited for the photographer to finish. Adamo
had told them the victim's name, and they stared with
more curiosity than the usual corpse generated. "Lieutenant Wolfard said he was coming down," said Stubbs.

"What the hell for?" Wolfard knew shit about homicide
investigations.

Stubbs shrugged, his dark eyebrows lifting in the oval of
his round face. Slightly taller than Wager, he had one of
those pudgy bodies, with narrow shoulders and wide hips
and a stomach that, no matter how much he worked out,
still pushed against his shirt with a soft billow. On the street,
his nickname had been Pumpkin. "He said to wait for him
here."

"We can do the neighborhood while we wait." At any
homicide, the detective interviewed witnesses while forensics went over the scene. Wager wanted to start knocking
on doors.

Stubbs glanced across the lot. Around them was the broken skyline of a neighborhood where commercial growth
had paused to leave homes not yet uprooted by the need
for more office space. At the far end of the block, two large
houses—now cut into apartments—sagged in weary dis-
repair and waited for their landlords to get the right price
for the more valuable land beneath them. Across the street,
in the long, yellowing façade of dusty, one-story row
houses, Wager made out three apartments that had a clear
view of the crime scene. Now a cluster of faces crowded the
chipped concrete stairs leading up to the tiny square
porches before each door. In the dark, with the constant

traffic and the unremarkable fact of one more car pulling to the curb, they probably noticed nothing. But they would have to be asked. Every door facing the street in this block would be knocked on by either Wager or Stubbs. And, if they were lucky, somebody might have seen something.

1748 Hours

He was finishing up his end of the row when the Cadaver Removal Service's black van pulled out from the cluster of marked and unmarked police cars and started for the morgue at Denver General. The woman he talked to leaned against the door frame behind a patched screen and balanced a round-eyed baby on her hip as she shook her head. A new fluff of cotton, pinned to the rusty screen like a bright, clean wish, waggled in the slight wind from the hot street in an effort to frighten the flies. She and Wager watched the van drive past; the baby watched Wager.

"No, Officer, I wasn't paying no attention to that place. Not until all the police cars come. Kids, they're always playing over there, you know. But I didn't notice nobody around it."

She hadn't heard anything like a shot, either—"except what was on TV." Wager thanked her and wrote another "Heard Nothing" on the Neighborhood Investigation Results form and turned back toward the cluster of automobiles that still crowded the curbs near the site. The forensics team had not left yet. The photographer would be shooting the ground where the body had lain; the others would be measuring and taping the distances to any and all foreign objects found in the area; labeling samples of soils, grasses, seeds from the bushes; taking spoonsful of bloody soil; sifting the dirt from where the body lay back along the most likely path to the curb. It was the familiar and time-consuming attempt to gather trace and fugitive evidence before it was too late. And, as Adamo said, with a death as important as this one, things would be done by the book— not for thoroughness' sake, but to cover ass. Wager expected the forensics people to take twice as much time as they did with the usual homicide, and he wasn't surprised that their familiar cars were still there.

The other cars were familiar, too: blue-and-whites of the district's Patrol and Traffic Control; the plain brown car of the medical examiner, who was just pulling away after pronouncing the corpse dead; the lieutenant's unmarked white car; and now the brightly marked station wagons and vans of the television crews and the tiny economy cars that the newspapers gave their people.

"Any luck?" Stubbs sprinted through the gap in the avenue's traffic and pulled heavily beside Wager. He grimaced as he spit out his gum and unwrapped another stick. "Jesus, I wish I had some water to rinse out my mouth."

That was one of the reasons homicide detectives tried not to puke. "No luck at all. How about you?"

"A possible on the car. A late-model Lincoln Continental—the kind with the spare-tire-hump molded into the trunk. Dark. Blue or black, possibly dark brown. It was there a little after eleven."

"The witness see anybody?"

"Just the car. She was up with a sick kid and when she looked out again, maybe an hour later, it was gone." Stubbs eyed the apartments across the street and then the weedy lot. "If that was the killer, he took a big chance. There are a hell of a lot more private places than this."

Wager thought so, too. Somebody took a chance that big because it was the only chance they had. "I think they were in a hurry."

"Speaking of which," said Stubbs, "we better be, too. The lieutenant's getting a little red in the face."

Every newsroom in the city monitored the police band and heard the lieutenant tell Stubbs he was coming to the crime scene. So the reporters had come, too; and even this far away and over the noise of passing cars, Wager could hear the garbled squawk of shouted questions.

Stubbs pushed ahead, his wide buttocks wagging slightly as he cut between the heaving shoulders and elbows of reporters toward the voice saying over and over, "We don't have a positive identification, yet, ladies and gentlemen, so

I can't say who the victim is. As soon as we know something, we'll have a statement. The next of kin— Stubbs, where the hell have you been?"

"Knocking on doors, Lieutenant."

"Wager with you?"

"Yessir."

The lieutenant shoved away from the crowd and past the picket line of uniformed police to find an almost-quiet circle of mashed grass near the tape. "Jesus, what a madhouse—God damn it, Sergeant, get that goddamned camera out of the crime scene. And keep those goddamned people back on the sidewalks!"

He stared hotly while two blue uniforms headed off a television crew and walked them protesting toward the crowd near the street. Then he turned to Wager. "Do you have a positive on the victim?"

Wager handed him the brown evidence envelope that dangled heavily with the victim's wallet. "City Councilman Horace Green."

"So it's true. God damn." He flipped through the plastic windows of the wallet. "Next of kin been notified?"

"Not yet. You told us to wait for you here," Wager reminded him.

Wolfard sighed and pulled his GE radiopack from the holster riding on his hip. "Definite homicide?"

Wager nodded.

The lieutenant keyed the microphone and called the number for Chief of Police Sullivan. The dispatcher answered that the chief had signed out for the day. "This is Lieutenant Wolfard in Crimes Against Persons. We've got a V.I.P. homicide and the press is already on it. It's something we want to keep the lid on, and the chief should know about it."

"Who's the victim, sir?"

"I'll give him a ten-twenty-five on that."

The ten-code was no longer official procedure, but most officers still used it; it marked them as veterans. Ten-twenty-five meant "report in person," and Wager wondered why, if Wolfard was going to talk to the chief anyway, he wanted the eavesdropping reporters aroused by radio.

Then he decided that the lieutenant, despite the stone face and outside calm, was sweating with nervousness because Chief Doyle, head of Crimes Against Persons, would be out of town until next week, and that left Wolfard holding the sack all by himself.

The dispatcher asked Wolfard to wait while he checked; then, a few minutes later, the voice came up to tell them the chief was on his way in.

"The Administration Building," Wolfard said to them. "Let's go."

They pushed toward their cars through the newly excited reporters crammed behind the police line.

"Wager— Hey, Gabe!" The shout jabbed through the rising volume of voices. "Wager, it's me, Gargan. Was it Councilman Green? Come on, Wager, was it?"

"Hello, Gargan."

A television camera swung toward him, its alert light a bright mark of interest.

"Wager, goddamn it, come on, man! This is real news!"

"Good-bye, Gargan."

The sedan's doors slammed against the still shouting voices and the steady, glassy winks of camera lenses. Wager bumped the horn a couple of times and then eased forward, the car's fenders nudging through dodging bodies.

"Jesus!" Stubbs wiped at his neck, his breath a mixture of fresh chewing gum and old vomit. As they pulled free of the shouting faces he rolled down the window to let out the trapped heat. "I hate those damned television cameras."

Wager pulled close behind the lieutenant's car as it angled across the lane of traffic toward the office towers that framed the vacant sky marking the old Brown Palace Hotel. In the rearview mirror, the television and newspaper reporters piled into their cars and darted after them. "That's why we have lieutenants and captains."

"You think it's funny, don't you?"

Wager felt the skin of his cheeks grow taut with a grin. "I could refer all questions to you, Stubbs."

"Hell, no!"

CHAPTER 2

That was also the lieutenant's warning when, after escaping the column of press vehicles by driving into the police garage under the Headquarters and Administration Building, they stood in the oversized elevator that carried the three of them up to Chief Sullivan's office. "Better refer all questions to me; it goes with the territory." Wolfard ran a hand through his thinning hair. "And God knows there's going to be a hell of a lot of questions about this one."

"Yessir." Wager smiled.

The thin chime of the elevator signaled the fourth floor, and they turned down the carpeted hallway lined with cases that displayed memorabilia to interest the chief's visitors: a series of badges dating back to the 1880s, assorted prison-made knives and daggers that looked clumsily efficient, a historical collection of handcuffs and other restraining devices, a roster of the state's hundred or so officers killed in the line of duty, and photographs of Denver's slain policemen. The only interesting police equipment in that case was a badge taped in black; that would be enough for any cop who glanced at the proudly stiff faces of the photographs. Civilians wouldn't understand, anyway.

The chief's large desk was backed by the standing flags of country and state, city and police; a scattering of upholstered furniture softened the lines of the room. Chief Sullivan, in civilian clothes and a shirt open at the neck, rose from the edge of his desk to shake hands with each of them in the formal way he had. Then he motioned them toward chairs. One of the stories about the man was that he had been appointed to the job because he looked like a movie star who played a cop on television. That might have been the case—to Wager, politics moved in strange ways and no mayor was unaware of images. But this wasn't television and every chief made changes, some good and many bad. In fact, a lot of the directives coming out of Admin were pretty dumb and seemed to be only for the purpose of making changes. But the office of Chief of Police was far above Wager's pay grade, and the games played there were generally on paper, so they didn't often have any real impact on his activities. Not until now, anyway.

"Want to tell me about it, Douglas?"

Wolfard told him about Councilman Green.

The chief's lean face turned to the sheer curtains that blurred the view across the roofs and toward the shiny gold dome of the state capitol up the hill. The window's glare etched baggy lines under his eyes and his head wagged once at some thought.

"Notify his wife yet?"

"We didn't," said Wolfard. "We came straight from the scene. We thought maybe you might want to do that."

The chief nodded. "Doyle's still on leave, isn't he?"

It was Wolfard's turn to nod. "He gets back Monday."

"That's right—Monday." A deep breath lifted and dropped his shoulders. "We'd better take care of notification. Some reporter's probably on the way over there already. . . ." He spoke briskly into the telephone, Wager catching a few of the murmured words: "City Councilman Horace Green . . . the mayor . . . police chaplain . . . two uniformed officers as soon as possible . . . No, now—right now." He added, "And have them tell her I'll be over as soon as I can." As he hung up, the light flashed, and he picked up the telephone with a note of irritation. "Yes? . . . No, tell them we have no comment yet. We'll call a press conference when we have some information." He set the receiver down. "They're calling already. Now, exactly what do you have so far?"

Stubbs glanced at Wager, who answered, "Not much. He was apparently killed late last night. One round to the back of the head. They'll probably do the autopsy tomorrow, but that's the only visible wound. The lab crew's still over there; they hadn't found much by the time we left. I don't think they're going to."

"Why not?"

"Just a guess. But I think he was brought there and dumped."

"Evidence?"

"It's pretty close to the street and to some houses, and nobody heard a thing last night."

"Motives?"

"None that we could see right there. His wallet was on him." Wager nodded at the envelope Wolfard still held. The lieutenant looked down at it with slight surprise and quickly set it on the chief's desk. "It looked like it had a couple hundred dollars. His watch and a couple gold rings were still on him—a big diamond ring with some kind of lodge symbol. There didn't seem to be any sign of a struggle, but the medical examiner can tell us more about that."

The chief's hand darted to the telephone again and buzzed the secretary. "Call the medical examiner's office and tell them we have a rush case and I'd personally appreciate it if they got on it right away." He covered the mouthpiece. "What's the case number?" Wager told him and he repeated it to the woman and then hung up. "Anything else?"

"No witnesses. No one living in the area saw anything last night or this morning. The body was found by a kid playing in the lot this afternoon."

The chief, perched on the edge of his desk, frowned at

the gray carpet. "No time is good for something like this. But with a fifty percent rise in the annual homicide rate already. . . ."

Wager knew the new statistics; both major papers had been full of them for a week: fourteen cars a day stolen, a rape a day, an overdose every sixth day, a murder every five days, three forgeries a day. . . . The list went on, and Wager—looking at the top of the chief's bowed head—wondered why, with that kind of jump in crimes, the man had promoted officers off the street to desk jobs. Even Wolfard could do more good on patrol. Perhaps, especially Wolfard.

The telephone flashed again and the chief picked it up with a clipped "Yes!" Then, with a slightly warmer voice, "No, Mr. Mayor, we have a positive identification by the investigating officers, but nothing else. I'm talking with them right now. . . . I think that would be a good idea; I suspect the press has already gone over there, so she probably heard about it from them. In about fifteen minutes—fine." He cradled the telephone and stared at them for a long moment. "You're going to be interviewing the family?"

It was a dumb question. Wager only said, "Yessir."

"You can put it off until after the mayor and I have a chance to express our sympathies. We'll tell the family to expect you a little later."

"Yessir."

Lieutenant Wolfard cleared his throat. "Chief? You want to take Lieutenant Elkins along?"

Elkins, one of the highest-ranking blacks in the department, served as liaison between the police and black community groups. The chief said, "Good thinking, Douglas," and punched another series of buttons on the telephone. Wager figured Wolfard had just gotten a leg up on his promotion to captain.

"You through with us, Chief?" Stubbs spoke for the first time and glanced at his watch. "We ought to get back—the lab people should be finishing up soon."

"Right." But his glance held them a moment longer. "You two keep the reporters out of this. Green was popular with his people. I don't want this blowing up into a riot, but a lot will depend on how the press plays the story. Refer all questions to Lieutenant Wolfard or to Chief Doyle when he gets back. I don't want you two making any loose comments to the press that might stir people up unnecessarily. Understand me?"

They understood.

The gray eyes shifted to Wager alone, and the eyelids drooped a little as they always did when the chief wanted his listener to pay particular attention. "You're the assigned detective on this one, right?"

"That's right."

The heavy-lidded eyes weren't sleepy; like a lot of politicians', they masked what the man was thinking. But Wager had a good idea what that was, and the chief's next words told him he'd guessed right. "You'll be very careful interviewing the victim's family members, Wager. And all politically sensitive witnesses as well. Very careful."

"Yes, sir."

"Keep Lieutenant Wolfard and Chief Doyle fully informed. And I will be very interested in the case, too."

On the elevator down to their floor, Stubbs's narrow shoulders bobbed. "Jesus. My first homicide. Why would I feel happier if Ross and Devereaux had gotten this one?"

"It's just another case," said Wager. "It's just like any other homicide."

"I hear you. But I don't believe you."

1915 Hours

The police lab detectives weren't ready yet to give them any solid facts. "We couldn't find the slug or any trace of it. What we've got, Gabe, is some cigarette butts, scraps of paper, crap like that. But most of it looks like it was already there. We'll know something for sure by tomorrow morning."

"The chief asked the medical examiner to do the autopsy right away."

"I get you. And we'll work on this stuff all night if we have to," said Adamo. "But we can only do so much so fast. When we have something, we'll call."

Finishing the paperwork that the preliminary report required, Stubbs glanced at the clock. "The city offices are closed. We'll have to do those interviews in the morning." He stretched and his stomach gave a little gurgle of despair. "In fact, it's four hours after quitting time—Nancy's stopped calling to find out if I'm coming home. You ready to hang it up?"

"Green's wife hasn't been questioned yet. The chief and the mayor should be there by now. They won't stay long."

Stubbs's face showed its weariness as he gazed a long moment at Wager. "Axton's got the night duty, Gabe. He can handle that interview."

"It's my case." Wager corrected himself, "Our case. And Axton's got about twelve homicides of his own."

"Who's got twelve?" Axton loomed in the doorway, his head dipping slightly as it sensed the lintel. "How you doing, Lester? Don't let this hard-charger talk you into working two shifts. He doesn't know when to quit." Max winked at Stubbs. "He's kind of loco about it, you know?"

Max wasn't the only one who thought Wager was crazy for doing what it took and sometimes more. He held up the report for Max to see. "Councilman Horace Green, recently deceased."

"Uh oh." The big man read the first two pages. "They hitting the panic button yet?"

"Still trying to find it."

Max glanced at the file drawer holding his "Open" cases. "What do you want me to cover?"

Wager shook his head. "I'm going over to interview the family. If I need help, I'll call."

Stubbs shoved back from his desk with a resigned sigh. "I'll go, too. What the hell, I'm supposed to be learning the business."

Max laughed. "You sure as hell got a good case to learn on. And a good man to teach you."

It was a quiet ride through the ebbing traffic. A few office workers still straggled toward the cooler lawns of the suburbs, and the first of the night traffic began coming back to town for dinner and the theatres. Overtime was nothing new to Wager, and Stubbs better get used to it, too. And he'd better get used to not being paid for it. Stubbs had called his wife and told her he would be even later than he thought, and to go ahead to his son's parents' night without him. He'd try to finish up in time to meet her there. "I can't help it, Nancy—it's the job. I told you what it might be like when I transferred, remember?" To Wager, he explained, "Kenny was hoping I could make this one. Being on the day shift, and all."

"I can handle the interview myself."

"I said I'd go. Let's do the damn thing and get it over with."

They swung onto Martin Luther King Boulevard and joined the column of automobiles speeding past the long islands of grass and low trees that separated the lanes.

"Got any ideas about motive?" asked Stubbs.

"No. But I have been wondering why, if he was killed last night, the family didn't report him missing."

"Did you check with Missing Persons?"

"I did. No report at all on an adult, black male." Just the usual teenaged kids who most likely were runaways, and two Caucasian females, neither of whom had been missing for seventy-two hours yet, so no formal report could be taken.

"You think his family might have something to do with it?"

The odds used to be that way: "Kith and kin killed one again." But the last year or two had seen a growing number of stranger-to-stranger homicides, usually in the course of a robbery or a fight. Sometimes impulse, or thrill, murders. Now it was only about fifty-fifty that a victim knew his slayer, and that made things a hell of a lot tougher for the police. "We'll find out."

"Yeah," said Stubbs. "But like the chief said, we'll find out very carefully, won't we, partner?"

"Sure." The way Stubbs said it hinted of stories the man had heard about Wager. But it wasn't something Wager was going to pursue, because he didn't give a damn what people told Stubbs or what the man feared.

"Here's Belaire up ahead."

Wager slowed for the turn, Stubbs's word *partner* still in his ears. Technically, the new man was right; he and Wager were partners because Wager was on the day shift this month and policy said to introduce new detectives to the day routine before assigning them to the less-supervised night duty. But for years Wager's partner had been Max— because, he was once told by an angry Captain Doyle, nobody else wanted to work with him. Which hadn't hurt Wager's feelings at all; he didn't like working with anyone else, and that sometimes included Max. Still, it felt different to have Stubbs ride beside him instead of the big man. With Max, the seat would be shoved against its backstops so Wager had to stretch to drive. And still Max would look cramped as he slouched in the rider's seat. Stubbs, leaning forward slightly to watch the houses pass, reminded Wager of his grandmother when she would get out for the occasional Sunday ride: too tense to sit back and enjoy, yet eager to show her children she was having a good time.

"I can't see one damned house number. There ought to be a law to have numbers on the curbs."

But it wasn't the numbers that told them which of the stately houses belonged to Councilman Green; it was the cluster of vehicles along the sidewalks halfway down the next block. The large, expensive homes had been built in the twenties and thirties, when the owners were trying to rival the Country Club district across town by creating a sprawling neighborhood of English-style estate homes. Gradually, as the black community settled in the northeast corner of the city and spread south, the rich whites began moving out and, for a while, the big houses hovered on the edge of collapsing into apartments and transient housing like so much of the Capitol Hill area. Then well-to-do blacks, who knew a good real estate value, began moving in and the homes were painted, long screen porches repaired, tree-filled yards cleaned and trimmed. Now, here and there, an occasional white family who could afford the cost was buying back into the area at three or four times the earlier, desperate prices.

"There's the chief and the mayor," said Stubbs. "They're just leaving."

Wager saw a stir among the group of reporters and photographers poised at the end of the sidewalk. A television camera hoisted to the shoulder of a girl in jeans and the hooded balls of microphones shoved forward. Wager pulled to the curb. "Let's wait a few minutes."

The mayor's hand lifted palm out toward the reporters—no comment—and he and the much-taller Chief Sullivan hurried past to the unmarked car that quickly pulled away, followed by a blue-and-white running cold. A television team tried to move down the sidewalk toward the silent house but a uniformed cop waved them back, their mouths opening in futile argument. After a few minutes, the guardians of the First Amendment decided there wasn't much excitement in staring at a silent house, and first a pair, then several, then the television crews began to leave.

"Who's that guy? The one staring our way?"

"Gargan." Wager sank down in the seat and turned his face away as Gargan's Honda Civic sputtered and paused and then pulled away sullenly. They waited until most of the press had left except for two or three who apparently had no other story to follow or who were paid by the hour. Then Wager drove down the block and parked.

They showed their badges to the pair of policemen standing guard at the edge of the deep front yard with its towering, shaggy blue spruce and the clusters of quivering aspen.

"How much you think this place is worth?"

Wager shrugged. "Two, maybe."

"I'd guess two-fifty, three-hundred thousand. It sure as hell ain't your usual ghetto."

"That's what America's all about."

Stubbs snorted. "Yeah. And he probably did it on food stamps." He pressed the bell, and a moment later a woman with cropped, white hair opened the door a few inches.

"Police officers, ma'am. Are you Mrs. Green?"

"No. I'm Mrs. Simpson, Hannah's mother. I'll tell her you're here." She craned to glance past Wager's shoulder at the street. "Those reporters gone yet?"

"Most of them, yes, ma'am."

"Thank the good Lord for that, anyway. Come in, please."

She led them into a large living room that held a variety of chairs and floor lamps and a grand piano, with its lid tilted open. Through the bay windows, they could see the shaded coolness of front lawn and, past an open double door, the corner of a formal dining room, with a long table and high-backed chairs. All the furniture looked carefully selected and expensive, and it reminded Wager of those Hispanics who got rich and moved away from the dusty streets of the barrio and, every now and then, would cruise the old neighborhood in their new car and wave at familiar, gaping faces. They brought more pride than envy to the barrio: If the Chavezes could do it, so could we—with enough money, accent or race or skin color made no difference. All you needed was enough money and you were equal.

A slender woman with puffy eyes and prominent cheekbones came through the double doors; the white-haired woman was close behind her. Wager showed his badge again. "I'm Detective Wager; this is Detective Stubbs. You're Mrs. Green?"

"Yes." That was all she managed to say. Wager could see the cords of her neck strain against what she was trying to stifle.

He wasn't asked to sit, but Wager pulled a chair close to the sofa where Mrs. Green wearily settled. Stubbs, as Wager had told him to do, strolled out of sight behind the woman, where he took out his notebook and waited.

"This is a bad time, Mrs. Green. But we need to know as much as we can, as soon as we can."

"I know."

"No time would be good, Mr. Wager," said the mother. "You go ahead. We understand."

"Yes, ma'am." They were the routine questions—when did you last see your husband? Did he mention anyone he was going to meet? Did he telephone you or anybody in the house later? But because they brought back the last time the widow saw her husband alive, they were painful ones for her. Wager had done his share of notifications, and he'd seen some of the explosions of grief, wails and screams to God and the unanswerable question "Why?" But surprisingly often, the response wasn't loud hysteria. It was a stunned numbness and even a kind of formality as if the person suddenly felt that any noise or emotion would be an insult to the moment. The deepest pain, Wager knew, would come later, in those silent times alone when the numbness faded and the loss was new again. Then would come the explosions of gut-shaking tears.

Mrs. Green's response was groping and dazed, and occasionally Wager had to ask a question two or three times and in different ways until, with gentle urging from her mother, the woman, licking dry lips, finally answered.

She had last seen her husband yesterday at noon when he stopped by for lunch on his way to a meeting downtown. No, she didn't know what kind of meeting—something to do with City Council business. She didn't know who it was with. Horace didn't seem upset or in any way apprehensive or worried. Yes—and the answer to this question was a long time in coming—he did occasionally come in very late, especially when there were so many political things going on and elections coming up in a few months. She went to bed around ten-thirty, after the news. She didn't know he had not come home until morning, when she saw that his bed hadn't been slept in. No, that did not happen often. Yes, she had been worried. She called the furniture store, but he wasn't there. That was around noon, when he sometimes went over there for lunch. He wasn't at his district office or down at the City Council offices, either.

"Poor thing was worried sick," said Mrs. Simpson. "That's when she called me and I came over."

"Yes, ma'am."

She had thought about calling the police, but it seemed silly. Horace was probably busy at a political meeting, or perhaps stayed overnight at a friend's, when he saw how late it was. Yes, that had happened once or twice before when he was too sleepy to drive home. But on those occasions he had called. No, there wasn't anything else she could think of at the moment.

Wager asked if the woman had been to Denver General to legally identify her husband, and she shook her head, lips tight as she stared at her twisting fingers.

"Horace's brother went, Mr. Wager." Mrs. Simpson's long fingers stroked her daughter's arm. "Chief Sullivan said it would be better if Hannah didn't have to see him yet."

He didn't even want to say "Yes, ma'am" to that; instead, he shifted topics. "Were your husband and his brother close?"

Mrs. Simpson again answered for her daughter. "Not like when they were children. But the families see each other a lot."

"May I have his name and address?"

She told him, and Wager went to the next item. "Did your husband have an appointment book, Mrs. Green? Something we might use to piece together his activities?"

"You sit here, honey, I'll get it." Mrs. Simpson's low heels made muted thuds on the Turkish carpet as she headed for another room.

"Mrs. Green," Wager asked, "can you tell me what kind of car your husband was driving?"

"The Lincoln."

"A Lincoln Continental?"

"Yes."

"What color?"

"Black."

"Do you happen to know the license number?"

"Yes—it's one of those vanity plates: HRG-1. Horace bought them. Mine's HRG-2."

"Do you know where his car might be now, ma'am?"

The car wasn't something that had been on her mind. "No . . . no, I don't." Then, with a faint hope of understanding, "Is that why it happened? Someone wanted that car?"

Stubbs jotted the vehicle's description to call into DMV as soon as they were in the patrol car.

"That's one possibility we'll look at," said Wager. He tried to think of an easier way to ask the next question but couldn't come up with one, and he wanted the answer while her mother was out of the room. "Did your husband have any enemies?"

"Enemies? Enough to . . . to kill him?"

"Yes, ma'am."

Her dark eyes, round and brimming with tears, stared deeply into Wager's, and she seemed to settle within herself as if something had been confirmed. "He was black."

Wager thought that over. "You think he may have been killed by a racist?"

"That's what that man on the phone said."

"What man? When?"

"The one who called just after the mayor and the chief of police left." The neck tightened again and the words came out slowly, like pebbles tossed one by one into an echoing bucket. "I didn't even know what he was saying at first. . . ."

"Now, Hannah—shhh, now, girl." Mrs. Simpson handed Wager a small leather-bound appointment book and sat close beside her daughter.

"Exactly what did he say, Mrs. Green?"

" 'Uppity niggers.' He said that's what happened to uppity niggers."

"Can you describe his voice?"

"No. . . . I just listened. I didn't really understand him until after he hung up."

"Did he say anything else? Anything at all?"

She nodded, swallowing hard to be able to talk again. "He said the rest of us were going to get it, too."

CHAPTER 3

It was long after twenty-hundred hours, and Lieutenant Wolfard, like everyone else who crowded into Crimes Against Persons during the day, was long gone. The desks were empty of all but the nightshift and a few strays like Wager. Stubbs had hurriedly signed out to sprint over to the school for his son's parents' night. This one was especially important, he apologized again; it was new-student night for junior high—you know, introduction of students and parents to the rules and the buildings and teachers before the next school year started. Kenny was nervous enough about moving into the larger and older group, and he really wanted his father to meet his teachers.

"You've put in your time," said Wager.

Stubbs glanced at the clock. "Ain't that the truth." He must have seen Wager's thought, because he added, "If there's something you really need me for, I can stay."

"There's always tomorrow," Wager told him.

And there would be plenty to do, he told himself as the man nodded and hustled down the gray carpet to the location board. Before leaving the Greens' home, they had warned the two officers on duty about the telephone call, and neither patrolman was happy to hear of it. "Holy shit, was it a bomb threat?"

"No. It was probably just your basic racist harassment call. But take a look around back every now and then."

"Yeah. Thanks."

They hadn't been able to report the threat to Wolfard, but Wager left a memo for him to see when he came in at eight. Then he wrote another for the Tactical Section of the Intelligence Unit. They were gone for the day, too; and Wager didn't have much faith anything profitable would come of it. But that was departmental procedure: Threats to public officials and their families, agencies, court witnesses, were reported to Police Intelligence so they could see if any kind of pattern existed. It was probably a crank call. City Council members had to vote on a lot of issues and some of the votes stirred up a lot of feelings. Wager hoped it was a crank call, because if racism was a motive in Green's killing, that brought even more pressure to solve the case quickly. Denver had a lot of prominent blacks, and the killer might not stop with just one.

When he finished logging and filing what little they had so far, Wager shoved his name across the location board to the OFF-DUTY slot. From one of the desks sitting under the empty, glaring fluorescence of the night watch came the familiar voice of Golding, who shared this tour with Max: "Orange. . . . That's right, orange-colored foods." The man looked up from the telephone and waved good night as Wager passed, his hand a wink of light from a lodge ring. "It's a social color—it carries Vitamin A and clears the mind and stimulates enthusiasm. . . . No, red food brings nervousness, she said. Stick to pomegranates, sweet potatoes, cantaloupe, and you get the stimulation without the nervousness."

Maybe, Wager thought, he should start munching carrots, because he could feel the letdown that came when the adrenalin began to ebb and coffee tasted like hot, sour water. It was that time of day when the body and even the emotions sagged, but the mind—ill-governed from weariness—was perversely active, stirring up old memories and re-creating past mistakes that you tried to keep buried under the day's tumult of business. As the elevator's musty quiet carried him down into the still-mustier and dimly lit garage, Wager kept his mind on the image of food even though his stomach hadn't generated the idea. He could use a little enthusiasm. In fact, he could use a little nervousness. But most of all, he could simply use something to focus his thoughts on besides Jo.

Nosing the black Trans-Am through the thinning traffic on Thirteenth, he pulled into Speer Boulevard, which straddled the shallow sand of Cherry Creek. The city had added bike paths down below the concrete abutments that walled the stream bed, and in the cool of the long evening, steady columns of bright-shirted bikers wove along the wide path. Some pumped hard to get the day's workout, others pedaled slowly to feel the breeze of their motion; both groups managed to keep pace with Wager as traffic lights periodically halted the flow of automobile traffic, while the bikes glided under the bridges. Slowing, Wager turned into the parking lot that served Racine's, a restaurant he had begun to like, not only because of its food and prices but also because the waitresses left you alone. Mostly he liked it because he had not come here often with Jo when she was alive. He'd found himself swinging wide of those places that held a lot of sore memories, and that meant a lot of once-favorite spots that he had enjoyed with her. He knew damned well he wouldn't enjoy them now; it was better just to leave them alone.

He had a glass of wine with dinner, a habit he'd picked up when he and Jo went out to eat or had a fancy meal at her place; and, as usual, the first sip was a silent toast to the memory sitting in the empty chair across the table. Followed by an equally silent snort at his sentimentality. The dead were dead, despite that little superstition or hope that returned to him in the long nights when he would think that maybe their spirits still lived as long as someone remembered them. A lot of people thought that, Wager knew; the cemeteries were full of photographs and fresh flowers and visitors on quiet Sunday afternoons. Maybe it was good that the river had never surrendered her body;

that way her marker was a place in the mind rather than a forgotten slab under a cypress. No, it wasn't better; at least with a grave, memory had a place to rest. Irrationally, her mother kept believing that she would return—that she had not drowned but suffered amnesia, and someday the doorbell would ring and there would stand Jo. But the dead were dead and no one came back, not even to help fill that breath-stifling emptiness that spread like black cancer in the middle of his chest when a picture of her smile or an echo of something she'd said crossed his mind. The dead were dead. When you realized that, you gradually came to believe it, and you could stop pretending to yourself that the world you lived in was only a temporary state between two realities: when she had been alive, and when she would return.

He paid the bill and slowly finished the last of a second glass of wine.

That was a lesson Mrs. Green was learning; it was a lesson most of us learned sooner or later, Wager was discovering. The dead were dead.

Sitting in the Trans-Am in the dim parking lot, Wager thought about that death to hold off thinking about the other: Mrs. Green's shock and sadness seemed genuine. Even if she had not told the full truth about the other times her husband stayed out all night, Wager would swear from his own knowledge of it that her grief was real. Slowly, he let the car's steering wheel take him where it would as his mind focused on the death of Councilman Green. Work was Wager's therapy, Golding had said once; and maybe the man was right. Even Golding could be right about something once in a while.

Wager wasn't surprised to find that the car, of its own, gradually worked its way toward nearby Denver General and the morgue, and he realized that somewhere in the back of his mind he had been counting the hours until the autopsy would be completed.

"Putting in overtime, Wager? Or do you have night duty?"

Doc Hefley, the department's forensic pathologist, peeled off the disposable rubber gloves and dropped them in the bag to be washed. That was another of the economies the hospital practiced now, reuse of items once thrown away. Except for two areas, a grinning Hefley told Wager: gynecology and proctology; their gloves were not reused.

He tossed the sheet half-over the cadaver stretched under the white lights of the dissecting room. It was a middle-aged Caucasian woman with no visible scars and an oddly featureless face that seemed to have a beard. Then Wager saw that the beard was really the woman's hair and her features were muffled beneath the glistening underside of a scalp peeled down off the skull and laid out of the way across her face.

"It's that V.I.P. killing. The one the chief's interested in."

"Tell me he's interested. He pulled me out of private practice this afternoon to work on it."

"Is the path report done yet?"

Hefley went to a tall filing cabinet in that part of the room partitioned off for a small office. "It may not be typed up. I told them to rush it, but you know how that goes."

"I know."

The doctor ran a finger along the thick documents and grunted happily. "What do you know—it's here." He handed Wager the heavy sheaf of forms and sprinkled talcum on his hands before pulling on another set of gloves. "Take it out to the lounge to read before you start asking questions, OK? I've got four of the damned things to cut up tonight and no time to waste being sociable."

Wager said OK, and Hefley strode quickly back to the cadaver to speak into the foot-operated recorder whose microphone dangled over the body. His voice was a lone, clinical benediction as Wager closed the door behind him. Then the small saw used to slice through the skull began its shrill whine.

A lot of the information in the pages of the pathology report wasn't any use at all to him; he scanned through the physical description of the dead man for any notations of something out of the ordinary. But there was nothing— Green had been generally healthy, with no indications of substance abuse or of any evident medical abnormalities in his organs. Death, the doc had concluded, was caused by a single, large-caliber bullet to the back of the head. The damage to the brain was detailed as the words followed the path of the bullet, which had gradually expanded from impact until it erupted out of the victim's face. No fragments of the bullet were found in the skull. The approximate time of death, and Wager started making notes in his own little green book, was between 9 P.M. and 2 A.M., and that fit with the witness seeing a car parked there around eleven. The stomach contents indicated that he had eaten chicken, peas, and rice some two to four hours before death—between 5 and 10 P.M., Wager figured. Coffee and a trace of alcohol were found, but no other abusive substances, including tobacco. The man's musculature . . . Wager glanced over the next few pages, which dealt with body fluids and internal organs in detail, and noted that all were checked as normal. He paused to study the section on lividity. The blood patterns indicated that the man might have been moved after he died, but no definitive analysis could be made. The blood had settled in the corpse's low parts as the body had lain on the ground, but there were indications of a secondary lividity of mild intensity. The doc offered no conclusions as to what all that might mean; all he did was list the facts and let them speak. But Wager knew the man would have some ideas about it.

The sheet was back in place, but the pungent sting of newly sawed bone lingered in the air. Hefley, sipping a cup of coffee at the small desk, put down a ballpoint pen and leaned wearily against the squeak of his chair back. "Well?"

"Was he moved or wasn't he?"

"Good question. I think he was, but it could be argued the other way, too: that the secondary lividity was the result of the body shifting as rigor set in."

Wager gave back the thick report. An orderly, his tennis shoes making wet, squelching noises on the waxed concrete floor, trundled the gurney and its load off the silver wink of a freshly hosed floor drain and out through wide doors. "Could somebody have put him back in the same position he died in?"

"If he was moved, then, yeah, I'd say that's what had to happen. It would have been natural for the body to fall forward—it was shot from behind. If he was moved, he was dumped in pretty much the same position he fell in initially."

"Why was he twisted up like that?"

"I don't know." Hefley thought a moment, gazing at the brown tiles of the wall. "For some reason, he didn't stretch out when he fell. Wasn't he found in an open field?"

"Yes."

"Well, he should have stretched out—the bullet killed him instantly, and his body should have kicked itself straight."

"Could he have been shot in a cramped place, like a car, and then stiffened before he was dumped?"

"If he was dumped, Wager—if. And no, not necessarily. In fact, I don't think so, but I'm only guessing. My guess is that he was either shot there and stiffened in that odd position, or—if he was moved—he was killed very shortly before he was dumped. The rigor was intact in all the toes and fingers. That's consistent with the body not being moved after rigor set in."

"Why's that?"

"Technically? Technically, because rigor depends on the pH of the muscle and its glycogen reserve at the time of death. Joints with less muscle mass set up more rapidly than heavily muscled joints. Fingers, toes, jaws set up before elbows or shoulders, and movement tends to break their rigor. For the rigor to remain intact in those small joints, the body would have to be moved shortly after death, before they set. The livor mortis could support this: not long enough for the blood to settle in any secondary cavities or uncompressed low spots. There are those traces of secondary lividity. We can't be certain of movement, but if so, the move was within an hour of death, and then the blood drained into the primary locations. But like I say, we can't be certain."

Doctors always moved from "I" to "we" when they weren't sure. "If he wasn't moved, how do you account for the traces of secondary lividity?"

Hefley's clean, short fingernails rasped in the bristles of his jaw. "Like I said, the body could have settled as it stiffened. Temperature, that could have some effect on lividity. There are half a dozen reasons why we can't say from this lividity alone whether the body was moved."

"What about its position? Would the photographs tell you something?"

"Maybe. Bring them by—let me take a look."

"OK. But say the body was moved, it was within an hour after the killing? You're sure?"

"Less than an hour, is my guess. Maybe less than thirty minutes. But I won't go into court with that." He thought a moment and then nodded. "I'd say it wasn't more than forty-five minutes, max, from the first position of death to where you found him. Any longer than that and the blood patterns would be more definitive. And the rigor in some of the small joints would probably be broken by handling."

"None of the neighbors heard shots last night."

"Well, that fits the possibility of movement, doesn't it? But all I can do is give you the medical facts from the corpse. You're supposed to make them fit with the other facts, right?"

"What about the size of the bullet?"

"Again, that's just a guess because the skull shattered at the point of impact. A .44 or .45. Anything smaller wouldn't be likely to exit the skull in a single piece."

"Magnum?"

"Possibly. I can't say. It was close-range—you saw that note about powder burns on the scalp?"

"I saw it." Wager asked, "You think the round hit him with full velocity?"

"What are you getting at?"

"A silencer. It slows the bullet a lot. Would it have come out the face like that going slower?"

Again the doc dragged his fingernails across the bristles. "I don't know, Wager. That's interesting, but there are too many variables, so I just don't know. That's a pretty big slug, silencer or not, and I don't really know what the impact might have been." He drained his coffee as the orderly shoved another sheeted bundle through the double doors. "I'll get the summary done tonight and over there in the morning. Good enough?"

It would have to be good enough, of course. Wager, feeling the numbness of the day's pummeling events begin to invade his mind as well as his body, guided the Trans-Am the dozen or so blocks up Sixth toward Downing and over to his apartment. Despite the welcome blur to his thoughts, questions began to arrange themselves like entries in his notebook: Why was the body dumped in a place as public as that? What happened to Green's car? Green's valuables were still on him, so more likely, it wasn't a robbery-homicide; the killer just needed wheels to put quick distance between himself and his victim. That fit with the big chance he took in dumping the body there instead of out in the country. Frightened? Was that the reason for the rush to get rid of the body? Green is shot in the back of the head and, within forty-five minutes, transported from X, dumped in that lot, and then the murderer, or murderers, drives off without bothering to make it look like a robbery. Just anxious to get rid of the body and be away from the scene. Anxious to get back to an alibi. Unplanned. That was the word Wager tentatively thought of: It looked like a hastily planned homicide, maybe even an impulse shooting—though it took a hell of an impulse to carry a heavy forty-five around before suddenly deciding to use it. Rage? Fear? Threat? A weapon that big, handy for use, but a rush to kill so that all the actions following the death—secrecy, escape, alibi—had not been clearly thought out.

He unlocked the door to his silent and dark apartment; the red gleam of his answering machine's light caught his eye. Before flipping the tape on, he went past the refrigerator for a beer and then into the bedroom to take off his tie and shirt and slip out of his hot shoes. Then, cooling feet splayed in the short nap of the carpet, he screened the message tape.

Most of it was blank, the caller hanging up without leaving word. Finally, a garbled voice stopped him and he reversed to get it from the start: "Wager, you know who this is. Call me now."

He knew who it was, but he finished the tape first, finding

the same voice two more times. Then he dialed a number from the back page of his little green notebook. As expected, a different voice answered, giving the name of the bar.

"Is Fat Willy there?"

"Who wants him?"

"Gabe."

"I'll see."

A minute later the lurch of the big man's breath came over the wire. "Wager, I hate that fucking answering machine of yours."

"It got your message to me, Willy. What's the problem this time?"

"The problem is I need to collect."

"Collect what?"

"What you owe me, Wager: a favor."

He didn't deny that he owed, but his question was, how much. "What kind of favor?"

"A couple of my people. They been busted. I want them out."

What Willy wanted and what he got were two different things. "Who's got them and what's the charge?"

"That Nick-the-Greek, son of a bitch. Papalopoulos, or whatever his name is. How come the Denver police ain't hiring Americans no more?"

Nick Papadopoulos worked out of Assault in the Crimes Against Persons division. Wager knew the man but not very well. "What's the charge, Willy?"

"Arson and assault. But that's only what the police say."

"They don't have to say a hell of a lot more than that. That's a couple of felonies."

"It's a bunch of bullshit, is what it is. You don't know nothing about it, Wager—I'm telling you it's bullshit and I want them out. You owe me!"

"Willy, you've got a couple cruds beating up on people and burning down their property and you want them sprung? I don't owe you that much."

"That's not the way it was, God damn it all!"

"If that's what they're charged with, I don't care how it was. They don't need me, they need a lawyer. Besides, if the charges have been filed, there's nothing I can do about it, anyway."

"They ain't been filed—they was just arrested. They being held for questioning—ain't no charges filed on them yet. That comes Monday." He added, "And don't give me no shit about you not being able to do nothing. I know and you know the police drops charges all the time, Wager. You owe me—you owe your ass to me. And now I want to collect!"

It was bound to come sooner or later, Wager knew. He'd used Willy and his information to solve an earlier series of homicides along the Colfax strip, and now the fat man was calling in his marker. "Have they been arrested before?"

"Who ain't?"

"Convictions?"

"That's the problem, man. They get convicted on this, it's the third conviction inside ten years. Shit, six more months and they be past the ten-year limit on their first one—that goddamn Papalopoulos!"

A third felony conviction within ten years meant an automatic twenty-five- to fifty-year sentence. A fourth felony, regardless of how much time passed, meant life. Willy and his people were right to be worried. "I'll ask."

"You do better than that."

"No, I won't. I'll see what I can find out. Then if I can help you, I will. If I can't, I won't."

"Damn you, Wager—"

"I know, you've told me: I owe you. I'll see what I can find out."

He dropped the receiver on another squawk and stretched against the stiff pull of his back. Slowly finishing his beer, he stood in the cool night air of the small balcony above Downing and gazed out without seeing the flickering restlessness of the city. Maybe, by now, he was tired enough to sleep.

There had been times when he was this tired that he and Jo would just hold each other, their naked bodies pressed tightly together beneath the thin protection of the sheet, not thinking sex but only wholeness. Together—her eyes even larger and darker in the room's dimness and only the twitch of lips against his cheek to tell him she was smiling. Those were times so good he didn't think they needed words, the union of their slow breath and heartbeat making the only statement. But he should have told her how nice it was; how—despite his silence—he found a kind of peace in those times that existed nowhere else. But he'd said nothing, until the chance for saying anything was gone.

CHAPTER 4

Lieutenant Wolfard called him and Stubbs into his office two minutes after he arrived. "What's this about threats to Mrs. Green?"

Wager told him.

The lieutenant swiveled his chair around to gaze out his narrow window and into the busy Friday traffic below. Wager had noticed that before—when administrators searched for words they usually did it without looking you in the eye. Maybe that way you wouldn't see they didn't know everything. "You think she needs further protection?"

"She'd probably feel better with it. And if something happened to her, there'd be a lot of questions about why she was given none."

"Yeah. Shit. Operations Division's so shorthanded they didn't want to let me have those two yesterday." He looked glum. "I know what they're going to say about posting a twenty-four-hour on her house."

Interoffice cooperation was the lieutenant's worry; catching the murderer was Wager's. He settled against the molded-plastic chair and sketched some organization to his morning while Wolfard talked mostly to himself. First the call to Motor Vehicles for the trace on Green's car. Then Green's associates: the furniture store, the City Council offices. Get the lab people's report on the crime scene. Forensic's report on Green's clothes and body. The afternoon would be for any leads turned up. And sometime early he should work in Green's brother.

"Well"—Wolfard swiveled back—"they won't argue with the chief. And I'm certain he'll say we should put some officers over there, right? Any idea when that pathology report's coming through?"

"The abstract's on its way this morning. I went over the preliminary last night." From the corner of his eye, Wager saw Stubbs's round face turn his way. "The cause of death was the shot in the head. The doc can only guess whether he was killed somewhere else. If the body was moved, it was within forty-five minutes of death."

"He can only guess?"

Wager shrugged. "He won't even go into court with that."

"Is it possible that we are dealing with a racist killing?"

"That phone call's the only motive so far, Lieutenant."

Wolfard tapped a sharp pencil against the wooden box that held a stack of blank memo sheets ready for use. It was that kind of desk, an orderly arrangement of papers with reference works placed at carefully measured distances, the most-used closest to the chair. Wager wondered if the man spent as much time working as he did getting ready for work. "Something like that could explode the whole black community. We could be right back in the sixties and seventies." Wolfard's pencil drew a series of precisely interlocked boxes on a blank memo sheet. He peeled off the sheet and folded it carefully before placing it in the wastebasket. "Are you sure that's the only motive?"

Wager had never met a saint, let alone investigated the murder of one; and he guessed that Green was as human as anyone else and as liable as anyone else to making enemies. But racism was the only motive so far. "We haven't had a chance to find out if there might be other motives, because all we've been doing is sitting here scratching our ass."

The man flushed and his pale eyes hardened as he stared at Wager's blank face. "Then why don't you just get off your ass and start working?"

On the way down the hall, Stubbs murmured, "Jeez, you really gave it to him."

"He wanted us to sit there and hold his hand." The anger that had lunged out from that ill-defined place in the back of his skull was slow to ebb, fired by another sleepless night and by the waste of his time at Wolfard's pleasure. "He's pulling the pay and he's got the rank. By God, he should do his own work."

"He's as new as I am in Homicide."

"Then he should know enough to let me do mine."

Stubbs fell silent as they passed the receptionist's desk where the civilian woman nodded and smiled, her ears alert to anything they said. In the elevator, just before they reached the basement, he asked, "What time'd you quit last night?"

"I don't know. Nine or ten."

Stubbs watched the light jump across the numbers to B-2. "Does Doyle want us to put in all that overtime?"

"I don't claim overtime."

"You don't? You put in a sixteen-hour day just for the hell of it?"

"It's the way I see the job. A lot of people see it that way." And it was something Stubbs shouldn't have to ask. If he wanted eight hours a day, five days a week, he should be a civilian. Or go back into uniform where a sly cop could manage to wrap up his paperwork right at the end of his shift. Axton, too, had made some comment to Wager about losing himself in the work: "You've been like this ever since you got back."

"Like what?"

"Trying to work yourself to death."

The anger had stirred then, too, and Wager started to tell the big man that it was his self and his work, and if Axton thought there was something wrong with either one, he was free to walk in and bitch to Doyle. But he didn't. Instead, he let the flare silently die back and reminded himself that Max had been his partner, and that he spoke because he cared. "It doesn't seem much different. I never did like to work by the clock."

"Yeah, I know. But there for a while, you know, when you and Jo . . . Well, you were a lot looser, then, Gabe."

"She's dead."

That, and the tone he used, said it all. Axton had gotten off the subject and Wager had been relieved by his silence. Just as he welcomed Stubbs's wordlessness, even if it was a bit sullen. He tossed the man the ring of car keys—it was his turn to drive. As they cleared the concrete walls of the police parking garage Wager keyed the mike for DMV and any luck they had looking for a dark Lincoln Continental, license HRG-1.

0848 Hours

Embassy Furniture was one of the smaller warehouses in the home furnishings district just off north I-25. Flanked by flag-bedecked buildings the size of hangars and advertising SALE ON ALL STOCK, Embassy's display windows showed samples of different rooms that featured a lot of dark wood and leather trim and beveled glass. Wager had half expected the store to be closed for mourning, but the only sign in the door stated the usual hours of operation. He and Stubbs were early—it wasn't yet nine—but Stubbs knocked loud and long enough to stir up a figure behind the glass. An attractive woman met them with a worried look. She had blond hair that tumbled in stiff curls and her makeup was precisely lined, like—Wager thought—one of those enameled-looking Texas blondes who were always entering beauty pageants. Before she could ask what they wanted, Wager showed his badge and identified himself. "Could we ask you a few questions?"

She was in her late twenties or early thirties and her age showed in sudden tired lines as her gray eyes stared at them for a long moment. Then she nodded. "Yes, of course. Let's go to the office." Turning, she called to someone out of sight among a forest of glinting mirrors. "Ray, will you watch the floor? I'll be in the office with these gentlemen."

A voice came back, "OK, Sonie."

Her name was Sonja Andersen but everyone, she said, called her Sonie. She had worked for Mr. Green for almost three years, first as salesperson and accountant and then as store manager after he was elected to City Council. Her voice was soft and reflective, as if she were telling herself rather than them what had happened. "When I heard about it, I didn't know what to do. I mean, whether or not to open the store this morning, or what." She shrugged and looked around at the silent gleam of oiled wood. "So I came down and opened up. I didn't know what else to do. . . ."

"How did you hear about it?" Wager asked.

"Last night. The news. It still doesn't seem real."

He waited a moment until her breath steadied. "Can you tell me when you saw Mr. Green last?"

"Yesterday afternoon. He always goes over the day's bank."

"That was after seven?"

"About then, yes. That's when we close at midweek. Fridays and Saturdays, we stay open until nine. And we're open on Sunday afternoons until five."

"So he left here some time after seven?"

She nodded and thought back. "A little after. I can't say for certain."

"He was driving his own car? The Lincoln?"

"Yes. He always drove that. He said it was one of his trademarks."

"Sounds like you work a lot of hours," said Stubbs.

"We rotate. Mr. Green makes it up to us. He's—he was—a very good employer." Her nose grew red and Wager saw tears tremble on her lower eyelids. "He was such a kind man. . . ."

"Did he seem upset in any way? Worried?"

"Not really worried, no. Tired. I think the City Council work was making him awfully tired."

"Did he say anything about it?"

"No. He'd never say if he was worried about anything; he wasn't that kind."

"Do you know where he went when he left here?"

The blond hair wagged from side to side. "A political meeting. He always had a political meeting to go to, but I don't know what time it was or where."

"Can you tell us the names of anybody he may have been meeting?"

"No. I just don't—didn't—know that much about that part of his life. Only what he told me now and then." She fell silent, staring at the Kleenex wadded in her fingers. Wager and Stubbs gave her more time to remember whatever she could. That was one of the things you learned about asking questions—not to move too fast, not to push a person off a topic too soon, because something may still be coming. "Mrs. Wilfong might know. She's Mr. Green's aide."

Wager jotted down the name. "Did he have a lot of all-night meetings?"

"All night? What do you mean?"

"Late enough so he wouldn't get home. So he might stay at a friend's house. Or maybe a motel."

"I . . . I really don't know. I guess he could. I don't know that much about his political life, so I suppose he could." She added, "The Council meetings go very late a lot of times, I know that."

"Did he ever say anything about a threat on his life?" asked Stubbs.

"Threat? No." The woman's hand went to her throat and Wager noted the absence of a wedding ring. "I thought—I just assumed—that it was a robbery. That someone killed him for his money."

"Did he usually carry a lot of money?"

"He always liked to have two or three hundred in cash." She went on, "He didn't like credit cards, which was kind of funny. We do a big credit business."

"The store's making money?" Wager asked.

"Yes. It's our line of furniture—Henredon, Thomasville, Ethan Allan—quality lines. The other stores," her hand waved at the walls and beyond, "they sell cheap stuff in bulk. But a lot of people want quality furniture now; the market's going upscale, and they don't mind spending a

little more for something that looks nice and will last. Horace—Mr. Green—believed in quality. That quality would
sell better than junk." The tears finally spilled in a silent
stream and Miss Andersen dabbed the Kleenex quickly,
splotching the heavy mascara from her eyelashes. "I'm
sorry."

"Can we talk to the other employees?"

"Yes—certainly." She sniffed. "There's Ray and Allie, up
front. Do you want to talk to the people out back, too?"

"Yes, ma'am. Everybody. It shouldn't take too long."

It didn't. Ray Coleman, a young man in a dark suit whose
teeth glinted whitely against the ebony of his face, said that
he had seen Mr. Green come in yesterday afternoon
around five, maybe five-thirty. No, he didn't seem worried
in any way—happy, in fact. He was always happy. Almost
always—sometimes he got pretty mad if somebody
screwed up, but that was OK because that's what a boss was
supposed to do.

"What time did he leave?"

"Sometime after closing. He and Sonie got back about
six-thirty, maybe. They were still here when I left at
seven."

"Got back from where?"

Coleman shrugged and looked from Wager to Stubbs and
back. "Coffee. Him and Sonie usually went out for a cup of
coffee."

"Do you know of anyone who might want to hurt Mr.
Green? Anyone who ever threatened him?" asked Stubbs.

"Nobody would want to hurt Councilman Green! He was
a man the people were proud of!"

"Can you think of any reason someone might kill him?"

"No. I swear to God I can't. A city councilman—a successful businessman. People looked up to him—we admired
him." The young man stared down at the gleam of his
pointed shoes. "I wanted to be like him."

He would be, Wager thought—we all would: dead. "Do
you have any idea where Mr. Green went last evening?"

Coleman shook his head. "No. He was always going to
some political meeting or council meeting or something.
That or home." The youth shook his head again. "There's

no reason for it. None at all. He was a good man, you know? Just plain a good man."

Good or not, Green hadn't gone home. "Do you know what kind of car he drove?"

"Sure. Everybody knows that showboat—big black Lincoln Continental. Even had his initials on the license plates. That's why he drove it, so people could see him coming. He'd toot the horn and wave and everybody'd yell back, 'Hey, Councilman!' "

"Do you have any idea where he might have been last night between nine and midnight?"

"No. Something political's my guess. It wasn't where I was, anyway."

"Where was that?"

"Movies. Over at the Mann on Colorado Boulevard."

Wager thanked Coleman, and he and Stubbs divided up the stockroom people. What little they added told them the same thing: Green was admired and respected by everyone and had no enemies that they ever heard of; he had arrived between four and five and was here doing paperwork with Sonie when the store closed at seven. If he was worried about anything, they didn't notice.

On the way out, Wager paused to ask Miss Andersen if she had been in touch with Mrs. Green.

"No. Not yet." Her makeup was repaired and she had herself under control. "I don't want to intrude."

0932 Hours

"That's a good-looking blonde," said Stubbs. "I got this thing for blondes. Maybe because my wife's a brunette."

Wager grunted some answer; his mind wasn't on Stubbs's preference in women.

"Where are we headed?" Stubbs steered the vehicle into the slow lane of I-25 and glanced at Wager.

"City Council offices."

The sedan picked up speed as it wove easily through traffic toward the Twenty-third Street off-ramp. The City Council chambers and offices were on the fourth floor of the

City-County Building with its façade of stone columns reaching out in two wings from a rotunda. Atop the tall center section was an odd cupola designed like the choragic monument to Lysicrates. Whoever the hell Lysicrates was. For some reason the phrase welled out of Wager's memory as he glanced at it. Jo had told him its name and why so many public buildings had the little doodad stuck up there. He wished he had asked her who Lysicrates was and what "choragic" meant. There were a lot of things he should have done when he had the chance. And things he regretted doing now that he had no chance to correct them. Maybe that was the cause of the taut anger that hung on like a fever and made him edgy and sore. Anger for those careless things done and not done. Anger for the easy assumption that the same sun would rise tomorrow for all of us. Anger for those debts thoughtlessly assumed in the belief they would never have to be paid. *La paz con otros comenza con la paz de sí.* "Peace with others begins in peace with one's self." One of the bits of philosophy his mother had offered from her family's store of sayings. But he remembered another of her sayings, too—one that usually came on a long sigh of weary exhaustion: "The only peace is in the grave." That was the trouble with living life by homily—there was more than one for every occasion, and they usually contradicted each other. And all they left Wager with was an ill-stifled anger born of self-contempt.

0947 Hours

"The agenda's set before Council meets—that's part of my job as chief of staff along with the council president." Mr. Fitch—Jeremy Fitch—was heavy-set but no taller than Wager, with a tuft of white hair that sprouted long on top and sagged over like a rooster's comb. It bounced slightly when he walked, sometimes dropping across a pair of horn-rimmed glasses that straddled his fleshy nose. He had the quick smile of a politician and the eyes of an insider who could tell you more than he was free to say. "After opening the session and taking care of the minutes and other routine items, they move into the conference room to go over items of motion and decide how they're going to vote. That's where they can say what they really think without it going into the minutes."

"They go out again?" asked Wager.

"That's right."

"Is it an open meeting?" asked Stubbs.

"Sure. The press goes right with them. The Sunshine Law, you know. That's where they talk over the business part of the agenda first so they won't waste time when they come back to the council hall. Usually, that's the most important and interesting part of the meeting, too. Sometimes some pretty harsh things get said in there that, you know, if they got in the minutes, might embarrass everybody later on."

"Did Councilman Green get into it with anybody?" asked Stubbs.

"Say, now, that's not what I meant—nobody gets wound up enough to kill anybody!" The hair bounced up and down as he shook his head quickly. "Don't go putting words into my mouth, all right?"

"That's not what I meant," Stubbs said quickly. "We're just trying to get a sense of who Councilman Green was. What his routines were. Anyone who was important to him as a friend or a political enemy."

Fitch led them from the stale air of the wide hallway with its gleaming walls of polished stone. Past the closed and dark doors of the members' offices, he hesitated. "You're telling me he was killed by a political enemy?"

"No, we're not," said Wager. "We don't know who he was killed by. We're just trying to get as much information on the man as we can."

"Politics gets pretty hot around here sometimes." The glasses aimed at Stubbs. "But there's nobody who'd go killing anybody over it. Their reputation, maybe—ha. But certainly not the man himself."

"I understand that, Mr. Fitch. And that's not my meaning."

"Just want to make that clear. A whisper in these halls is heard a long way, and a wrong word can do a lot of damage." He opened a glass-paneled door that said CHIEF OF STAFF and led them into the office whose single window seemed to dwarf the small space. Through the opening, Wager glimpsed a gray stone wing of the same building. "I sure wouldn't want it getting around that the police insinuated things about City Council."

Although the budget was the responsibility of the mayor's office, the council had approval of that budget. Including the police line. Fitch made certain the two detectives remembered that, and Stubbs understood and looked worried.

"Did you see him at all yesterday?" Wager asked.

"Once in the morning, once in the afternoon." The man's eyes were guarded by puffy flesh that had squinted against tobacco smoke and the glare of fluorescent lights far more than against the sun. "We had three committee meetings here yesterday—Health and Social Services; Recreation; and Zoning. He's on the last two. He might have spent some time in the council offices, too, but I didn't see him."

"Did he show up for work every day?"

"Unless they have their district offices here, council members don't come around except for meetings. Thank God."

"How many committees was Green on?"

"Councilman Green," Fitch corrected him, "was on five standing committees and had several special assignments."

"Five?" Stubbs glanced up from his notebook. "How many committees are there?"

"Twelve. Got to have twelve so each councilman gets to chair a committee. Thirteen councilmen, twelve committees. The council president chairs the council meetings and sits on all the committees." Fitch added, "Gets paid more for it, too."

"Whether the city needs twelve committees or not?" asked Wager.

Fitch didn't smile. "They're all busy committees, Officer."

"Can you list his committees for us?" Stubbs asked.

The man rustled through a tray of papers and pulled out a blue-and-white brochure labeled DENVER CITY COUNCIL: COMMITTEE ASSIGNMENTS. "This is part of the press packet. It has this year's members and their committees and special assignments."

Green was vice chairman of the Downtown Denver Development Committee, and a member of the committees on Recreation and Culture; Housing, Community, and Economic Development; and Transportation. He chaired the Zoning, Planning, and Land-Use Committee. His special assignments included liaison with the County Corrections Board, the Downtown Area Planning and Steering Committee, and Urban Drainage and Flood Control. "Why are so many council members on the Transportation Committee?"

"That's Stapleton Airport—there's a lot of receptions and trips for council members from the airlines. All official business, of course."

Wager grunted. "He didn't have a desk here? Any place he would keep papers?"

"No. He has a district office. Over on Colorado Boulevard. The address is in that brochure."

"Who appoints his replacement?" asked Stubbs.

"Nobody. It's by special election, and it'll be very interesting."

"Why's that?"

"Well, for one thing, it's got to take place inside sixty days, by law. So the candidate who can get organized fastest has the best chance. That takes backing—money, people, contacts. You know who has that kind of organization ready to go right now?"

Wager didn't.

"The mayor! His honor himself. But the current council's run by people opposing his downtown development plan. Green was against it, you know. So he's not likely to help out somebody in that camp, and my guess is he's already for a candidate who'll vote his way for election support. Yessir"—Fitch's hair bounced once and his eyes lit with a gleam of icy laughter—"it'll be real interesting."

CHAPTER 5

Friday, 13 June, 1021 Hours

Green's district headquarters was in a line of single-story shops facing the crowded lanes of Colorado Boulevard. Flanked by shoe repairs on one side and a barber shop on the other, a wide blue-and-white sign in the plate-glass window said HORACE GREEN, YOUR CITY COUNCILMAN, and underneath that, DISTRICT HEADQUARTERS. Another sign dangling in the glass of the recessed doorway said OPEN. COME IN. They did.

"Anybody here?" Stubbs wandered past the well-worn leatherette chairs and couches that formed a kind of lobby separated from the back by a plywood partition painted pale green. Wager recognized it as the same uneasy color that decorated so many of the city's office walls. On a small table a glass-covered coffee warmer steamed slightly and a stack of styrofoam cups stood ready. Above it, offering approval to whatever voter poured himself a free cup, the familiar face smiled down from a large poster that said ELECT GREEN. Across the room on another table stood small piles of brochures and handouts, and a stack of frayed magazines. A rack held today's newspapers and a series of government information pamphlets, the kind with small type and long columns of print and no pictures. These looked fresh and unthumbed.

Stubbs came back from sticking his head through an open doorway in the partition. "The place is empty."

"Try the bathroom?"

The desk in the back office was littered in a kind of chaos that reflected haste and a lot of different jobs to do. Here and there a neater pile of memos or receipts stood like islands in the wash of loose papers, as if someone made periodic attempts at organization. A multiline telephone sat silent amid strewn pamphlets; and, within easy reach of the swivel chair, a large calendar tacked to the wall held scrawled notes in the white squares for each day of the month. Wager began to read the cramped writing.

Stubbs came back from the small hallway that led to the bathroom and rear entry. "Nobody."

In the square for Wednesday, the eleventh, Wager found "Recep—Vitaco 7–9," "PDC," "Call Dengren/Collins," and a list of half-a-dozen first names with times behind them. It was far more detailed than the few entries in the leather-bound appointment book they had received from Hannah Green's mother. The only notes in that had been the long-scheduled meetings of council and the routine dates that could be projected a year or so in advance: quarterly tax payments due, birthdays, anniversaries. Wager guessed that the leather appointment book had been a Christmas present and Green had dutifully made entries in it to show the giver how useful it was. But his real schedule was kept on this cluttered calendar.

"Can I help you gentlemen?"

In the office doorway, a bakery box sagging in her hands, stood a large woman whose hair was clipped into a billowing Afro designed, Wager guessed, to make her wide face seem smaller. She was in her thirties and wore a neat, pale-blue suit that had a band of new black silk pinned around the left sleeve. "Something you gentlemen want here?"

Stubbs showed his badge. "We're police officers. Do you work here?"

"Yes. I'm Julia Wilfong, the councilman's administrative assistant." She set the box on a corner of the desk and slowly tore the paper tape that sealed it. "I went out for some doughnuts. I keep expecting people to come by to pay their respects. But so far nobody's come."

Her manners had a formality that emphasized her self-possession—as if, Wager thought, she was one of those people who had been through enough to fully understand her own weaknesses and strengths. "Have you worked for Councilman Green long?"

"Ever since he was elected."

That would be over two years ago, when Green ran a campaign against the incumbent who had been accused of accepting bribes for awarding city contracts. Though nothing had ever been proven, the rumors were enough to turn the election. "Can you tell us when you saw the councilman on Wednesday?"

"Once in the morning and then that afternoon. He came in as always, about eight or so, and we went over the day's schedule. Then he met with some constituents. That afternoon we had the Zoning Committee meeting. He's committee chairman and I take the minutes."

"What was his schedule for Wednesday?"

She told him, pointing to the calendar and explaining its abbreviations. In addition to routine committee work, meetings, and functions, he had a dozen-or-so visitors to talk to.

"Is that usual?"

"A few more than some mornings, but not that unusual. People are always after something."

"Any idea what they wanted to see him about?"

"Of course. They all check with me first—I'm the administrative assistant. Most of the time I can help them out and they don't have to bother the councilman. Some of them want to anyway, though. Sometimes the councilman himself has to do it."

"What about these names? What did they want?"

Wilfong took a pair of glasses from her purse, the kind with large round lenses that dwarfed her face and seemed to weigh on her nose. "This first one here, Rollo, that's Rollo

Agnew. He wants a permit to rent out part of his house."
She explained, "The zoning says no multifamily dwellings."

"Wouldn't the city zoning office handle that?"

"They already told him no. That's why he came to the councilman—to get the zoning changed."

"Did Councilman Green help him?" asked Wager.

"He told him the exact same thing I told him: It's a local zoning regulation and if the neighborhood wants to start renting out, they can petition for a change. Rollo just had to hear it from the councilman."

"So he didn't change the zoning for him?"

"No. Councilman Green wasn't about to stir up that whole neighborhood for the likes of Rollo Agnew. He didn't vote for him, anyway."

The woman detailed the other names on the list of appointments: complaints about a dangerous intersection that the city had done nothing about, an elderly woman whose sidewalk assessment wouldn't leave her with enough money for food, a bar owner whose liquor license was threatened with suspension, an ex-serviceman who wanted a job with the city. It was, as Wilfong said, a parade of people who wanted; Wager figured it was the kind of petitioning that every councilman heard, and none of it seemed serious enough to rate a bullet in the head. But the questions had to be asked.

"Did Councilman Green help all these people?"

"Most of them. And the ones he couldn't help understood why—he was good that way. Even when they didn't get a thing, they went out of here satisfied that somebody had listened to them. Even Rollo Agnew."

"So you can think of no one who might have a grudge against him?" Stubbs asked.

"Enough to shoot him, you mean? No, sir! He was a good man and a good councilman, too. He stepped on some toes—you got to when you make decisions. But he was a good soul, Officer. A good one!"

Wager said, "Somebody didn't like him."

Wilfong slowly folded her glasses away. "I don't see how it could be any black person. They respected Horace Green—they admired him." Her dark eyes glanced at

Wager, a flash of smoldering heat deep in them. "What about that telephone call to Mrs. Green? The one from the racist who threatened to kill more of us?"

"You've heard about that?"

"Everybody's heard about it, Officer. Question is, what are you doing about it?"

"Mrs. Green has police protection," said Wager. "And a lot of officers are working on the case, including us. Can you think of anyone at all who ever threatened Green or who might have disliked him enough to kill him?"

"Whoever made that phone call, that's who. God knows, there are people like that around." In her low-heeled shoes, she was almost as tall as Wager, and her angry eyes looked levelly into his. "And if that's who it was, there's going to be some real trouble."

Stubbs said, "It could have been a crank call, Mrs. Wilfong."

"It could. And that's what I've been telling the people when they ask about it." She began arranging the doughnuts neatly on a tray, using a paper napkin to protect them from her fingers. Then she unfolded another napkin and laid it precisely over the even rows. "But then again it might not have been."

Like most black citizens, she didn't want a riot, either. But the sting of old insult and anger lay close to the surface. "You made out the councilman's schedule?"

"The important things. A councilman doesn't have time to be bothered by all that paperwork. Once a day he either came by or called, and we went over the agenda for that day and the next." A calendar sheet showed the day-by-day and hour-by-hour spaces for appointments. Most of them were filled. "Every Friday, we went over the next week's calendar. That was the routine—the councilman wanted to make sure he didn't miss anything important he had promised to attend."

"Have you worked for other councilmen?" Wager asked.

"No."

"And Green—Councilman Green—was in his first term?"

"That's right. He was coming up for reelection next time."

"He was planning to run again?"

"We hadn't discussed that—it's a bit early. But I'm sure he was."

"You have any idea who'll run for his seat?" asked Stubbs.

"No, I do not. The man is not even in his grave, Officer."

"He wasn't thinking of running for mayor?" asked Wager.

"No—that was just newspaper gossip. I don't know where the newspapers get that bull. The mayor's in the same party. You're not going to have somebody in the same party run against a strong incumbent." She spoke like a schoolteacher explaining the obvious to ignorant kids. Which, Wager reflected, wasn't too far from the truth: They were ignorant of a lot of the city's behind-the-scenes politics.

Councilman Green's last day, Wednesday, had been a typical one. Wilfong showed them a page whose letterhead said CITY COUNCIL, CITY AND COUNTY OF DENVER, complete with the city shield and a column listing the representatives of the eleven districts and the two at-large. All the headings and names didn't leave much space for messages, but a paragraph listed entries for yesterday's meetings, beginning with the Health and Social Services Committee at 9:15, the Recreation and Culture Committee at 10 A.M., a noon construction briefing and luncheon at the city airport, a 3:30 special Zoning, Planning, and Land-Use meeting that Green chaired. All council members were invited to a buffet reception at the Brown Palace Hotel, beginning at six and hosted by the Prudential Development Company.

"They get a lot of free meals," said Wager.

The woman frowned. "They earn those meals. They get briefed on things like construction proposals and land development—the kind of things there's no time for in the rest of the day."

"It's a busy schedule, all right," agreed Stubbs.

"More than just what's in the *Bugle.*" She pointed to the page in Green's open appointment book. His day had started with a 7 A.M. conference with CCC, and some time had been blocked out for the morning's petitioners at the district office. He had a 2 P.M. meeting with AFS, and the last item of the night—7:30 to 9:30—was the Vitaco reception that Wager had earlier noticed inked on the wall calendar. What wasn't penned in, of course, was Green's final appointment with whoever killed him.

"What's Vitaco?"

Wilfong tilted her glasses to read the entry. "Oh, yes— that's the company that wants to expand its manufacturing operations. They're in our district."

"They need a zoning change?"

"No. More water taps. That's the purview of the Denver Water Board, which has its own authority apart from the City Council. But a lot of times they listen to what a district councilman has to say."

"Did he go?"

"I believe he did."

"You don't go with him to these things?"

"Very rarely. If I'm invited."

The Vitaco reception would have been after the Brown Palace buffet. "Can you tell me who Dengren/Collins is?" asked Wager. He pointed to the 4:30 time slot that held the two names.

"That would be Mr. Douglas Dengren and Mr. Rick Collins. They wanted to discuss the neighborhood improvement policy. They're the co-chairmen of the Northeast Denver Action Committee."

"Did the councilman make that meeting?"

"I don't know. I personally have very little to do with that group. They prefer to act outside the party structure, and I prefer not to be identified with them in any way. They're trying to build a support base in the popular mind by playing on the people's grievances."

"Do you have their telephone numbers?"

Silently, she thumbed through a Rolodex for the names and then told Wager the number.

"What about this seven A.M. meeting with CCC?" asked Stubbs. "Who was that?"

"That, gentlemen, is your own sheriff's office. One of the

councilman's special assignments was liaison with the City-County Corrections Board. They meet at seven in the morning once a month." She glanced at Wager. "A breakfast meeting."

He pointed at the two-o'clock line. "What about AFS?"

Her brow creased with thought. "I don't recognize that abbreviation, and the handwriting's not mine." Then she nodded. "American Furniture Service—that's probably what that is. The councilman wrote it in himself."

"Are they in your district?"

"No. They're wholesalers. In addition to full-time employment for the city, the councilman also had to run his business."

"I thought Miss Andersen ran the business for him," said Wager.

"Not by herself she doesn't."

"Do all of them have personal businesses?"

"Mostly, yes. They can't stop their businesses for the duration of their terms as councilmen."

"Did you help with his personal business, too?"

"No."

"But as an aide, you covered the city business when Councilman Green was tied up with his own?"

"That's right. The administrative assistant's job is very important and very time-consuming. There are many details and many items of business that the councilman himself doesn't have time to negotiate."

"You do city business in his name?"

"Routine matters, certainly. Office accounts, answering correspondence, researching issues pertaining to the district. Occasionally, I help draft motions and resolutions, but most of that's done by the council staff."

"That would be Mr. Fitch?"

"And his analysts and assistants, yes."

"So you didn't see Councilman Green or hear from him again after that zoning meeting on the afternoon of the eleventh?" Wager asked.

"No. He left the committee meeting and I came back here to type up the minutes."

"About what time was that?"

"We usually get the work done in the time allowed. Councilman Green was proud of that; he liked to run a brisk meeting, so I suppose it was close to four-thirty when we adjourned."

She was interrupted by the rattle of the door as an elderly couple entered and, seeing the two white men, hesitated.

"The constituents are beginning to arrive to pay their respects, gentlemen. If you need nothing more from me . . ."

Wager held up a finger to keep her attention. "Was it usual for the councilman to stay away from home all night?"

"What do you mean?"

"He was killed Wednesday night. He wasn't found until Thursday afternoon. Did his wife call yesterday to find out where he was?"

Wilfong thought back. "Yes—she did call. But she just asked if he was here. She didn't seem worried."

"Wouldn't you be worried if your husband was out all night?"

"I'm very glad that my ex-husband is out of my entire life, Officer. I don't know anything about the councilman staying out all night or what his wife might or might not have thought of it." She lifted the napkin from the doughnuts and folded it before dropping it in the trash. "If you will excuse me now, I have to talk to the constituents."

1056 Hours

In the car, Stubbs whistled a little off-key tune and kept time with a forefinger bouncing on the steering wheel. "You're really hung up on Green's staying out all night."

It was one of those loose threads that kept snagging his attention: why Green's wife didn't make an effort to find her husband when he didn't come home. "I figure either Mrs. Green knew where he was or she didn't care."

"But she said he did it before, and that's why she wasn't worried." He angled down off I-70 and into the maze of streets that served the businesses beneath the elevated highway.

"That's what she said."

"You don't believe her? Why not?"

Wager put it into words as much for himself as for Stubbs. "We have a victim who has almost every hour of his day scheduled. Day after day, somebody knows where he is. If his wife ever needs to get in touch with him, all she does is pick up a phone and make a call or two. To the furniture store—to the district office. But then he's gone all night, and the wife calls nobody until almost noon the next day. Why? Wasn't she worried? Or maybe she didn't have to call to know where he was?"

"Well, she did call around."

"After he was dead."

"You think she knew he was dead?"

"I'd feel happier if somebody else told me Green stayed out all night, too. And where he stayed."

Stubbs whistled another few notes. "If we stir up a lot of shit about a city councilman and his wife, we could get splashed on."

"We go where the evidence takes us."

"Sure—yeah. That's the job, I guess. But we'd better go real carefully. If you think the councilman had a little something doing at night and the wife did a little something to get even, let's be damned careful how we dig into it."

Wager looked at the man's worried profile; the downward slope of loose flesh under his brief chin matched the slope of his forehead. "This isn't a parking ticket, Stubbs. It's murder. We catch murderers."

"Don't play the hard-ass with me, Wager. I've put in my time on the street. I know damned good and well how much backup a cop gets when he stirs up crap about some V.I.P.: none. You want to stick your neck out, go ahead. But don't drag me along with you."

"You chose Homicide, Stubbs. If you can't take the heat, move on."

"Don't worry about me. I can take more heat than you can. But I was warned about you, man. They told me you got a thing about fucking up your career. Well, don't fuck up mine, that's all. That crap you handed Wolfard this morning about sitting around on our ass. Now you're coming up with some shit about a city councilman and his wife. I don't want to get burned because of you, man."

So Stubbs had been warned against him. By "them." Screw Stubbs. Screw them. Screw all of them together. Wager knew what good police work was, and you didn't get it by sucking around afraid to do the job. "Just do what you're supposed to, Stubbs. Your ass'll be covered."

"Yeah—right. Just trust you." They rode in tense silence for a block or two. Finally, in a quieter voice, Stubbs said, "Besides, there's still a dozen possibilities, and we're just getting started on all the guy's contacts. Let's check them out before we start saying the guy was screwing around on his wife."

"That's what we're doing."

"How many contacts you figure he had? Two hundred? You figure he talked to two hundred people the day he was killed?"

"Maybe."

"It'd be a hell of a lot easier if the guy'd been a hermit."

That was true; a victim who had as many contacts as Green made things tough on detectives who were trying to trace the frayed ends of his life. The easiest way, of course, was to start with the last known sighting of the dead man and work back, and that's what they were doing now. Wager peered down the street cluttered with commercial trucks and a few signs identifying the various buildings. It was a region of light industry, the kind of area that had a lot of one-story square buildings set back behind chain-link fences of varying heights. On weekends and after working hours, the street and the parking lots would be deserted; now, in late morning, the lots were filled and more cars and light trucks sat at odd angles just off the pavement, while heavy trucks growled slowly to and from loading docks. Little money was wasted on advertising for the stray retail customer, and less on placing street numbers where they could be seen.

"Is that it?" Stubbs pointed to a dun-colored building that

sat behind its own fencing. A sign half-hidden under a leaning slab of plywood said -ACO.

"Let's try it."

Stubbs swerved onto the graveled apron that served a
long series of high, square doorways to coast past a line of
vehicles and stop at a door that seemed to lead to an office.
A small sign on the door repeated the name, VITACO.

"Yeah, help you men?" A black youth with a pencil behind his ear looked at them across the counter and
scratched at something on a clipboard.

"Are you one of the company officers?"

"What?"

Wager repeated the question and the young man
laughed. "Naw, I'm the head shipping clerk; this is the
shipping office. You want the business office—that's around
on the other side."

They followed his directions to a quieter hall of the building and a boxy office. Just inside the entry, two potted
plants caught what sun spilled through the small windows
beside the doorway.

"May I help you?" A thin white woman looked up from
the desk. Her long, straight hair draped like parted curtains
past her face to accentuate its narrowness.

"Can we talk with one of the company officers, please?"
Wager showed his badge.

"Mr. Yeager's in. Let me see if he's busy."

They waited while she spoke into an intercom; then she
nodded at an open door. "Go right in, please."

The sign on the desk said Arnold Yeager, and the man
himself was just coming to meet them. "This is about Councilman Green?" He was stocky and the fringe of dark beard
made his face even heavier; his solidity seemed to match
the oak paneling dotted with framed certificates and
plaques and photographs of people smiling and shaking
hands. There were a couple of plants in here, too—broad-
leafed ones that looked like small trees.

"Yessir. We understand he was at a reception you gave
night before last."

Yeager nodded. "He came in a little late. He got here at
about . . . eight forty-five, I guess. Maybe a few minutes

either way. I remember we were waiting for him, and about eight-thirty, we started getting kind of nervous. He was the main guest, so to speak."

"Why was that?"

"Well, we want to expand our plant and we need additional city water to do it. We do high-intensity plastic molding for electronics components, and the shop's just getting too small." There was a note of almost surprised pride as he glanced at the paneled wall with its Rotary Club wheel and scrolls of membership in civic and service organizations. "We hit it at the right time, I guess. This'll be our third expansion in five years."

"Did Councilman Green say he'd help you get the water tap?"

"Oh, he was very friendly—he promised to talk to some people on the Water Board. It means more jobs for his district, and we're one of the local leaders in minority hiring." A worried note came into his voice. "Now, of course . . ." His head wagged once. "A terrible thing. Really terrible."

"Can you tell us exactly what happened at the party?"

"Sure. Like I said, the councilman came in around eight forty-five and there were some drinks and sandwiches and hot snacks. And a lot of people."

"Who was here?"

"We invited the entire plant staff—about a hundred and fifty people showed up, I guess. Most of the workers live here in the councilman's district. We figured it would be a little more effective that way; he could see how important Vitaco is for his district."

"He talked to a lot of them, I suppose?" Stubbs asked.

"He shook a lot of hands." The beard parted in a brief grin. "Election's coming up, you know." The grin faded back into the hair. "I guess that's not important now, is it?"

"Was there anybody he spent a lot of time talking with?" asked Wager.

Yeager tugged at the fringe where an occasional glint of gray mottled the dark hair. "He talked to Barbara Jackson for a while. She works on the assembly line. And to Tony Purdy. And . . . well, maybe two dozen others. The councilman knew the names of a lot of the people in his district and went out of his way to shake hands with all of them. But except for those two, I don't recall anyone he talked to more than a minute or two. He was good at that—a word to everybody and not too long with any one person. I hadn't seen him in action before, but he was good at it—a real politician."

"When did he leave?"

"A little after nine—quarter after, maybe."

"Did he seem worried in any way? Or anxious?"

Yeager shook his head. "Seemed real happy to be here."

"Who was the last one to see him go?"

"I suppose that would be me. I went to the door with him and thanked him for coming by."

"Did he say where he was going?"

"No."

"Did he leave alone?"

The man nodded.

"Did anyone follow him out?" asked Stubbs.

"No. But the party started breaking up about then, so it's hard to say." Yeager's brown eyes blinked once or twice. "You're not thinking that someone at the party followed him. . . . No, my people wouldn't do that."

Wager turned from reading one of the plaques on the wall. "You have some ex-convicts on your payroll, don't you? I see this award for the Second-Chance Association."

"Well, yes, but they're some of the best workers I've got. Those people are grateful for their second chance, Officer. I can't imagine a one of them who'd do what you're suggesting."

"I'm not suggesting anything, Mr. Yeager. I'm just asking questions."

"Yes, but your implications . . . I just can't believe any of my people would do something like what you're implying."

Wager spelled it out for him. "Councilman Green was on the Corrections Board. That's the board that oversees the parole process and monitors halfway houses and other community corrections efforts. It just may be that one of your second chancers had a grudge against the councilman. It's a possibility we have to check out."

Yeager looked from Wager to Stubbs. Under the dark hair of his mustache, the pink tip of his tongue wiped across his lip. "You're serious, aren't you?"

"I'd like a list of the ex-cons you've hired. And the names of any who were fired or who quit lately."

A long moment passed and, in the silence, Wager could hear the creak of the man's dry throat as he swallowed. "All right." He leaned to speak into the intercom and looked up when he finished. "But it's like I'm betraying them. I tell them when they're hired that I won't bring it up if they don't make me bring it up. So many families in this neighborhood have relatives who have gotten in trouble. All they want is a chance to straighten out. And now it's like I'm betraying them."

"The ones with nothing to hide have nothing to fear," said Wager.

Stubbs softened it. "We'll go over the list for any probables, Mr. Yeager, and only interview the ones who might have some cause. Maybe none of them will."

The thin woman had the list waiting when they went out. At the top were half-a-dozen names of ex-employees and the dates of termination; below that was the roster of the still-employed ex-cons. Stubbs looked at it. "Twenty-seven more names," he said.

The secretary told them how to get to the employee lounge, a brightly painted room dominated by vending machines and molded-plastic furniture. A few minutes later both Barbara Jackson and Tony Purdy wandered in, puzzled at being called off the line. Neither had much that helped; Jackson talked to Green about the problem of noisy and dangerous dogs in her neighborhood, and Purdy complained about the beer drinkers who congregated every weekend in the small park across from his house. "They don't even live in the neighborhood. Kids, you know? Drive around and get somebody to buy beer for them, and then park their asses across the street and raise hell all night with their goddamn boom-boxes."

Neither knew Green personally, neither had ever been to his district office, neither knew if he spent much time with any of the other guests or if he seemed worried or if he left the party with anyone. In fact, they couldn't remember for sure when he did leave.

"For a famous man, he sure got invisible," said Stubbs.

Wager grunted an answer and turned to the next possibility on the list, the Prudential buffet. If they were lucky, something might turn up there. If not, they would go back to the four o'clock meeting, the one marked Dengren/Collins. A telephone call to the Prudential Development Corporation went through a series of operators, receptionists, and secretaries, and finally ended at the voice of an assistant to a vice president: "Councilman Green didn't make the reception, Detective Wager," she said.

"He didn't show at all?"

"No, sir. We have name tags for all the guests and he didn't pick his up."

"Could he have forgotten to?"

"I don't think so. I'm the one in charge of receptions, and I usually have a table at the door. Everyone who comes in goes past me."

"That's what you did on the eleventh?"

"Yes, sir. It's company policy to know who attends our functions."

Wager held the line open while he thought. "Did anyone else miss the party?"

"Only Councilman Green, thank goodness. I mean it was a pretty important function—at least we thought so. If too many councilpeople stand you up, well, that means a lot more work at the hearings."

"Did he call to say he wouldn't be there?"

"Just a moment." It was longer than that, but the voice finally came back. "No, we don't have him on the RSVP list at all."

"What time did the buffet end?"

"Eight. Six to eight."

"Thanks."

Stubbs looked over the notes in his own book. "Sonja Andersen said he left the furniture store at around seven-fifteen, latest. Yeager said he arrived maybe eight forty-five, maybe a little later."

"That time of night," said Wager, "it's a twenty-minute drive at most. More likely, fifteen."

"He could have stopped for gas, take a piss, whatever. But that still leaves almost an hour."

That was true. And though there might be plenty of common-sense explanations for the gap in time, Wager still wrote in large print on the leaf of his notebook: "Prudential buffet? 7:15–8:45 P.M.?"

CHAPTER 6

Friday, 13 June, 1133 Hours

The headquarters of the Northeast Denver Action Committee was a small house set among other small houses in one of the crowded residential blocks pushed against the fringes of downtown. Douglas Dengren had hazel eyes and could have been either white or black, but he chose to wear a high Afro and a small, elongated wooden head that dangled from a leather thong around his neck.

"I read about it this morning. There's a lot of anger among the people about it. Horace Green may not have been the finest councilman we've had, but he was one of us. We won't forget what happened to him."

"What did happen to him?" asked Wager.

"You're the police. Don't you know?"

"We're the police. We're trying to find out."

Stubbs stepped forward. "We're trying to trace his final activities, Mr. Dengren. We understand he had a meeting with you and Mr. Collins Wednesday afternoon around four-thirty."

"That's right."

"Care to tell us what it was about?"

"It was about progress. And the lack of it. It was about this neighborhood and all the others in his district like it. It was about the city's promises to its citizens and the breaking of those promises—promises that Horace Green made and promises that Horace Green broke!"

"You had a fight with him?"

"We had a discussion. For all the good it did."

"A discussion about what, Mr. Dengren?"

"About the people! About why Horace Green was betraying his own people to those who would reverse the gains we have fought so hard for in the past. About why he would help the exploitation of the poor and downtrodden, and why he would step on people whose only crime is their poverty and the color of their skin. That's something you whites"—his eyes shifted to Wager—"and you browns don't understand."

Wager listened to the cadences of the man's voice and wondered if he had a collection of Jesse Jackson records at home. "If you're talking about the mayor's downtown development plan, I thought Green was against that."

"He said so, didn't he? He said so in public I don't know how many times. But when it came time for the vote, you saw how he voted."

Wager hadn't seen. "How did he vote?"

"For the money—the *white* money!" Sixteen houses— homes to sixteen families who can't afford anything better than what the slumlord rents for twice what they're worth. But that was all those people had and now those houses are coming down, Mr. Policeman. They already got the wrecking crews over there. Not even twenty-four hours after the City Council voted, they got the wrecking crews over there, so white people can have a place to park their cars when they drive in from the lily-white suburbs. Sixteen black families out on the street for that!"

"This happened recently?"

"Monday night came the vote. Tuesday morning came the eviction. Wednesday morning came the wrecking crews. Oh, it was legal—Councilman Green saw to that. He saw to it that nobody would notice on first reading, four weeks ago, or on final reading, Monday night. A minor zoning change, that's all—nothing to call attention to. A quick little motion from Councilman Green's committee— two quick, little routine votes—and sixteen families were quickly shoved on the street. You didn't read about it in your racist papers, did you? It wasn't news like a black man holding up a white liquor store. No!"

"Where are these houses, Mr. Dengren?" Stubbs asked.

"Down on Tremont. Nineteen-hundred block of Tremont."

Wager made a note of the address. It wouldn't be the first time a politician said one thing and did another, and it was the kind of deal that mingled the odor of corruption with the perfume of profit. "What time did Green leave you?"

"About ten minutes after he got here. It was a short meeting—the good councilman didn't have much to say. Wasn't much he could say!"

"That would be about four-thirty? Four forty-five?"

"Just about."

"Did you see Green again after your meeting with him?"

"Did I have the opportunity as well as the motive to murder the man? Is that what you're asking me?"

"Did you see him any time later in the day or evening?"

"No. I don't travel in the same circles as Councilman Green, thank the Lord."

"What did Green say about the evictions?" asked Stubbs.

"He said he'd 'see what he could find out.' Find out! It come through his committee, he voted for it twice on the council, and then he starts saying he'll 'find out' about it. Now, that's a politician for you."

"Did the evicted people blame Green?" asked Wager.

"That is a good question. I made sure they knew whose fault it was. I made sure they knew the name of the Judas who sold out his own people. There's an election coming up."

Sixteen new names.

"But if you're thinking one of them did it, you're wrong. They're kind and decent people who just happen to be poor and black. God knows I wouldn't blame them if they did kill the Judas, but they're not that kind. They bow their heads under this latest injustice and cry out 'How long, O Lord!' "

"Do you have any idea who might have killed him?"

Dengren hesitated. "Word is, it was somebody who wanted to kill niggers. But I suppose you haven't heard that."

"Where did you hear it?"

"Around. It's what the street's saying. But of course the racist police will deny that, won't you?"

"If you have some facts to back that up, Mr. Dengren, we'd like to hear them," said Stubbs. "Do you know any-one—any names at all—who ever threatened to kill the councilman or any other Negro?"

"You never heard of the White Brotherhood?"

"That's a prison gang."

"That's where it started. It's outside the walls now. They have a chapter right here in Denver—hardshell honkies ready and eager to do the work of a racist society. They see the advance of the people toward justice and equality, and they are jealous. They see the growing power and might of those they despise and they are fearful! And yes—they have made threats, Mr. Policeman. Their very existence is based on that threat. You find them. You find them and you will find the killers of Councilman Green who, despite all his faults, was still one of the people. A leader of our people. And a target for those who would keep our spirit in bond-age. Find them, Mr. Policeman. If you got the guts!" He turned away.

"Salaam alaikem," said Wager.

1151 Hours

Stubbs had just turned the car toward downtown and the Administration Building when the radio popped their call number. "Lieutenant Wolfard wants to know your ten-twenty."

"We're on our way back now."

"Check with him as soon as you get in."

"Right."

Wolfard was waiting, his door open to the hallway's long axis so he could see which detectives headed where. "Come in, Les. Wager. What's turned up?"

From the top of the building, the low groan of the emergency siren began rising into its screaming wail—noon and the monthly test of warning equipment throughout the city, a reminder of weapons angled toward Denver from some concrete launch site far beyond the northern horizon. It wasn't something you thought about often: the mechanical ease with which an anchored, concrete city and all in it could be vaporized. Like the shifting, thin crust of the earth itself, like the fragility of life on the high desert around Denver, like your own death, it wasn't something you thought about. But every now and then something reminded you, and a fissure opened at your feet and you stared for a long moment into its blackness. The three of them held their silence through the aching shriek almost— it crossed Wager's mind—like a moment of prayer, and he remembered the weekly drills as a schoolchild crouching more in solemn meditation than fear beneath the thin protection of his plywood desk with its wads of old gum and occasional streaks of dried snot. He wondered if children were still doing that or if, like everyone else, they simply waited for the scream to end, trusting that it was only another pointless interruption in a world whose continuance was guaranteed.

When the siren's final groan died, Stubbs answered, telling the lieutenant about the Vitaco reception.

"No one saw him leave?"

"A Mr. Yeager. He walked him to the door. He said Green left alone."

"What about the list of ex-cons?"

"We'll get on that this afternoon."

Wolfard straightened a blank yellow tablet so that its edge matched the desk blotter. "I've had calls from the *Post* and the *News* about this. I suppose you saw the headlines this morning."

Both papers had bannered CITY COUNCILMAN SLAIN and filled over half the front pages with story and pictures. Wager had spotted himself in the background in one of the photographs of the scene, and the reporter—Gargan—had implied that the police were being uncooperative with the press. "Yes."

"The television people are bugging me, too. One of the reports floating around is that the killing's racially motivated. Did either of you people say anything to anybody about that threat to Mrs. Green?"

"No, sir," said Stubbs.

"Well, somebody put the word out on it. I've been getting calls all damned morning. What have you turned up from that angle?"

Stubbs told him.

"The White Brotherhood?"

"Dengren said that."

"Jesus—that's all we need for a race riot." Wolfard straightened his desk calendar. "Pressure, gentlemen. There's a lot of pressure to get this one cleared up as soon as possible, and not just because he was a councilman. The race issue . . ." From down the hallway, a sudden pause in the noise of telephones half drew Wager's attention for its oddness; then the ringing began again and filled in the background like distant crickets. "We don't want to go back to the sixties and seventies, do we? 'Burn, baby, burn' and all that."

Wager figured the lieutenant was working around to something instead of just wasting time. He hoped the lieutenant was working around to something.

"Pressure," he said again. Then, "Do you need help on this?"

"Right now, Stubbs and I can handle it, Lieutenant. Anybody else, we'd just be tripping over each other."

"You're sure? Les is a good officer, and he's learning fast. But he's new."

Wager was sure.

"Well, that's a relief, anyway. We're shorthanded as hell. Ashcroft's on temporary assignment and Ross has his leave coming up." He leaned back and gazed at them and Wager saw that the man was becoming painfully aware of the distance that his new administrative rank had carried him from the street cops. "The chief called again this morning. I didn't have much to tell him."

They waited.

"Well, drop everything else and take what overtime you need. If anything comes in, turn it over to Devereaux or Golding—their caseloads are the lightest right now. Let's focus on the racist angle—that's the most explosive possibility. Check with me later this afternoon and let me know what you have."

1206 Hours

The homicide detectives' desks were around the corner from the lieutenant's office, just out of sight but close enough for voices to carry, and Wager had the feeling of Wolfard's ear stretching out behind them.

"What's next?" Stubbs, a fresh cup of coffee in his fist, settled with a sigh at his desk and noted the papers and memos beginning to pile up.

"Get the landlords of those apartments—find out the names of those sixteen families who were evicted."

"The lieutenant said to work on the racist angle."

"They're black, aren't they? That's racial, isn't it?" Wager pushed away from his desk. "I'll be over in Assault, then upstairs in Intelligence."

Nick Papadopoulos was eating a brown-bag lunch at his desk, one of two tucked into an almost-quiet corner behind a partition framing the shift sergeant's office. He looked up when Wager came around the corner. "I got your note." Stuffing the last bite of something that looked like a meat pie into his mouth, he licked the juice off his fingers. "What's it all about?"

A lanky man with a bald patch running back from his forehead, his glasses made him look more like a teacher than a cop. Wager hadn't worked with him but heard from other people in Assault that he was pretty good; he consistently had one of the highest clearance rates in the section. "What's that you're eating?"

"*Spanakopittas*—spinach and meat pie. The wife makes them. They're good." He began cutting hunks off a slab of white cheese and reached into a small plastic bowl of black olives. "Want some? *Feta* and *kalamatas*. A lot of energy and not much in calories or bulk."

Wager shook his head and wondered if he ought to introduce Papadopoulos to Golding. Maybe they could develop a line of color-coded ethnic food. "What's the rap on Franklin and Roberts?"

Papadopoulos rattled an olive pit into his wastebasket. "Arson, assault with intent. Those are the big ones."

"What'd they do?"

"The complainant, one Matthias McKeever, states that said Franklin and Roberts first threatened to burn down his place of business and subsequently attempted same. And that when he reported their attempt to the police, said defendants did assault him about the head and shoulders with their fists and further attempt to terminate his life in a most painful manner."

"They're out on bond?"

"Said Franklin and Roberts haven't been formally charged yet—I want to fill in some holes in the paperwork. They're still in the pokey." He spit out another olive pit. "What's your interest?"

"I want to know how hard it'll be to spring them."

Papadopoulos's jaw stopped moving and he leaned back to look up at Wager. "Goddamned hard. They're a couple of cheap punks who were shaking this citizen down. They take this fall, they have a third felony inside ten years. Career criminals—and they're off the streets for a long time."

"It's McKeever's word against theirs?"

"Yeah. Plus the testimony of Mr. Bruises and Mr. Contusions. He didn't get them falling down stairs." He popped another hunk of cheese into his mouth and spoke around it. "Why do you want them out?"

"They work for somebody I owe a favor to. I told him I'd see what I could find out about it."

"That's a big favor."

Wager shrugged. "I owe him that much. I don't owe him my badge."

Papadopoulos shook his head. "I want these two off the streets. And I don't owe your friend a damn thing."

The rest of it was that he didn't owe Wager anything, either. "That's what I'll tell him, then."

The Intelligence office was on an upper floor and removed from the steady bustle and jingle of Crimes Against Persons. Wager stifled his irritation at Papadopoulos's abruptness by reminding himself that Franklin and Roberts got their own tails in that crack, and he couldn't work miracles no matter what Fat Willy thought he was owed. And, by God, Wager really didn't want to—it sounded like they were getting what they deserved. But he had stuck his neck out and asked; if Willy wasn't satisfied with that, to hell with him.

Through the door's glass panel, he could see the long row of filing cabinets and extra computer terminals that cramped the space, and he had to knock loudly on the security door to get someone's attention. Finally, a head popped around the corner to look and a buzzer cleared the lock.

"Gabe—don't tell me you want some intelligence?" Marty Martinez, another of the patrolmen like Adamo who had made the grade to detective two or three lists ago, unlocked the door and shook hands. He had been a first-rate patrolman, and Wager was glad to see the promotion.

"If I ever took some, you wouldn't have any left. How's Lynette and the kids?" He never could remember children's names.

Martinez, leading him past some desks to his own, told him, and then asked Wager about his health and life. "I heard what happened to Jo," he said. "She was good people. I'm sorry."

"So am I." But sorry never brought anyone back. "What do you know about the White Brotherhood?"

"Not much. If it wasn't for business, you wouldn't come by here, would you?"

"I've been meaning to—busy, that's all. Do you have anything on them?"

"Let me see what we've got. How soon do you need it?"

"Ten minutes ago."

"Yeah—right." He pointed to a stack of brown dossiers marked with bright sensitivity codes. Beside them, a half-eaten sandwich and a cup of steaming coffee said that he, like Wager, was working through his lunch hour. "I got a deadline on this, too."

Wager wouldn't have said it was a rush job if it wasn't, and he thought Martinez should have known that. "It's a V.I.P. homicide. Councilman Green."

"You're on that?" He heaved a deep breath and pushed back in his chair. "OK—the whole goddamned department's running around like a bunch of chickens with their heads cut off over that one. So why not me, too?" He carted the folders to a safe and locked them away, turning up the green side of the cardboard flag that straddled the dial. "Let's punch it up—if they've got the mainframe on line, yet."

Wager followed Martinez to a computer terminal and watched while he clattered a series of code letters into the machine. A few seconds later the reply lined across the screen and Martinez began typing again. On a bulletin board near the terminal, someone had tacked up a wanted notice for "Dudley Doberman, height 2′4″, weight 85 lbs., eyes brown, hair red and brown, alias Dog Face." Two blurry photographs showed a Doberman pinscher dressed in a coat and tie, wearing a hat, and dangling a cigarette from the corner of its mouth. The rap sheet listed "K-9 rape, impersonating a human being, and flight to avoid the animal control officer." Someone had scrawled under one of the photographs, "Hansen—he looks like your sister." Squad room humor hadn't changed since Wager was in the Marine Corps.

"OK," said Martinez. "Now let's run it." He pressed another series of buttons and the printer began to chatter. The top of the sheet held a date stamp and a notice: CONFIDENTIAL. Beneath that were "Reliability Code B" and "Content of Report 2." Wager recollected from some long-past training session that the heading meant the information could be shared with law enforcement officials on a need-to-know basis, that its source was known and reliable, and that the material itself was probably true. A few moments later, he and Wager read the printout:

The White Brotherhood is a loose federation of chapters advocating white supremacy. Apparently originating in California at San Quentin, it is a reaction to several gangs of blacks who had banded together to take control of the institution's illicit activities and to intimidate the white prisoners. Affiliated with the Hell's Angels, chapters began to appear in other prisons that held members of the motorcycle gang. The chapter in Colorado's Canyon City Maximum Security Prison was founded around 1972 and, like other chapters, now includes a large number of white prisoners not known to belong to patch gangs. A recent disturbing trend is the expansion of chapters from prison into the civilian population. Released and paroled members maintain their prison contacts, and it is probable that the outside chapters serve as means of supplying drugs and other contraband for chapter members to sell inside. The Denver chapter dates from around 1980. Previously reliable informants state that the current number is around twenty-five active members with an undefined number of affiliate members, both men and women.

Wager began jotting names and addresses from the list of known or suspected members, and he recognized a couple of them—Benjamin ("Sonny") Pickett, whom Wager had busted for pushing heroin almost ten years ago; and Jerome H. Davis, a.k.a. "Big Nose Smith." Davis had been a suspected triggerman in a gang killing four years ago. Suspected, hell, he did it; but nothing could be brought into court to prove it because all the witnesses were gang members.

"I didn't know Big Nose was back in town."

Martinez, looking at the name, shrugged. "I haven't been

following them. That's Norm Fullerton, but he's off-duty now."

"When's he in?"

"Tomorrow—he's got the weekend."

Wager finished copying the list of members and put Fullerton's name in a little circle above them. Martinez walked him to the security door and pressed the unlock buzzer.

"Let's go for a beer sometimes, Gabe."

"Sounds good."

"I mean it, man. Be good to talk with you."

Wager meant it, too. But by the time he reached the elevator, his mind was already lining up the afternoon. He found Stubbs back at his desk with a telephone stuck to his ear and waited for the man to hang up before he showed him the list of White Brotherhood members.

"Another twenty-five people? Holy shit, Wager!"

"We won't have to talk to more than a couple, Stubbs; they'll all have the same story."

He sighed and wagged the telephone. "I called one landlord for the names of tenants. I've located six of the families; Elaine's working on the other landlords."

That was one of the civilian secretaries hired to relieve officers of as much routine work as possible. It was the kind of job she liked, and even now Wager could hear the nasal voice, smug in identifying itself with the power of the state, "This is Elaine Spiska with the Denver Police Department, Mr. Goodrich. You were the owner of some rental properties in the nineteen-hundred block of Tremont? Would you mind answering a couple questions about your tenants?"

"Wager!" Wolfard's voice snaked around the corner to pull him into the lieutenant's office. "I thought I heard you out there—I just got a call from Councilperson Voss. She wants to talk with you about the case."

"It's a current investigation. It's confidential."

"I realize that, Wager. But she's also the president of the City Council. That's not somebody you just say no to."

He could have reminded Wolfard that a lieutenant was supposed to intercept crap like that so the detectives could do their jobs. But the pinch of worry between the man's eyebrows told Wager that it wasn't something Wolfard wanted argued.

"I told her you'd be over to her office in ten minutes."

"Thanks."

"You, ah, have any idea why she asked for you?"

"What do you mean?"

"I mean do you know the woman?"

What he meant was what kind of political clout might Wager have. "Sure. We're old buddies."

"I see." Wolfard rearranged his pencil cup. "Check with me when you get back, OK?"

He wasn't an old buddy of the council president; he knew only her name and picture from the newspapers, but it wouldn't hurt Wolfard to wonder a little. A cop who chose to leave the streets for administration should pick up a few distinguished gray hairs. In fact, as he walked across a busy Fourteenth Avenue toward the granite-colored block of the Civic Center, Wager was puzzled, too.

1250 Hours

The elevator doors closed on the echoing clatter of voices and shoes that filled the tall hallway of the first floor. It was the noisy and nervous shuffle of citizens drawn into the business of the City and County of Denver: court appearances, marriage licenses, traffic hearings—a steady swirl of curious eyes and preoccupied faces that Wager had long since grown used to. Less familiar was the hushed vacancy of the fourth-floor corridor whose polished aggregate seemed larger and more solemn because of its emptiness. A sign in one recessed corner said SHERIFF'S AREA, DON'T LOITER, marking the holding rooms for prisoners waiting trial in the downstairs courtrooms. Across from the elevators, a bulletin board lit by fluorescent lights was mostly empty and dwarfed by the dimness of the high ceiling. It held the current agenda of the council, notes of the last Water Board meeting, and a bulletin from the Citizens Advisory Board. A maintenance man in a light-blue shirt with an I.D. badge pushed an oiled mop far down the gleaming corridor, and in the quiet, Wager could hear the rhythmic pop of the man's chewing gum.

Shiny black paint spelled ELIZABETH VOSS, COUNCIL-WOMAN-AT-LARGE on the frosted glass of a large door, and behind it the yellow light showed a vague shadow move across the room as Wager knocked.

"Come in. You're Detective Wager?"

"Yes, ma'am." The councilperson was brisk and brunette, with a firm handshake. Somewhere in her late thirties, she wore a dress that reminded Wager of a man's gray business suit. He closed the door to the office whose ceiling seemed as high as the room was long and sat in the chair that Voss nodded toward.

"You're the homicide detective investigating Horace Green's murder?"

"One of them. Yes, ma'am."

"I didn't realize you were a minority. Your name, I mean; it's not Hispanic."

"Does that have something to do with Councilman Green's death?"

The woman's dark eyes hardened and Wager had a sense of what she might have done to win her seat on the City Council. "It might, Officer Wager. It just might, indeed."

She leaned back in the padded swivel chair to look out the single window that opened to the muted light of an air shaft and another window just like it. "I've heard rumors that Horace's death was racially motivated."

Wager hesitated; here was another administrator looking out another window. The woman might be a city official, but she was still a civilian, and the proper person for her to talk with was the chief. Or even Wolfard. "That's one of the possibilities we're investigating."

A slight smile momentarily lifted one corner of her mouth. "Do the police memorize lines like that?"

There was nothing funny about it in Wager's mind.

And the glint of humor passed quickly. "If there is truth to that rumor, I don't have to tell you how serious something like this could be for our community."

"No, you don't."

"You're a minority. You can understand how our black minority must feel. And how a few intemperate individuals—black or white—could quickly destroy all the progress we've made in the last few years."

Wager didn't consider himself a minority; he was an individual. And he wished she would quit wasting his time with her platitudes. Stubbs probably had a complete list of the evicted tenants by now, and would be sitting around until Wager got back to tell him what to do next. They still had to chase down the White Brotherhood. Today was Friday, and about one minute after five those people would be on their motorcycles and gone for the weekend.

"And conversely," she went on, "if Councilman Green was killed for some other reason—some reason that reflected . . . adversely . . . on his role as a leader in our black community—that, too, could harm race relations."

"What was that?"

"I'm not talking for my own pleasure, Officer Wager." She folded her hands in front of her face; a large diamond glinted on a right finger, but her left was bare of rings. "This is a delicate issue and I expect the courtesy of your attention."

"Yes, ma'am. What do you mean, 'some other reason'?"

"As president of the City Council, my job is to oversee its activities in the broadest sense. I ensure that the city's business gets done effectively and expeditiously, and that council members, despite wide differences of opinion or personal philosophy, contribute to the welfare of Denver's citizens."

Wager wished the damned woman would quit sneaking up on whatever she was trying to say and just state it. " 'Some other reason,' ma'am?"

She took a deep breath. "I have heard from a confidential source that Councilman Green may have been involved in a possible malfeasance."

"What kind?"

"I said possible. The information—well, it's no more than a rumor. But it came from someone who seemed genuinely worried. And," she rocked forward in the chair and turned her face to the desk, "to judge from some of the facts, it's conceivable."

"A homicide's involved, Councilman Voss." Wager cited the familiar phrases from the Manual, "If you have information or evidence pertaining to a felony, it's your duty to reveal it. Failure to do so could bring a charge of accessory." He added, "With a homicide, that means a Class Five felony."

The woman's dark eyes widened with heat. "I know damned well what it means, Officer. And I also know something about privileged communications and disclosure. And I would not have called you over here if I had any intention of withholding information." She paused to let that sink in. "What I am trying to impress on you is the delicacy of this. We are talking possibility and rumor, not fact. And we are dealing with a man who is a symbol—a highly emotional symbol—for a large segment of our city."

"We're also talking murder. And information that might lead to arresting a killer."

Voss swung her chair toward him and looked at him with an icy interest. "I wonder if this was a mistake," she said half to herself. "I thought I was doing the right thing, and that I was doing it the right way. Now, I'm not so certain."

"It is the right thing to report what you know about a crime." But Wager understood her question and had one of his own. "Why didn't you go to the chief with this?"

"Because I want as few people as possible to know about it. The chief would have to give you the information, anyway. I decided to cut out the middleman." The dry tone slipped into anger, "But you seem intent on charging in at full speed, making as much noise as you can. Tell me, Officer"—the chair swiveled back—"is pig-headedness issued with that badge?"

The Spanish lilt that came when he was angry colored his voice. "My sworn duty is to locate and apprehend criminals, Councilperson. Sworn to the city and its people, not to you. That's what I do, lady, and I do a good job at it." It was Wager's turn to let things sink in. "I don't want to start a race riot, either. And I don't want to ruin Green's or anybody else's reputation. But I do want his killer. And I'll tell you this: If we don't find him—and soon—there's a lot bigger chance of a riot. Now, why don't you tell me what you know so I can carry out my duties."

The woman's mouth was a tight line of something stifled, but Wager didn't care much about that. And if *she* cared, she hid it for a later, more advantageous time; she took another deep breath and the anger left her voice just as quickly as the humor had earlier. "Do you know what committee the councilman chaired?"

"Zoning, Planning, and Land-Use."

She seemed slightly surprised that he would know. "Then you can understand the pressures that property owners and developers bring to the members of that committee."

Wager could. Depending on the proposed zoning change or usage planning, a fortune could be made—and split among several pockets. There were checks and balances to guard against that kind of profiteering—public hearings, published records, review by a series of other committees and boards as well as by the mayor's office and staff. But, as Dengren had implied, certain favors could be done. "He was manipulating something?"

"That's the problem; it's not all that clear. All contracts of a value of over $500,000 need the City Council's approval. If someone out at Stapleton Airport, for example, wants to sell ice cream on city property, and if their gross receipts are over a half-million, they need a vote by City Council to do business. Usually, these are fairly routine; the appropriate committee holds its hearings and reports its findings to the council, and the council generally votes to support the recommendation of the committee. But some issues get a lot of discussion; land use is one—a zoning change or application that brings a lot of traffic to a neighborhood. Nonetheless, a large number of proposed changes are routine, and if, on first or second reading, no one raises a fuss over it, the council tends to pass it. Especially if the councilman whose district the change affects is in favor of it, and if the Zoning Committee is in favor of it. When you add up the number of zoning or land-use changes referred

over a couple of years to the committee, it involves a tre-
mendous amount of money."

"You're telling me the councilman was getting kickbacks
for helping people get zoning changes and city contracts?"

Voss ran her ringless hand through medium-length hair
and nervously shook a tangle out of the large curls. "As
council president, I appointed Horace to that committee.
One of the things at the back of any council president's
mind is the integrity of the people she appoints to key
committees like Zoning." A wry smile. "It's never mentioned, of course. A person who becomes a councilman is
assumed to act in good faith—sort of a baptism by election. But only a fool wouldn't ask herself that question before appointing the chair of Zoning. And I had no doubts
at all about Horace's honesty. I'm not sure I do now . . .
but . . ."

"But somebody told you something."

"Someone told me something."

"What?"

"That Horace . . ." She paused. "Will you promise to keep
this to yourself?"

"The lieutenant knows you called me over here. He'll
want to know why."

"I don't want him or anyone else to learn about this. If
word gets around that Horace Green is being investigated,
people are going to scream that the police—and the city—
are trying to cover up for a racist killer. And if it comes out
that there were no grounds for suspicion after all, the city
and the police are going to lose completely what little trust
we've earned among the black community."

Wager often had the feeling that the fear of losing trust
was a kind of blackmail; he'd heard police administrations
speak of cops doing things that would cost the trust of a
minority group. And then heard from members of that
group—Chicano, black, Native American, Korean, Viet-
namese, whatever—cynical laughter about manipulating
the cops and never trusting the sons-of-bitches anyway. But
the belief was a truism now, and, on very rare occasions,
Wager had seen results: the Chicano kid who offered a
sweating traffic cop a glass of lemonade, the letter from a

black whom Wager had put in prison, thanking him for helping his wife and daughter get through a hard time. Besides, Councilperson Voss wasn't going to tell him a thing if he didn't go along with the party line. "I can tell the lieutenant you wanted to ask about the investigation. I don't have to say you wanted to tell me something, too." A half truth was good enough for a half-assed lieutenant, anyway.

Again that little smile. "Perhaps you should think of politics, Officer Wager."

"I'm thinking of Horace Green, ma'am."

The smile died. "Yes. You would, of course. Well, then, I was told that he had received a fee for a zoning change that made a certain contractor a large amount of money."

"I'll need names."

"I wasn't told any names."

"You don't know who the contractor was?"

"No."

"Do you know which job?"

"Not for certain. Something in his district, though. As I understand it, the contractor needed a down-zoning change to erect some kind of multiuse building in a residential area. It was in Horace's district and he reported it to the committee. He supported the change and it went through. But—and here's the real issue—the data he used to get it passed was apparently slanted and even perhaps untrue. There have been recent questions from the City Planning Office about the water and sewer capabilities, as well as powerlines and setbacks. But that came after construction was well underway. The original proposals and specifications reported made no mention of these potential problems and, equally importantly, de-emphasized neighborhood reaction to the proposed change."

"What makes you think it was Green's fault and not the contractor's? Wouldn't the contractor provide all that information?"

"That's one of the gray areas. The contractor does provide the plans and specifications; they're reviewed and verified by the city inspectors before any hearings are held. The City Council staff researches the overall impact of, and the neighborhood response to, the proposal and packages everything for the councilman. He makes his decision and goes to the committee with any recommendation he may have."

"This one didn't follow the usual route?"

"The city inspectors raised some questions about the plans—I checked that out with the informant before calling you. But their documents were apparently lost somewhere between their office and the presentation to the committee. The rest of the presentation was highly favorable and Horace spoke for it."

"The inspectors don't sit in on the hearings?"

"Only if they're called."

He weighed what she told him. "So Green may or may not have been aware of the misrepresentation?"

"I don't think he was. I can't think that."

"You said something about a payoff?"

"There's no proof. But a contractor with that much at stake is likely to want some insurance. And I was told there had been a payoff."

"Who's your informant?"

"I'm not at liberty to say." She added, "But it's someone who would know. And they think it's probable."

She didn't have to tell him. Not now, anyway. But in the back of his mind, Wager was thinking Grand Jury. If they asked the questions, Voss—council president or not— would be answering. Unless some lawyer got her off the hook and hung him in her place.

"Can you give me some idea of people I can talk to for a start?"

Again that caution, but finally she said, "Ray Albro might be someone worth speaking to. He's vice chairman of the Zoning Committee. And Horace's aide, of course, Julia Wilfong."

Wager jotted the names down under the heading "Voss."

"But for goodness' sake, please remember how sensitive all this is. And please don't tell them who referred you."

"Yes, ma'am." He asked something that had been itching at the back of his mind. "You went to the Prudential buffet Wednesday night?"

"Yes."

"Did you see Green there?"

She thought back. "I can't remember seeing him. But there were a lot of people—I really don't know if he was there or not."

"Was it important that he be there?"

"It was an important presentation, yes. Especially for the Zoning Committee. Prudential wants to develop part of the old railroad yards, and they had a model and slide show of the project. He should have been there."

Wager stayed for a few more questions and then rose to go.

"Please remember that it's not only Horace's reputation and the effect such a disclosure would have on his family, but also the impact it might have on the black community. You must be very careful with this information."

"I understand." And he understood, too, that it wasn't only Green's reputation but her own that would suffer. Which was probably why she hadn't gone to the D.A.'s office with it: City Council had a lot more control over the Police Department than over the D.A.'s office.

CHAPTER 7

Wolfard had his eye on the hallway when Wager, hoping that Stubbs had finished his chore, hustled back.

"Wager—in here." Wolfard waved him to a seat with a forefinger. "Well? What was all that about?"

"She wanted information on the investigation—if we had any suspects yet, that kind of thing."

"That's all? She could have asked me that."

Wager shrugged. "She said she wanted to cut out the middleman."

"Middleman? Me?" The lieutenant sagged back in his chair. "That's a bunch of crap."

"Her words, Lieutenant. Not mine."

"Jesus. So what'd you tell her?"

"I gave her what we have. It didn't take long."

"Did she make any comments?"

"She's worried about race relations. She told me how important Green was to the black community."

"Yeah, well, that's what I've been saying. But that's it? That's all she wanted?"

Here came the outright lie and Wager kept his face and eyes still and unblinking as he gazed back at Wolfard's pale-blue ones: "That's it."

With a curt nod, the lieutenant dismissed him and Wager went quickly around the corner to the detectives' office. Stubbs had his lunch spread across his desk and was chewing an apple and grunting into the telephone. He saw Wager and pointed at a list anchored by a small can of tapioca pudding. "Tenants," he said away from the telephone, and then into the mouthpiece, "Yessir. Davis, Jerome H. That's right. Thank you."

The taste of the lie was still sour on Wager's tongue as he read down the names of those evicted by Green's vote. The list wasn't complete, but it had most of them, and Wager was pleased that Stubbs had been busy.

The man hung up the telephone. "I wasn't sure when you'd be back, so I called the parole board about those White Brotherhood people, the names Martinez gave you. Sonny Pickett's p.o. tells me he's working construction over on East Colfax. I can't get a thing on Big Nose Smith—he's off parole. What happened over at the CC building?"

"I'll tell you in the car."

He did, most of it. Stubbs's foot lifted slightly from the accelerator, and the unmarked cruiser slowed a bit in the surge of traffic between red lights. "Some kind of payoff?"

"Maybe. Maybe not. The source wasn't all that clear about it."

"That puts you way out on the end of a little bitty limb, Wager. And me with you."

"Just me. I never told you about it. And you won't tell anyone else."

"Right, sure. But holy shit, Gabe, you didn't have to promise one damned thing to whoever told you. You should have stopped them right there and told them to save it for the chief."

"I don't think the person would have told anybody. Then where would we be?"

"We wouldn't be up shit's creek."

"It's only a rumor. That's the whole point."

"I understand that. But what it means is they want it

looked into. They want it done without getting tied to it. If something pops, they'll deny they ever told you or anyone else a thing."

That was true.

"It's politics, Wager!"

That was true, too. But there was one other truth that outweighed all that: "It's also a lead."

The construction job was more a destruction job, at least so far; a crew was slowly dismantling an old hotel that had served as a nightclub and whorehouse to rebuild it into a combination retail and office building. It was a "historic landmark"—for some reason Denver's preservationists wanted future generations to admire old churches, breweries, and brothels. A few blocks east of the state capitol on Colfax, the site was marked by a façade of rawly stripped brick and cast-concrete ornaments, and by sheets of flopping plastic over the glassless holes of windows, to protect the busy street from the dust and occasional explosions of splinters and chips. Stubbs set the cruiser in a yellow zone and flipped down the visor with its police identification; Wager found a slit in the mesh fence and went past a sign that warned against trespassing. A springy plywood ramp led up to a ragged hole in the brick wall and into a barnlike first floor whose steel piers showed where partitions used to be. Above them, on the other side of thick planks that formed the floorboards of the second story, the brief ratcheting clatter of an air hammer was followed by a startled hoot and a loud crash and a cackle of high-pitched laughter.

"Wouldn't you know Sonny could find a job where he'd be paid for trashing a place?"

Wager stepped carefully over a splintered two-by-four that lay with long nails aimed skyward. Another ramp, this one lined with strips of lath, led to all the excitement above.

A young man in a yellow hardhat and stained muscle shirt wrestled a wheelbarrow load of old brick toward another hole in the back of the building. "Below!" he called without bothering to look, and dumped the load into space. Turning, he was surprised to see Stubbs and Wager watching him. "You looking for Mark? He's out back, in the trailer."

"Who's Mark?" asked Wager.

"Foreman. Who you looking for?"

"Sonny Pickett."

"Pickett?" The man, in his late teens or early twenties, was coated with brick dust that had channels of sweat carved down his chest and ribs. "No Pickett on this crew."

"He's a big guy," said Wager. "Beard, tattoos, the whole bit."

"Great big?"

"Right."

"Must be the guy working on the elevators. I don't know his name, but goddamn, he's big, all right." He gestured across the open floor toward a cluster of beams that formed a kind of open cage. "He's working in the shaft, down in the basement."

Wager peeked down the hole surrounded by the skeleton of iron. Far below, the white glare of an unshaded bulb lit a hulking figure humped over a tangle of greasy metal. Even from this distance of three stories, he recognized Sonny.

They went back down and stopped at the top of a ladder dropping into a square hole in the concrete floor. "Pickett?"

A broad, bearded face looked up. The hairy flesh over the cheekbones swelled with gristle that dwarfed the man's tiny, snub nose and made his eyes look smaller than they were. "I know you."

"Detective Wager, Denver Police. I busted you a few years back. I'd like to ask you some questions."

The face turned back to its work, showing Wager a sweaty tangle of long black hair that wasn't much different from the front. In no hurry, he hooked his hands under the shaft of a large electric motor and, with a fluid motion that was surprisingly quick, stood to heave the machine to his shoulder. Then, ponderously, he turned and climbed the ladder, each step swaying the creaking two-by-fours that formed its rails. They stepped back to let Pickett out, first the broad hand and forearm gripping the barrel of the motor, then the hairy head canted against the weight, then the rest of him, a cannonball of a man whose bulk beneath the sleeveless overalls looked fat but was really solid flesh and bone. He tilted the elevator motor off his shoulder and swung it heavily to the scarred wooden floor.

"What's that thing weigh?" Stubbs asked.

Pickett kicked it thoughtfully with the toe of his motorcycle boot. "Three-fifty, four, maybe." He looked from Stubbs to Wager, eyes sleepy beneath the wet ringlets of black hair. "What you want to ask?"

"We want to know about the White Brotherhood."

Pickett grunted and reached to scratch one massive arm with a finger that left a smear of grease across a tattoo. An eagle, it looked like, wings spread and a banner in its beak reading "Liberty or Die." "Yeah. I'm a member. So what?"

"So did the Brotherhood have anything to do with the death of Councilman Green?"

"Who?"

"The city councilman who got shot a couple days ago— the black councilman."

Pickett looked down at Wager. "What the hell kind of question is that, man?"

"The word going around is that it was a racist killing. The White Brotherhood's racist. What do you know about it?"

"I don't know shit about it. And I don't care. One less nigger, fine. But don't lay it off on me."

"I looked over your jacket, Sonny. You're on probation for another eighteen months."

"So?"

"So you can go back in if I don't like the way you look."

The shape seemed to grow wider and Pickett swayed forward like a leaning tree. "Why you hassling me, man?"

Sonny wasn't all that dumb, but like a lot of big men he acted dull and brutal to heighten the sense of threat and to mask the vulnerability of intelligence. It reminded Wager of a high school football player's act. "To get answers, Pickett. If you know something, tell us. Because it's your ass if you don't."

"I never heard of that son of a bitch."

"The Brotherhood hates blacks. Maybe somebody decided to stir things up."

The eyebrows pinched together under their fringe of damp ringlets as he traced Wager's meaning. "You want me to fink? Is that it? You want me to be one of your fucking 'confidential informants'? That what you want?"

"That's it."

"No way."

"Eighteen months, Sonny. All I do is blink my eyes and you go up for a year and a half."

The large head that seemed to rest directly on the thick, sloping shoulders wagged once. "No."

Wager held out one of his business cards with a penciled number on the back. When the man's arm didn't move, he tucked it into the front of the greasy overalls. "If it was some of the Brotherhood and you find out about it, it's you or them. If you don't tell us and we find out—it's you and them."

They left the man staring after them and scratching vaguely at the place where the card had fallen inside his sleeveless overalls. In the car, Stubbs shook his head. "He's not going to turn, Gabe. Doing eighteen months is nothing for him; hell, he can hold his breath that long."

"The way it smelled, he should. But his jacket says he just had a baby daughter and he's buying a house out in Commerce City. It's not just his ass hanging in the breeze and he knows it."

Stubbs was doubtful. "If word gets out he finked, he'll be just one big target. He's not going to do it."

"Maybe not. But we'll see. If anything's there, he just might shake enough dust to make somebody sneeze."

1522 Hours

Stubbs had the list of names and addresses of the evicted tenants, and now he and Wager would probe to see which might hold a grudge against Green. By this time most had scattered into other housing in the neighboring North Capitol Hill and Five Points areas; some had disappeared, leaving no forwarding address, no telephone numbers where bills might catch up with them. But many of the families who had just moved were single women with children who needed their ADC checks and made it easy for the mailman to find them. Most had no idea that Councilman Green had any responsibility at all for the eviction—"They going to put up a parking lot, so they made us move, that's all"—and a large number did not even know who Councilman Green was. A few knew and were angry.

"I heard what I heard. That Councilman Green, he voted to throw us out, that's what I heard."

"Have you ever met the man or seen him, Mrs. Dent?"

"No, and I sure don't want to. I'm not sure what I'd do to that man."

"You know he was murdered?"

"He what? Somebody killed him?"

"Yes, ma'am." Wager studied the broad face as she seemed to hear the news for the first time. Behind her in the tiny, hot apartment that opened from a door roughly chopped into the side of the frame house, a girl about fifteen sullenly nursed a heat-sprawled child.

"Well, he didn't deserve that."

"Do you know anyone who might have thought he deserved it? Anyone evicted who said anything about getting even?"

"No. And nobody would around me. I'm a church woman, praise be the Lord." She spoke over her shoulder, "Claudine, you hear what this man say?"

"Yes'm."

"You know anything about it?"

"No, Mama."

"You sure now? We talking a killing here, girl. One of the Lord's Commandments already been broke around here and I don't want you breaking another being a false witness."

Wager was unsure which Commandment the woman was talking about—killing or adultery—but it made little difference; the sullen girl shook her head. "I don't know nothing about it, Mama."

The questioning dragged into the dinner hour when the heat and odors of cooking began to seep through the open doors and mingle with the smell of the heavy Friday afternoon traffic. The sun was still three hours above the jagged outline of the mountains west of town, and it would be longer than that before its weight began to lift and the cramped and airless rooms started to cool. Now, the inhabitants sought relief on porches and on steps that caught a strip of shade, the men still in their work clothes or peeled to undershirts and pulling on a can of beer, the women stepping away from the heat of stoves to take a deep breath. Everywhere, impervious to the heat, children flowed in clusters, their voices high, birdlike sounds sharper than the steady rush of the traffic they dodged through.

They were two-thirds of the way down the list when Stubbs pulled to the curb in front of a small, brown-brick house sandwiched between two apartment buildings. He and Wager got out, an assortment of kids drawing back from the curb to eye them in curious silence. Even the six- and seven-year-olds recognized detectives, and cops meant some kind of excitement, and maybe even trouble for somebody.

On the porch, in silent suspicion, a gray-haired woman rocked slowly and stared at them. Beside her, two young men in grimy tank tops sat and stared, too. Wager caught the eyes of the one he recognized, and the man blinked and slowly tilted his head to spit something between his feet.

"Denver Police," said Stubbs. "We're looking for Mrs. Bliscomb."

"What you want with them?" The woman kept rocking, the unhidden anger in her eyes making them dark and wet.

"Ask a few questions. I hear she moved in with you."

"She ain't done nothing." The woman added, "Officer."

"She's not wanted for anything," said Stubbs pleasantly. "We just want to ask her some questions."

"About what?"

"That's between her and us, Mrs. Wells." Wager glanced at the larger of the two youths whose closed faces said how much they hated cops. "How are you, Edward? Keeping out of trouble?"

"I'm doing all right."

Which meant he hadn't been caught. The Wells brothers and their mother were familiar names in the burglary division; the kids did the stealing, the mother did the fencing. The two sons had long juvenile records, though the oldest, now that he had turned eighteen, had become cautious. Beyond the water-starved hedge at one end of the porch, Wager saw the bobbing heads of children sneaking close to see what was going down—to find out what the police wanted with the Wellses this time so they could carry the story breathless and get the attention of the older kids and grown-ups at home. Wager remembered the awed and scary feeling he used to have as a kid when the Gonzales family, who generated a lot of whispers among the grownups in the Auraria barrio, used to be visited by the Anglo police. Pato Gonzales would always look for a fight after the cops came to get one of his older brothers; it was his way of telling Wager and the other kids he wasn't afraid of them or Anglo cops or anybody. The last Wager heard, Pato was in jail in Texas.

"It's about a homicide," Stubbs explained. "A murder."

"Who she supposed to kill?"

"Nobody. We just want to ask her some questions. Is she here?"

The woman's eyes flicked to her younger son, Edgar, and he heaved himself carelessly off the stone of the porch wall. A few moments later, a woman came nervously onto the porch; Edgar leaned silently against the door frame and watched.

"Mrs. Bliscomb?"

"Yes."

"Denver Police. Can we ask you some questions?"

"I reckon." She wore an apron that clenched tightly around her hands and a bandanna tucked over her hair in a way that Wager thought of as Southern. He hadn't seen that often in Denver. They went through the list of questions, Mrs. Wells rocking in the background and listening intently.

"You don't know Councilman Green?" Wager asked.

"I heard of him, I think. But we haven't lived here long—we came up from Galveston only a while ago."

"You're living with Mrs. Wells now?"

"We rents a room. Me and the children. Until we can find another place of our own."

"You've got a job?"

"Yessir. We getting by. I just wish they'd of left us stay where we was at."

"Were a lot of people mad when they had to move?"

"Mad? I reckon some, maybe. Most was just worried. It's hard, you know, when you got a place and then they takes it away from you. I just put up some curtains, too."

That was the god called Progress worshipped in the name of Profit. It had a way of abstracting people into percentages and norms so their faces couldn't be seen when they were uprooted and—as in his old neighborhood, the Auraria barrio—the bulldozers scraped away their homes and memories both. But Wager was paid to deal with the faces; he couldn't hide them behind computer printouts or the fake-leather binding of planning documents. Developers did that, and lawyers, and even city councilmen. "Did anyone make any threats against Councilman Green for voting to rezone the apartments?"

"No, sir. Not that I heard."

They thanked her and turned to go down the cracked brick steps. The sound of Mrs. Wells's rocking chair stopped. "That what you trying to do?"

"What's that, Mrs. Wells?"

"You trying to blame the people for Councilman Green's killing?"

"We don't have anybody to blame yet."

"You are, ain't you? But we heard already—we know."

"Know what?"

"We know he was killed by a white man. We heard what happened."

"We don't know who killed him. If we did, we'd have an arrest."

"You want us to think he was killed by a Negro, don't you? Well, we heard what really happened—it wasn't no

Negro killed Councilman Green!" Behind her, staring with
the same hatred, her two sons were poised shadows.

"Where'd you hear that, Mrs. Wells?"

"We heard. We know." She added, "We know what we
gone to do about it, too."

In the car, Stubbs gave his short, tuneless whistle. "We
found him yesterday and the rumors are all over the street
today. Even if they didn't like him, they hate Whitey
worse."

Wager could understand the feeling. It was one thing to
fight among your own, but something else when an out-
sider came into the barrio to kill. And it wasn't just hate;
there was a lot of fear, and that was far more infectious than
hate. It gave an easy excuse to those who sought revenge
and could weld the noncomitted to the bringers of violence. "We can't prove it's not a racist killing."

"Yeah, right. But we haven't had that kind of trouble in
so long, it's hard to realize how close to the surface those
feelings still are."

A bruise was always touchy, Wager knew, even when it
wasn't visible. Maybe you had to grow up in a barrio or
ghetto to know that. But some, no matter where they grew
up, were always seeking revenge. "She just hates, Stubbs—
black, white, everybody." It was the others: her sons, their
friends, the kids who ached for a chance to play their role
as rebellious victims, who would fill the streets. "Head back
to the Admin Building—the lieutenant's probably wetting
his pants waiting for us."

He wasn't; Wolfard had left shortly after five with the rest
of the administrators. But a note in Wager's box told them
to telephone him at home. Wager did.

"So far, nothing, Lieutenant. We talked to one of the
White Brotherhood—an overgrown meatball named Sonny
Pickett. He claims he didn't even know who Green was."

"That's not very damned surprising. Who else in the
Brotherhood did you run down?"

"Nobody. They'll be hard to find on a weekend. They get
on their bikes and go."

"So we have to wait until Monday to trace this out?"

"I didn't feel Pickett was lying. But I twisted his arm to

come up with whatever he could. Maybe we'll be lucky."

"Maybe doesn't cut it, Wager. I heard from the chief this afternoon; he's under a hell of a lot of pressure from the mayor's office to clean this up ASAP. There's rumors all over the place about Green being killed by a racist and what the blacks ought to do about it. I told the chief I assigned you and Stubbs to this full-time, and he wanted me to put even more people on. Hell, you two are one-fifth of the entire homicide section right now, so he went along with it. But he's thinking of bringing in the CBI and maybe even the Feds if we don't come up with something soon. People have been knocking on his door all day long, and if we don't produce, he's taking it away from us."

"We also talked to twelve of those sixteen families evicted from the apartments. Nothing there."

"Damn it all, Wager, I told you to stick to the racist angle! That's what those rumors say and that's what I want you to spend your time on. Not any goddamned long shots like that!"

In a killing, any possible motive needed checking out. Wager shouldn't have to tell Wolfard that. "Yessir."

"You and Stubbs are on duty tomorrow, right?"

"That's right."

"Well, keep after that White Brotherhood. I want to know who and what they are and if there's any possible chance one of them might be involved. Any chance at all."

"Yessir."

"And keep me posted."

Wager leaned back and stretched against the back of his chair and gazed around the homicide offices without really seeing the pale walls and the clutter of gray metal desks. The television set mounted high in a corner flickered with a sitcom where a large black woman leaned threateningly toward a slender youth whose eyes widened with mock innocence as he held up his hands palms out. The sound was turned off but dialogue wasn't really needed; the emphasized gestures carried the familiar story and defined the equally familiar characters, and you didn't really need to suffer through whatever they were saying. In some ways, it was like this case—the kinds of actors were already known, and all the lieutenant wanted Wager to do was supply the names and faces to play those familiar roles. The trouble was, of course, life wasn't a sitcom, and there might be a few players whose roles as well as names were neither predictable nor clear. Political players, maybe, such as the one who could have paid off Green for a favorable vote.

CHAPTER 8

Stubbs had gone for the night, the long tour pressing on his shoulders to make his walk heavy. The only other figure in the office was Golding, who shared the night shift with Max. As usual, he was on the telephone talking to someone about improving the spiritual side of life; this time it was by moon-phase dining. "Well, it sounds kind of weird, yeah, but she said to try it for a couple of months. And when you think about it, there's some sense to it—you know, the moon regulates the tides and a full moon brings all sorts of weird calls. Even the birthrate goes up. So I thought I'd try it. . . . No, what you do is pick foods that coincide with moon phases—receptors, she calls them."

Wager tried to ignore the list of full- and quarter-moon foods as he shuffled through the papers that had piled up in his mailbox during the tour, routine bulletins and notices that went to every detective in every section whether or not they were pertinent. He did not use the computing service, so it made no difference to him that new limits had been put on mainframe access, but the notice was there, anyway. What did make a difference was the memo stating that all computer terminals would shut down between 2 and 3 A.M. every morning, so Denver General, which shared the same equipment, could run their bills for the day. That meant the police had to stop chasing criminals while the city chased its dollars. A newsletter from the Police Brotherhood complained about long hours and understaffing, both of which had been around for as long as Wager could remember, and a hell of a lot longer than the PBA. But they were right: The numbers of crimes committed, especially burglary, had leaped, while the number of cops to investigate them stayed the same. The result was fewer minutes to spend on each crime, so you went after the ones you had a chance of clearing fast. What that meant was the professionals—the burglars who made their living with occasional big hits—were safer from arrest than the busy amateurs who tended to make small scores and big mistakes. But the brass went by stats and an arrest was an arrest. So you tried for the easiest bag.

He found a reminder that he was due to pop a few caps this month, and he'd better make time to get out to the range for that—it was a silly way to lose pay. Finally, the forensics package on Green—an envelope wrapped with a short string and sealed with a CONFIDENTIAL label. He opened it and slid the pile of forms and pages onto his desk. As Wager began reading the insistent buzz of Golding's voice faded from his consciousness.

Much of what the pathology report told him, he already knew—the manner of death, approximate time, and so on. Nothing in the official document mentioned the possibility that the body had been moved—Doc Hefley was cautious about committing himself to that idea. But Wager forced his way through the familiar facts one more time, making occasional notes as stray ideas came up. Then he turned from the medical to the investigators' reports. Walt Adamo's survey of the crime scene turned up several patterns of footprints that had not been attributed to witnesses or investigators walking the scene. The prints were described in the appendix and Wager studied the paragraph that told him most of the unattributed prints seemed to be from either tennis shoes or street shoes. One set of tracks going to the murder scene and back out again looked promising: the deeper imprint of a narrow, tall heel, like the heel of a cowboy boot. The depth and distance between strides going in implied that the wearer carried a heavy weight; the few prints found exiting were shallower and the stride longer, and that could mean the burden had been dropped. The distance between exiting strides indicated a person approximately 5 feet 9 inches, medium build, and normal walk. Casts had been taken of all prints that had been found; however, the friability of the dry earth made identifying characteristics difficult to determine. "See item #151."

Wager looked down to that entry: "Occasional scrapes ran parallel to the line of heel prints (Item #122) possibly caused by the victim's shoes dragging toes-down through the dirt. Marks on the toes of the victim's shoes were consistent with being dragged (Item #202)."

He was dead before he was dumped. That's what those marks told Wager: Green was hauled in by someone who draped the victim's arm over his shoulder to carry the weight. Someone wearing heels like cowboy boots. That was hypothesis, of course, not fact—the only facts were the prints and the scrapes in the dirt. But now those facts were starting to speak.

Wager turned to the itemized survey of the victim's clothing and personal effects that had been tested in the forensics lab. Green's pockets contained a wallet, handkerchief, comb, a dollar and seventy-three cents in loose change, a small pen knife, and nothing else. Wager thought about the things in his own pockets and the everyday things that should or should not be in Green's. Keys. No keys. Everybody had keys: car, home, office. But no keys on Green. That reminded him to call MVD again about the missing car, because the keys would have been used to drive away in that car. The wallet had been gone over for forensic evidence, too. Nothing unusual there: only Green's prints on the various cards and photographs in the plastic windows. Wager scanned the list of contents for other pockets and found nothing notable. A glasses case and a pair of sunglasses found in the jacket's inside pocket, a matching gold pen-and-pencil set also found in the vest pocket. That was it, and Wager leaned back to gaze at the ceiling and turn over those items in his mind.

Nothing that shouldn't be there. . . . Only one thing that should be. . . . Somewhere at the edge of his concentration, Golding hung up the telephone, shrugged into his coat, and said something to Wager as he left the office. Wager's mouth said something back, but his mind didn't register what, because it was again counting off those footprints and scrapes, those things found on the victim. He jotted another note and then turned to the lab analysis of Green's clothing. According to visual inspection, the suit was recently pressed; recovery of trace materials from the pockets, pleats, and seams was hampered because of removal of the victim's clothing at the morgue. However, a lab analysis of the underwear revealed traces of semen and vaginal fluids, indicating that the victim had sex and apparently dressed rapidly after the act so that the fluids on his flesh were still damp enough to smear.

He found corroboration further down in forensic's detailed study of the corpse. Skin swabs of the crotch and penis indicated heterosexual activity, and combing of the pubic area resulted in hair samples different from the victim. Wager read that entry and then ground the heels of his hands into his tired eyes and read it again. The samples were from a blond Caucasian woman.

A wife who wasn't too surprised when her husband was gone all night.

Two periods of missing time.

And Sonja Andersen had not called her condolences because she was unsure whether or not Mrs. Green would want to hear from her.

Making a longer entry in his notebook, Wager finished reading Adamo's survey of the forensic findings: The site offered little conclusive evidence of the perpetrator's identity, but enough soil and vegetation samples had been collected to provide links to the clothing of any future suspect. The pathological analysis of the victim's clothes revealed sexual activity probably on the same day he died.

Replacing the sheets in their envelope, Wager leaned

back and thought for a while. Then he jotted a few more lines in his notebook and began finishing up the rest of the notes and notices in his mail. Near the bottom of the pile, he found a telephone slip with a familiar number and a request checked: "Call as soon as possible."

He dialed and listened to the tone rattle twice before a man answered with the bar's name. "Is Fat Willy there?"

"Who wants him?"

He was sure the bartender knew his voice by now, but the ceremony never changed. "Gabe."

"I'll see."

A few seconds later the wheezing voice came over the wire. "Thought you forgot all about your friends, Wager."

"I've been busy."

"You been busy, shit. You been running around in circles, you mean."

"All right—I've been busy running around in circles."

"Uh huh. What's the word, my man?"

"Nothing doing. They're up for two felonies and Papadopoulos wants to put them away as habituals."

"Shit, Wager—you owe me! Goddamn it, you owe!"

"I owe what I can pay, Willy. Not what I can't. McKeever complains they threatened to set his store on fire, and then the damn fools did it. Then they beat him up because he fingered them. Nobody can help a couple of turdheads like that."

"That ain't the way it was! That McKeever—you know him? You know what kind of scumbag he is?"

"Never heard of him."

"You about the only one. He set fire to his own store, man. Insurance scam. He set fire to it and then laid it on Franklin and Roberts. They went over there to make him stop that crap and he come after them with a forty-five— wasn't a damn thing they could do but take it away from him. Assault? Shit!"

"He must have had some reason to blame your two choirboys, Willy. Or did he just pick the names from the telephone book?"

Willy's lurching breath measured a second or two. "All right, here it is—straight. That McKeever, he runs a numbers game out of that two-bit candy store. Numbers, a little cards, and craps on the weekend, you know. He likes to lay off a few bets with me now and then." He paused. "Personal wagering—friendly bets—all legal, you understand."

"I understand real well, Willy."

"Yeah. Anyway, McKeever, he got no luck. He's one of them people got no luck at all. He always loses and he loses big. He owes me, you know?" He waited for Wager to say he knew, but there was only silence. "Well, he owes me. So I send Franklin and Roberts over to talk to him—see what they can find out about when he's going to pay up."

"And if he doesn't pay, they burn him out?"

"No, shit, man—they don't say nothing about that! That's what I'm telling you—they burn down his store, how's he going to make money to pay me? They go over and look mean and that's all. God damn, Wager, I know what their records is. I use muscle, it ain't going to be somebody got three falls against them."

"So you're telling me McKeever burned his own place for the insurance and blamed them."

"Yeah—turns out I wasn't the only one he owed. That eedjit got into his own crap game and lost. His own game! I told you he was unlucky. Except he lost to a crazy man— Wall-Eye Oates, the one spent too much time down in Canyon City. Wall-Eye, he say he going to pocketknife McKeever if he don't pay up and pay up now. McKeever believes him. Hell, I believe him. So McKeever burns down his own store, and he knows damn well he can't make it look like nothing but arson, so he blames Franklin and Roberts."

Wager knew of Wall-Eye; he'd interviewed him once in the emergency ward of Denver General when what was left of the man had been hauled in after a knife fight. He was crazy—that much of Willy's story was true. "All this can come out in court, Willy. That's grounds for a not-guilty plea."

"I don't want it to get that far. Them two, they got long records and it's only their word against McKeever. You think a jury or judge going to listen to what they say?

McKeever knows that. He ain't had a charge against him in twenty years. My men don't want to take a chance in court and I don't blame them. You heard what Nick-the-Greek said he do."

There was a lot more that Willy wasn't telling him, additional reasons why the fat man was so worried about Franklin and Roberts. "Those two've worked for you a long time, right, Willy?"

"What's that got to do with anything?"

"They know about your business. They said if you don't get them off, they'll trade what they know for a lighter sentence, right?"

Another heavy breath, something like a sigh. "Maybe."

Wager, too, gave something like a sigh. "I'll tell Papadopoulos what you told me about McKeever. But I don't think it'll do any good. He likes the simple truth of Franklin and Roberts shaking down McKeever." And so would a jury.

"Well, damn it, do some good! What the hell we paying our taxes for?"

"You don't pay taxes Willy. You know that."

"Maybe I don't, Wager. But I pay in other ways. I paid for this in advance—I saved your pimply white ass that time, and you goddamn owe me for it."

"I'm also goddamn working on a homicide right now."

"Don't hand me that shit, Wager. You know who killed Green; it's all over the street."

"Who?"

"Who! Who! You know who: that White Brotherhood shit, that's who."

"I don't know that, Willy. I don't know that at all."

"You the only one! That's the word that's out, Wager. Everywhere."

He gave it a try. "What can you find out for me about Green?"

"Say, what?"

"Green. Find out everything you can about him."

"You asking for another fucking favor? You tell me to kiss my own ass about Franklin and Roberts and then you turn around and ask for another fucking favor? Man, you got the most . . . You are the biggest . . ."

He groped to think for a word that fit, and in the pause Wager said, "If you come up with something worthwhile, it's leverage. The chief might be willing to shrug off Franklin and Roberts if it means getting Green's killer."

". . . Oh, yeah?"

"It's a chance. But it has to be soon. They go up for charges on Monday. After that, it's in the court's hands."

Willy muttered something under his breath. "What I hear, Wager, is Green was straight. Somebody the people are proud of. That's why they so pissed."

"See what you can find out, Willy. The name of the game's information right now. With it, maybe we can do something. Without it, we'll take a little longer."

"Yeah, a little. Forever, you mean. I'll see what I can do. And Wager—your best ain't been too good; you do better than that, you hear me? And one more thing, my man: You got some calls from me on that shitty answering machine of yours. Maybe if you ever went home sometime, you'd get your messages."

1911 Hours

The reason Wager did not go home was that he knew what was waiting in the silence of his apartment and he wasn't yet tired enough to be able to ignore it. He had considered moving, leaving behind the echoes and shadowy things that hovered at the corners of his eyes and, when he turned to stare at them, congealed into a familiar lamp or a chair or a bathrobe hanging from a half-open door. But to leave it required an energy he didn't feel, and something else, too: a willingness. He did not know that he was willing to strip himself of those memories even though they were a source of pain. He did not want to lose the only thing that remained of Jo—the pictures in his mind of moments that, for no clear reason, had been captured and which for reasons equally obscure came back now. Her smile as she held the flowered coffee cup in both hands, elbows propped on his table after a quiet dinner; her shadowed profile as she looked up at him with her hair spread in wild grace across the pillow; a favorite phrase she used when some minor thing went wrong and that even now brought a half smile to his lips. He remembered especially the baggy way his bathrobe wrapped her after they swam in the apartment pool, and how it emphasized her smallness and gave her an appearance of vulnerability that she never admitted to. He felt again the eager happiness she brought to him when they went cross-country skiing that first time, and her laughter as he learned to ride a horse. But the memories that ached deepest were of those times for the two of them alone, times marked by a quiet smile or a glance or the touch of his flesh on hers. These memories, mixed with the magnitude of their loss, would be waiting for him at home, and he wasn't yet ready to face that.

Instead, he flipped through the pages of his notebook until he came to the number he sought and dialed, unconsciously counting the rings until a young voice answered with an eagerness that faded when the call was for the child's father. A few minutes later, Wager was mingling with the throbbing traffic of Friday night and angling across town toward the northern edge of District Two.

The resemblance between Ovid Green and his brother wasn't noticeable unless the two were side by side or, as Wager had done, you stared at enough photographs of the city councilman to carry his face in memory. Four or five years older than Horace, Ovid had the same heavy build and large but fragile-looking jaw. But his eyes were different—larger and set closer together—and the flair of his nose above the thick mustache was wider. He stepped back from the glare of the porch light and asked Wager in. "I don't know what-all I can tell you. My brother and I didn't see that much of each other. Especially since he became a city councilman."

"I'm just trying to learn anything I can, Mr. Green." He sat on the couch Green gestured toward. From beyond the living room and past the open dining area came the tinny laughter and music of a television set. Wager guessed there was a family room at the back of the split-level, one that opened to the fenced yard through a sliding glass door. The click of toenails scratched the hardwood floor and a large German shepherd padded into the room to sniff with interest at Wager's shoe before ambling over to Green's chair and falling with a weary grunt beside it.

"We weren't all that close. As kids I was, well, four grades ahead of him. That means a lot when you're that age, you know. I was in junior high while he was still in grade school; then when he moved up, I was in high school." The dog's brown eyes watched Wager unblinkingly. "In fact, we were closest when Horace got out of the Air Force and came back to start up his furniture store. I was still working as a loan officer at the bank and Horace was busy getting started. We saw a lot of each other then." He said modestly, "I helped get his loan through."

"How long ago was that?"

"Lord, ten years I guess—" He counted back over the years. "Eleven. He was twenty-six when he started that store. Only twenty-six, can you believe it? Of course, it wasn't in the same place as the new one and he's upgraded it a lot."

"He just moved out to I-25?"

"Four years ago, maybe."

"He's made a good living from the store?" Wager glanced around the small home and Ovid Green understood.

"Done better than me, that's for sure. But then he went into business for himself. That's where the money is. It sure isn't in being a bank officer, unless you get to the top." His large hands tilted up in acceptance. "But Goober took the risks, he deserved everything he made." One hand waved at the room. "He sold us our furniture at cost—saved us a lot of money on that."

"Goober?"

"Horace. That's what we called him when he was a kid—Goober. He was the color of a peanut when he was born." The dark eyes settled on Wager. "He was a good boy, Officer. I've been thinking of that a lot since I saw what was down there at the hospital: the kind of a kid he was, and the things he used to do. He didn't deserve anything like this. You think you're going to be able to find who shot him?"

"We've got a good chance, Mr. Green. And we're doing everything we can." They had, according to the latest statistics put out by Admin, a four-out-of-five chance. That was the percentage cleared by homicide in Denver: 80 percent. Of fifteen cities similar in size, Denver, with the fewest number of investigators—eleven—was just about in the middle on clearances. "What made him run for City Council?"

"Tell you the truth, I think he was getting bored with that store. That's not what I'm supposed to say, I know. What I'm supposed to say is he ran because he wanted to serve the people. Because he wanted to put honesty back in the office, that kind of thing. And that's true—he did. But I think the real reason was he was plain bored by that store. Last few years, he couldn't lose money on that place and it just ran itself."

"Is that why he hired a manager?" Wager asked. "Sonja Andersen?"

Green nodded. "Yeah. He couldn't run the store and run for office, too. So I guess it didn't really run itself."

"Did you ever hear of anything going on between your brother and Miss Andersen?"

Green studied the dog's head as he tugged idly at its ear. "You think she had something to do with it?"

"What do you think?"

The dog, rising sleepily against the feel of Green's hand, yawned widely, the teeth a glimmer of ragged whiteness in the pink of its mouth. "You know something about that? Him and Sonie Andersen?"

"I know he had sex with a blond woman on the day he died."

"I see." Green turned back from the dog. "I don't know for sure about her. I really don't. But it could be true— Horace liked women. Black, white, brown, you name it, he liked it. And they liked him, too. He was a good-looking man. Women were all over him like flies on syrup. He just took his pick of what he wanted, and after he got on the City Council, man, didn't he strut."

"How did his wife take that?"

"Who was going to tell her? I mean none of it meant anything, you know? It wasn't his fault women climbed all over him."

Maybe Green was in training for national politics. "So it happened often?"

"Often enough, I guess. But I didn't keep score. They just wanted a quick lay, and so did he."

"And that's what Miss Andersen was for him—a quick lay?"

"I don't know. If so, he was a fool to mess around with an employee. I told him that when I saw her the first time. I said, 'Little bro, you hired yourself some trouble.' He just laughed and said he could handle it." Green shook his head. "Well, he didn't, did he?"

"You think she could have done it?"

Green's voice grew shaky with the memories Wager's questions had stirred. "I don't know! How do I know who could have done it? Nobody could have done it, but somebody did!"

"His wife didn't know about any of these women?"

"Aw, I guess she figured things out. You know how a wife is, they got noses on them better than this dog here. But as far as I know, she didn't ever say or do anything about it. Like I say, we didn't see much of them after a while, especially after they moved down to South Park Hill and that big house."

"Did your brother ever talk to you about City Council business?"

"How do you mean?"

"Bills and acts—the Zoning Committee business, that sort of thing."

"Some, sure. He had some fine stories about the councilmen and the damnedest things they say and do. Makes you wonder how the city ever gets anywhere. And just what all this tax money's going for, too."

"What about Zoning Committee business? Did he ever talk about that?"

Green thought a few seconds and then shook his head. "Not that I remember. When we saw each other we talked family, mostly. A few stories and laughs, sure, but we didn't talk business much. There just didn't seem to be time for that stuff."

CHAPTER 9

Friday nights were often busy, but last night set some kind of record. On his way home, Wager had heard the dispatcher call patrol units to half a dozen outbreaks of civil disturbance. Most of them were in the northeast quadrant, but even as he finally flicked off the monitor and closed his burning eyes against the room's darkness, he heard the locations shift toward the northwest sector—the predominantly Chicano neighborhoods of District One. This morning, the Headquarters Building still held remnants of the night's action, a heavier-than-usual number of cars parked in the private vehicle lot, and a residue of official sedans and vans still at the curbs and in the no-parking zones. Even inside the building, the hallways, usually empty of administrators on Saturday and Sunday, showed an ebbing tide of baggy-eyed faces that were beginning to sag as they lost the adrenalin that had carried them through the night of extra duty.

"Jesus, Gabe, what a tour." Golding stretched as he finished a final page of a report. Beyond him, Max, slouching over his deskful of papers, lifted a weary hand at him and turned back to the sheets. "I lost count of the ten-fifteens," said Golding.

"Anybody hurt?" Wager had already seen the morning headlines: the *Post* that stated blackly, UNREST OVER GREEN SLAYING; and the *News*: FIVE POINTS RIOTS!

"No, just a couple of civilians hauled down to emergency. Some of the good guys have lumps, but that's about it."

"The papers made it sound pretty bad."

"Yeah, well, they always do. That's what sells. Most of it was gang crap—an excuse for the little bastards to trash out a couple stores and steal what they could. Fucking animals." Golding wagged his empty cup at Wager. "It's all yours now—hold the fort." Carrying the cup into the small sink area, he rinsed out the fragrant herb tea with cold water, and hung it to dry from a peg. From down the hall and the duty sergeant's desk came a mutter of voices as the shift changed there, too, and bright, rested faces brought a pulse of fresh blood into the stale building.

"How've you been, partner?" Max finally began stacking the papers and he, too, stretched against the morning's weariness. "Anything on Green yet?"

Wager shook his head. "Some leads—not many and none good."

"I hope to hell we come up with something soon. We managed to keep the lid on last night, but I don't know how long that'll last. Tonight . . . tomorrow night . . ." He shook his head and paperclipped the sheets together. "How's Lester Stubbs working out? You teaching him the business?"

"He'll pick it up, I hope."

"That's not very enthusiastic." The big man's voice dropped and he glanced through the open door to see if any ears stood nearby. "Trouble?"

"You see what time it is?" Wager pointed at the wall clock, whose minute hand made its tiny jump past the hour.

"Not everybody spends their whole life here, Gabe."

"Right, fine. But this is a big case and a lot's riding on it. He should be here by now."

"Yeah, I know. It's too bad it came when you're breaking in a new man. Listen, if you need help, just call. Wolfard can assign more people to this one. In fact, I'm surprised he hasn't already."

"He hasn't because I told him Stubbs and I can handle it."

Max nodded and wrapped the string around the cardboard buttons of the inter-office mailer. "That's what I figured." He added, "But like you say, it's a big case, and it involves the whole squad. Hell, the whole department."

"I'm the investigator of record."

"And half the department was running all over District Two last night, and it'll get worse tonight. If you need help, Gabe, ask—that's all I'm telling you. I know what the work means to you since Jo drowned, but this one isn't therapy, partner. It's dynamite."

Wager looked at his ex-partner to see if he was serious. "That's what you think? That I'm using this assignment for goddamned therapy?"

"Yeah, I do."

Well, maybe there was a little truth to that, though it wasn't the way Wager would put it. "And you think I'm not doing it right?"

"I didn't say that. What I am saying is that Wolfard's new on the job and he doesn't know ass from teakettle yet. If Doyle was here, half the squad would be on this thing already, and you know that. There are a lot of cops whose asses will be dangling if we have riots because of Green's homicide; and one man can only do so much, I don't care who he is. So if something pops and you need help, ask. That's what I mean: Don't let that orgullo, or whatever you call it, get in the way of the case."

"If I ever do need help, I'll ask. So far, there's nothing I need a damn bit of help with." He smiled at his ex-partner. "And don't worry about my orgullo."

"That's not what worries me, Gabe; it's you. I wish there was some way I could convince you: You can't blame yourself forever for Jo's death."

"That's my private life. It's got nothing to do with the job."

"Don't get huffy with me, partner. We've been together too long for that."

Behind him, he heard Stubbs's voice in the hallway say

good morning to the civilian receptionist. Her voice trailed him down the hall with the tired joke, "Help, homicide, my phone's dead!"

"The case isn't developed enough to need more man-power. If something comes up and I need help, I'll ask. I hope that's enough to make you happy, Axton."

The big man yawned widely and pulled his jacket across his shoulders and tossed the mailer into the OUT basket. "Happiness is going off duty, Gabe. But I can't help worrying about you a little bit even if you don't want it. Paternal instincts or something." He winked at Wager. "You blame yourself for too much, partner; you're not the badass you think you are. Hi, Lester. How are you getting on with this sawed-off cactus?"

"Morning, Max—Gabe." Stubbs nodded briskly, freshly shaved and eager for action. "What's the latest?"

Max waved good-bye as Wager handed Stubbs the forensics report that had come in last night.

"Anything worth looking at?"

Wager blinked. "The whole damned thing. It's the forensics report on a homicide."

The man's eyebrows lifted with surprise as he took the envelope. "What's the matter, no sleep last night?"

He ignored Stubbs and poured the shift's first cup of coffee and settled at his desk to outline the day. He should have been able to sleep last night; God knows he was tired enough. But something had brought him out of his dreams about two-thirty and he'd tossed and writhed until almost five before easing once more into sleep. The dreams themselves, perhaps, had wakened him. The one he remembered clearly was the familiar fight to reach for Jo's hand as a foamy curtain of water closed around her and sucked her away. That was when he woke up fully: when her eyes—wide and pleading as they stared at him—were blotted out by the water and her hand flickered from his stretching fingers. There were other dreams before that, too, that he half remembered as a chaotic mixture of Jo's death and the images and scenes of the Green slaying. The face of Green's wife, Hannah, looking at him with eyes as wide and lost as Jo's; Sonja Andersen's wan face swirling in the river where Jo's should be. If he'd been Golding, Wager would hustle over to a dream analyst and see what it meant for his karma. But he wasn't Golding, and he didn't need Max or anyone to tell him that he still felt guilt for Jo and that he was fretting over Green, trying even in his sleep to pull some sense from the bits and pieces that had turned up so far. What did puzzle him, however, was the ease with which those women merged into his dream's-eye vision of Jo. The only explanation was his feeling that the loss, the guilt that he knew for himself, was something they had sampled, too; that, like him, they had lost something deep and vital and now it was his job to compensate them for what was missing.

But that was the world of dreams and personal problems, both of which had to be pushed away; he wasn't collecting his pay to sit here and waste time with ill-defined crap like that. Let the dream world take care of itself; he was stuck in this real one and facing a homicide whose reverberations not only echoed in street violence, but also in the memos on his desk: "Wager, call me at home after 9 A.M., Wolfard." It wasn't after nine yet, and he didn't have anything substantial to report, anyway. Besides, a few other calls were more important.

Stubbs's voice broke into his thoughts. "So he really was killed somewhere else!"

Wager nodded. "I figure the killer shot him in the car and then wanted to dump him fast."

"Cowboy boots. All we have to do is arrest everybody wearing cowboy boots."

Which was probably about half of Denver. Wager was dialing the Motor Vehicle Department when Stubbs looked up again from the wad of papers. "A blonde?"

Wager nodded, talking into the mouthpiece. "That's right: HRG-1, registered to Horace R. Green." He spelled the last name. "A dark Lincoln Continental, a year old." It was the third time Wager had called to see if MVD had turned up the vehicle. Each time they needed another full description, and each time they asked the same questions. "No," said Wager, "he's not a felon; he's a homicide victim and that car could be material evidence—that's why. All right, thanks." Nothing. The car could be anywhere, parked on a public street until the tickets piled up deep enough to attract attention from the city impound lot, or, more likely, parked on somebody's private land—an empty lot, an unused driveway, a pay lot—and left there until the neighbors complained maybe a month or two from now. Wager had alerted the patrol division to look for it, too, but that was hit-or-miss; they had a lot of other things to worry about besides a parked car. And he didn't need Wolfard to tell him that there wasn't enough reason to assign a special detail of scarce patrolmen to a city-wide search. A dark car at the crime scene, Green drove a dark car, his dark car was missing. It all added up to a possible lead, but if they didn't find it, it wasn't worth a fart in a whirlwind.

"Gabe, Green had sex with a blonde?"

"I read it."

Stubbs flipped through the next few pages of the report. "That's all it says." He turned back to the notation. "Any idea when?"

Wager looked at the little column of figures he had in his notebook. "There are a couple possibilities. First, he left the furniture store a little after seven and turned up at Vitaco a little before nine. Or, after he left there, after nine. He was killed as early as then or as late as two the next morning. The witness saw a dark car parked at the curb around eleven. If that was the killer, maybe Green had a hundred and twenty minutes of bliss before he died."

"Which means the sex could have happened at the time of death?"

"That's what it means."

The man shook his head. "We're getting a hell of a lot of motives all of a sudden."

"Like what?"

"Now it's jealous women—a jealous blonde, a jealous wife. Maybe even some other woman who was jealous of both of them."

"Don't forget he spent part of the afternoon with a blonde." Wager's pencil tapped the column of numbers. "He was with Andersen from about four-thirty to six-thirty."

"They were at the store."

"They went out for coffee."

Stubbs stared at Wager. "Sonja Andersen?"

"Know any other blondes in his life?"

"No. But that doesn't mean there might not be."

That was true, but one of the basics was that you started with the knowns and givens of a case and worked out from there. You didn't waste time or create confusion by chasing down vague possibilities unless that was all you had to go on. "We'll begin with Andersen. If that doesn't work, then we'll look for other blondes."

Stubbs glanced at the wall clock. "The furniture store doesn't open for an hour, but I've got her home address here." He showed Wager a page in his notebook. "We could swing by."

"We'll wait until the store opens. We'll want to talk to the other people again, too."

And there were other phone calls to make. Wager dialed the four-digit extension of Intelligence and asked for Norm Fullerton. "This is Gabe Wager in Homicide, Norm. What can you give me on the White Brotherhood?"

"What's your need-to-know, Gabe?"

Wager sighed and played the game. "They may figure in the Green homicide."

"I see." The line buzzed and hummed a moment. "Better not tell you over the phone. You downstairs?"

"Right."

It took him a couple of minutes before he came in, walking quickly, with the look of a man who had too much on his mind and was trying to figure how to handle it all. But that was the way he always looked, Wager knew, even when he was only chewing gum. As he did now while pouring himself a cup of coffee from the Silex. "Hi, Lester. Wager. You think the White Brotherhood's involved in the councilman's death?"

"It may be. We talked to Sonny Pickett; he said they weren't. But then he wouldn't be likely to tell us they were."

"Sonny Pickett! Now there's a body you don't forget. I

can't say that about his face—I never saw it. He still working on elevators?"

Stubbs nodded. "With one hand, while he holds up the building with the other."

"He's a big boy, all right. But he's only one of the soldiers." Fullerton, frowning deeper with effort, told them what they already knew about the history of the Brotherhood, then began on what they wanted to hear. "Pickett's usually the sidekick—kind of a sergeant at arms when they have formal meetings. He could be more important if he wanted to, I suppose, but he never was in the center of things."

"Who's the leader?"

"Leaders. It's a collective leadership. Sometimes three guys, sometimes four. They're usually the same but not always. They come up with a plan and the rest go along or don't, depending on how they feel about it. It's a gang, but it's not really as tightly organized as some."

Wager and Stubbs waited through Fullerton's explanation of several models of group structure, and the differing definitions of "collectivity" and "gang" and "organization." "The membership's more consistent and formal than a collectivity, you see, but the internal structure's not nearly so rigid and clearly defined as an organization."

Wager smiled politely and tried not to notice the clock's minute hand take another tiny bite out of the morning. "Who's the leaders, Norm?"

"Well, that's what I'm trying to explain—there's no specific leadership. It varies. But there's a nucleus of figures who seem to be in on most of the major decisions most of the time. From the technical point of view, it's really a very interesting structure."

"Names, Norm?"

"Oh, let's see . . . Big Nose Smith, Leon Oakland, Little Keith Brownell. They're three of the most central. Billy ("Two Fingers") Marshall and Big Al Turner are involved a lot of times. Wiley Kreuger, Stinky Malone—there's some others, but those are the ones I'd concentrate on if you want the nucleus."

Stubbs looked up from making notes. "Have you heard of any ties with the Green killing?"

"Only from you. Where'd you get it?"

"It's on the street. All over."

"That's kind of a surprise."

"Why?"

"Well, they talk a lot about race war and so on, but most of the real activity's running contraband into the prisons at Canyon City and Buena Vista. That and cornering the dope market in the topless-bottomless joints where their women work. I can't imagine they'd want to stir things up by knocking off a city councilman even if he is black. I mean, you've already come down on Sonny, right? Those people are smart enough to know they're going to get hassled for something like that."

"You have an informant in the gang?"

Fullerton got cautious. "Our information's reliable. That's all I can tell you."

"Can you have him find out what he can?"

The man frowned even more deeply. "I'm not going to jeopardize sources, Wager. Our sources are protected— that's from the top—and I'm not about to put any heat on any informant for you or anyone else."

"I'm not asking for heat, just for an ear. I've already put some heat on Sonny, but he's not going to turn. What he might do, though, is stir something up that your informant can catch."

"I did not say we had an informant in place."

"Right—I understand. But you understand this, Norm: We've got a murdered city councilman. And he's black. And we've had one night of ten-fifteens and we have a whole weekend to go."

"I know, I know. And if you had something concrete, I'd be willing to risk making contact. But all you've got is a rumor. You want me to take a chance with a source it took us years to develop—to have that source nose around on nothing more substantial than a rumor. I'm not going to do it."

"I want you to get in touch with him and ask him to listen, that's all. Just tell him what to listen for, that's all. We've got to start getting some action on this thing soon or all hell's going to pop. That's from the top, too. The very top."

Fullerton drained the coffee and pulled the paper cup from the plastic holder and crumpled it into a waste basket. "I'll ask him to listen. That's all I can do."

"That's all I want you to do. That, and tell me as soon as possible if he hears anything."

"All right."

When he was gone, Stubbs glanced at Wager. "What he says makes sense, Gabe. The Brotherhood doesn't want all this heat."

Wager saw it that way, too. But a lead was a lead. "I wouldn't call those bastards the sanest bunch of citizens in the state, would you? Besides, Wolfard wants us to investigate the Brotherhood, we investigate the Brotherhood. Among other things." He reached for the telephone again.

"Who're you calling now?"

He had been going to call Julia Wilfong to see if she'd heard anything about a payoff to Green, but that was an aspect of the case he didn't want to spread any wider under Stubbs's nose. "The furniture store to see if anyone's there."

A tape recording said they were closed on Saturdays until 9 A.M. But if the caller would leave his name and number, a representative would return the call as soon as possible. Wager tried the home number that was in his little green notebook, beside Andersen's name. Another recording simply said he had reached that number and after the tone leave name and number and any message thank you.

The clock said 0845; he figured Sonja Andersen was on her way to work. "Let's give the store a try."

The graveled parking lot in front of Embassy Furniture was empty, but a large red sign on the door said OPEN. Employees probably parked around back, using a rear door. Wager and Stubbs passed through the electronic eye that set off a faint chime somewhere behind the shadowy forest of headboards and tall china cabinets, and a moment or two later, Ray Coleman—the young salesman—came out of the gloom. When he recognized them, his face shifted from a smile to inquiry. "Can I help you officers?"

"Is Miss Andersen in?"

"Back in the office. This way."

He led them past groupings of furniture to the small alcove whose light, blocked by a partition from the rest of the store, was a hard fluorescent glare.

"Sonie, those detectives are here again." The young man disappeared beyond a cluster of rolltop desks.

Under the harsh light, the woman's eyes looked puffy and masked by heavy makeup. Wager nodded hello and he and Stubbs refused a cup of coffee from the glass pot steaming on a hot plate. On the desk, invoices and receipts, wholesale catalogs, and brochures sat in loosely organized piles. The woman seemed to be groping toward some kind of classification of them rather than doing anything as concrete as making ledger entries or filling out orders.

Wager sat in a chair placed beside the desk for customers. From this angle, the light bounced back off the strewn papers and he could see her face clearly. "Can you tell me what kind of key ring the councilman carried?"

"Key ring?" If she had expected any question at all, this wasn't it.

"Yes, ma'am. We found no keys in his pockets. Just about everybody carries keys."

"Oh . . . I see. . . ." Two creases folded in the pale skin between carefully shaped eyebrows. "It was a key ring with a gold nugget. A small one on a little chain—you know the kind?"

"Real gold?"

"Yes. But not very big. He didn't like his pockets bulging out with keys."

"There weren't many keys on it?"

She shrugged. "Maybe four or five, I suppose. I really don't know."

Wager nodded and asked the next question. "Did he see a lot of furniture jobbers, Miss Andersen?"

She followed Wager's gaze to the glossy covers of the brochures. "Jobbers? No—he saw a few, I mean. But generally they deal with me now. His schedule, you know."

Wager nodded. "Those that he did see, were any of them women?"

"There are a few women jobbers. But I can't remember any who . . ." She finished the sentence with a shake of her head, the blond hair glinting in the artificial light.

"You can't remember if any of them had blond hair?"

"No. Why?"

"The autopsy report, Miss Andersen. It shows that Horace Green had sex with a blond woman sometime before he was killed."

She stared at Wager. "They can do that?"

"They can even tell who it was with. If necessary."

The rush of blood from her face left it ashen in the brittle light and she swayed toward a faint. Then she gripped the desk tightly and forced herself to inhale a long, shaky breath. "I didn't kill him. I swear I didn't kill him."

Stubbs pressed a bubble or two of water from the large bottle in the corner and handed her the paper cup. "Why not tell us about it, Miss Andersen?"

She took the cup, her eyes shifting from Wager's flat, alien stare to Stubbs's kind smile. Sometimes, usually with Hispanics, Wager and Max played it the other way: Max was the blue-eyed gringo angry with suspicion, while Wager showed he understood and even sympathized with the oppressed victim of an Anglo police state. But Stubbs's round face had a softness to it that blurred any sense of grim duty, so Wager told him to play the friend.

"I loved him!" She spoke to Stubbs. "I did!"

The man nodded and sat in the upholstered chair placed so customers could talk over prices and terms before moving to Wager's seat to sign papers. Wager leaned back to leave her with Stubbs.

"Just tell us what happened, Miss Andersen. You and Horace were lovers, is that it?"

Lips pressed tightly together, her hands fumbled blindly for something among the piles of paper on the desk and her eyes blinked rapidly to fight the sting of tears.

"All you have to do is tell us the truth, Sonie." Stubbs laced his fingers like a father confessor and leaned closer, his voice a low murmur against the steady buzz of the overhead lights. "You're the blonde he made love to, aren't you?"

"Yes."

"It happened after work, didn't it? On Wednesday."

"No. In the afternoon."

"What time?"

"I'm not sure. Around five. Five to six. That's the time we usually—"

"Did he force you to do it?" asked Wager.

"No! It wasn't that way!" The tears spilled over and she said "Damn" and found the packet of Kleenex under a sheet of paper. "I promised him—I promised his memory—I wouldn't cry. Damn!"

They waited while the woman's shoulders twitched with stifled breaths in a futile effort to stem the tears. She finished with a tiny, cramped blow of her nose and wadded the Kleenex into a fist.

"It wasn't that way. We . . . we loved each other. I knew he was married. I knew he couldn't get a divorce—his political career, the gossip. . . . But we loved each other."

They waited for her to go on.

"He was so . . . so alive. And bright. And gentle. And he had such a good, fine sense of humor—we'd find so much to laugh about. Despite . . ."

"Despite what, Sonie?"

"Despite knowing we could never be anything but lovers. That even if he could get a divorce, people would never accept the two of us together."

"Because he was black?"

She looked startled, gazing at Stubbs as if seeing him for the first time. "No. Because I was white! He could never be elected to anything if he had a white wife. He ran such a risk to be my lover! If anyone had found out, his political life would have been over."

"How long were you lovers?" asked Wager.

"A year and eight months. Seven months after I came to work here. It just happened—we fell in love long before it happened, and then one afternoon . . . we touched. That's all it took—that one little touch of our hands."

She was speaking more to a memory she had replayed over and over rather than to either of them. They waited.

"After that first time, he offered to find me a job anywhere I wanted. To pay my salary until I found one I liked. He thought he had taken advantage of me because I worked for him." The golden hair wagged from side to side in remembered surprise. "He was so apologetic. I told him over and over I didn't want to work anywhere else. That I wanted to be with him."

Which probably wasn't exactly what Green wanted to hear. "You knew at the time he was married?" asked Wager.

"Yes. But it didn't make any difference." Her eyes turned angrily to Wager. "And it still doesn't, except for his . . . for Mrs. Green." A spasm of fright chilled the eyes wide. "She doesn't need to be told, does she? She doesn't need to be hurt by this, does she?"

Stubbs smiled and shook his head. "We're not interested in his sex life. We're after his killer."

"I don't know who could kill a man like that. He was a good man—really. A good man."

"Do you know if he had other girlfriends, Sonie?"

"No." The Kleenex went back to her eyes, blotting the damp mascara. "No, he didn't. I know what you're thinking—a cheap, sordid office romance. But it wasn't. I was the first—the only—other woman he had since he was married. And we both knew it shouldn't have happened."

The words were coming easier now. Wager had seen it before: The pent thoughts and worries held in silence for so long suddenly spilling out when there was someone, preferably a stranger, who would listen and not dispute. And the survivor's willingness to ignore the faults of a dead loved one—to believe that he or she was capable of nothing but good. What wasn't clear to Wager was whether the saintliness of the dead was the result of grief or an intensifier of it, a means of honing guilt and loss into a luxuriance of pain. He had seen it in others; maybe he even had a touch of it himself.

"He wanted to go into politics—the City Council was the first step—and he could have been a great leader. We would have to be very strong, he said."

"Why's that?"

"Because of his plans—the politics. We couldn't let any-

one even think we were lovers. And someday"—she gathered herself together again—"someday we couldn't even
be lovers anymore. That's why we had to be strong."

"Tell us what happened Wednesday afternoon, Sonie."

Wager leaned forward to study her face and eyes and to
hear the soft voice better. As she began to answer, the radio
pack in his holster gave a loud pop and his call number and
pulled her face toward him, startled at the reminder of who
these two men were and what they represented. Keying
the reply button two quick times, he muffled a curse and
stepped around the partition into the shadowy display area.

"Ten-six-nine," he answered with his call number. "Go
ahead."

"Lieutenant Wolfard wants you to report by telephone as
soon as possible."

"Will do."

"He wants to know when."

"As soon as possible, God damn it."

He turned off the radio, another violation of regulations,
and returned to the office in time to hear Sonja Andersen
say "That was the last time I saw him."

There were a few more questions, mostly designed to
establish names and locations that could be used in further
investigation. Her previous job was as an account processor
for Reliable Savings and Loan. She had lived in Denver for
almost five years. Her home was Chadron, Nebraska—a
farm about twelve miles north of town. She lived alone in
Denver. No, she did not have any other boyfriends.

"What did you do Wednesday night after work, Sonie?
The eleventh."

"I went home."

"Did anyone come over to visit? Did you talk to anyone
on the phone?"

"No."

"You were home alone all evening?" asked Wager.

"Yes."

"Horace Green didn't come over to your place between
nine and two in the morning?"

"No." She looked puzzled. "He had I don't know how
many political things to do. He couldn't come by."

"Did he come by often?"

"Sometimes. Not often. It's a long drive."

Maybe she meant miles, but Wager figured the real distance Green had to travel had been psychological—certainly the distance from wife to mistress, perhaps the distance from black to white. And he wondered if Sonja Andersen knew just how long those distances could be or if, because she loved, she assumed he did, too. Or if she really loved as she said she did and as she wanted Wager to believe.

On the way out, they found Ray Coleman staring silently through the plate glass at the empty parking lot and the traffic flickering past on I-25 beyond.

"Mr. Coleman, can I ask you a few questions?"

"Sure. You guys come up with anything yet? About Mr. Green's killer, I mean?"

"Not much, so far. But maybe you can help." Wager opened the door and motioned for the young man to step outside. "Did you ever hear any rumors that Councilman Green was stepping out on his wife?"

Coleman's eyes slid away toward the traffic, and he fingered the thin line of hair on his upper lip.

"Did you, Mr. Coleman?"

His face darkened with embarrassment and the finger moved off the mustache to scratch at the corner of his full lips. "You mean . . ." he finished by jerking his head toward the office.

"What can you tell us?"

"They had it on, I guess. Thought nobody knew."

"Green and Miss Andersen?"

"Yeah. She was all over him from the first day she was here."

"Who else knew about it?"

"I don't know. I sure wasn't going to tell anybody. I felt . . . I don't know, it just didn't seem right, you know? Here he is, somebody the people really respect—a city councilman, a deacon in the church, and he's sneaking around with this woman. A white woman."

"How long did it go on?"

He shrugged, but it was more with disgust than carelessness. "A year maybe. Maybe longer. First time I heard it, I didn't believe it. I didn't want to believe it. But she was having him, anybody could tell."

"A lot of people knew about it?"

"The whole store, that's all."

"What about his wife?"

"Mrs. Green? You mean did she know about it? I sure didn't tell her, man! I wouldn't do a thing like that."

"Did Mrs. Green ever visit the store?"

He looked down at the pointed tips of his glossy shoes and flicked a piece of gravel with his toe. "A couple times, yeah. But she didn't come down a lot."

"Did she ever meet Miss Andersen?"

"Sure. She had to. The bitch's been running the place for two years, now."

"How did they act together?"

"Act? I guess that's the word for it, all right." The head jerked again. "On her part, anyway—smiling like a damn Halloween pumpkin and taking Mrs. Green on a big tour of the store."

"They were friendly?"

"If you want to call it that. Sonie was as nervous as a whore in church, but Mrs. Green was cool, man. If she knew anything, she wasn't letting on."

"Did Green care for Miss Andersen?"

"Care for her? I don't know. I don't know why he did it in the first place. I mean, she's not all that good-looking, and she's white, you know? I mean, what the hell did a man like Horace Green want with that? I just don't understand it, that's all."

"Did a lot of people feel that way?"

"What way?"

"Angry at Green for having a white mistress."

"I don't know. I didn't talk about that to nobody. And I don't know if angry's the word. Sad, maybe. There was no reason to do it—a white woman, for gosh sakes."

"Did anyone ever mention the affair to you?"

"Pee Wee told me about it."

"Who's that?"

"Pee Wee Crawford. Him and James Mellor work in shipping."

Wager remembered interviewing them briefly on his first trip to the store. "You talked it over with them?"

"Talk it over? No—Pee Wee came up one day and told me he saw them kissing. He couldn't believe it. It shocked him, you know? So he had to tell somebody and he told me. I wish he hadn't. I liked Councilman Green. He was doing things I want to do. I mean having his own business and being on City Council—not that other stuff."

"Did James Mellor feel that way, too?"

"No. He just laughed. Said a man should be able to dip his wick wherever he wanted to. He likes white meat, he said—a touch of honey."

"You kept working here, even though you didn't like what was going on?"

"It's a job, man. Jobs are hard to get. And Mr. Green was a good man—that's what I can't figure out. Except for this, he was a real good man." He glanced at the passing cars. "She won't be around much longer, anyway. I bet Mrs. Green fires her ass right after the funeral."

0958 Hours

In the car, Stubbs whistled dimly as Wager steered through the still-heavy morning traffic on the major north-south interstate. "That kid sure doesn't like whites, does he? I thought they were all drooling for honky quim. But I still can't see that as motive enough to kill a man, Gabe."

Wager had only been thinking aloud. "If Ray Coleman felt that strongly about it, why not someone who felt even stronger?" He'd seen it among the Hispanics: a pride that rejected, sometimes violently, everything Anglo—values, language, products, women, even a mixed-breed like himself. As a kid, he used to puzzle over the thin line between racism and that kind of pride.

"Like Mrs. Green?"

That, too, was possible. But it wasn't exactly what he was

trying to formulate. "Like someone who felt betrayed by Green. Someone who wanted to punish him for not being perfect."

"Or someone who thought the affair was over and didn't want it to be? We're getting a lot of motives and damn few suspects. A racist killing, jealousy, now some kind of weird justice. And everybody keeps saying what a good guy he was."

"Don't forget the vote-selling."

"Jesus. His elements were mixed, all right."

Whatever the hell that meant. Wager swung with heavy traffic around the Mousetrap and east on I-70 headed for Colorado Boulevard.

"Are you certain you want to talk to Mrs. Green now?"

"It's not a question of wanting," Wager reminded him.

"I guess not."

Everyone did agree that Green was a good man. But even a good man could have a lot of shady areas in his life, things that at first seemed like harmless fun or, even if verging into the illegal, seemed like minor sins at first. Far less than what everyone else was getting away with. So why not give it a try? Perhaps Green was on that gentle road and someone saw it more clearly than he did and resented it. Or perhaps Green had looked up and seen how that road, without his really noticing, had slanted down below the level of the one he had long ago believed himself traveling. And so he wanted to get off. To get back up to the ideal level he and his people's vision of him thought he should be on. And someone had not wanted him to.

"You want to do the talking or do you want me to?" Stubbs stared at the big home, dim and still behind the spruce trees.

"I will."

Mrs. Green herself answered their ring. The initial shock had worn away and left her with the sunken, tired look of deep sadness. Although they had not called to say they were coming, she did not seem surprised to see them. She opened the door and stepped back, a hand loosely indicating the large living room. "Come in, Officers."

"I'm sorry we have to bother you again, Mrs. Green. But

we need a little more information about your husband."

"I understand. Would you like some coffee?"

"No, ma'am." Wager and Stubbs waited until she settled onto one of the straight-back upholstered chairs before seating themselves on a couch. Its heaviness anchored the room's window-brightened lightness and seemed to suit what they came for. "Mrs. Green, exactly how well did you know your husband?"

Her eyes, red over the dark circles of flesh, stared at Wager for a long moment. There may have been a stir of anger, but it was quickly buried under pain and resignation. "He was my husband, Officer."

"Yes, ma'am. But sometimes men have lives their families know little about."

"Just what are you trying to tell me?"

After a moment, Wager said, "I'm trying to tell you your husband was unfaithful. I'm telling you this to find out if it's a motive for his murder."

This time the tears came, but the woman did not move. She didn't even seem to breathe.

"It's not something everybody knows or something they should know. But—"

"But you think I might have killed him."

"I don't think anything yet. I'm just trying to learn as many facts as possible."

"You've learned that one. I don't see what more you have to ask me."

"You did know about it, then."

"Of course."

"Were you estranged by it?"

" 'Estranged'? Did we become strangers, you mean?" She thought that over. "I felt it. I certainly felt it, Officer. But we never talked about it. I kept hoping that if I said nothing, let him suspect nothing, he'd come to his senses. For the sake of the children, for the sake of what we shared together. 'Estranged'? Yes. On those nights when he didn't come home and I was alone, wondering—knowing—yes, I was estranged."

"But you loved him, too."

"Yes."

"Did this happen often?"

"No. I mean I don't think so." The tears had stopped flowing, but the last of them trembled on her cheek as if she didn't know she cried. "I really don't know, anymore."

"Did he ever say anything about a divorce?"

"No."

"Did you?"

"I've already told you, Officer, I said nothing."

"Do you know who the other woman was?"

Her eyes moved from Wager's to the double French doors that shut off one end of the living room from a glassed-in sun porch beyond. Through the second barrier of glass, Wager could see the bright warmth of flowers in a sheltered garden. "I figured it out."

"Did anyone ever mention it to you?"

"You mean, how many other people knew about it?"

"Yes, ma'am."

"I don't know. I hope to God it wasn't many. Not for my sake."

"But nobody spoke to you about it?"

"No. They wouldn't."

"So you don't know if anyone might have strongly resented your husband. . . ."

The eyes turned back to his with a spurt of mocking, angry laughter. "I did, Officer. I resented it very strongly!"

"Yes, ma'am. But would anyone see it as a motive to kill him?"

"You think I wouldn't?"

Wager and Stubbs held their tongues.

She stared at them with all the hatred she had stifled against her husband, because they insisted in poking into those places where hurt lay. And because they, too, were men.

Then her narrow shoulders quivered in a deep shudder. "You're right. I wouldn't. I thought about it—God forgive me, I thought about it in those long nights. But I loved him. And he was a good man despite that." Her fingers folded inside each other and she studied them for several moments. "He didn't love her. I think it was . . . the competition. He was one of the most competitive men I've ever known—he wouldn't have been a good businessman or politician without that. But you have to understand something about black men, Officer, and white women; even when they won't admit it—the men—it's a way of getting even. It's showing the white man who's the more macho. It's a mix of anger and fear that they have to face somehow. Even with black women . . . many black men feel angry toward black women because their families were dominated by women. It's a way of asserting their manhood."

Wager heard that tiny shift in her voice that told him she was no longer saying what she really felt but repeating something she had read or heard somewhere and elected to believe. Something she found comfort in thinking might be the explanation.

"You can't remember anyone who might see the interracial thing as a motive for killing your husband?"

"No."

"Mrs. Green"—Stubbs spoke for the first time—"have you had any more threatening calls?"

"No."

And Wager had one last question. "When he didn't come home on the night of the eleventh, you thought he was with Miss Andersen?"

She nodded, lips clamped against the woman's name as she stared at her hands.

On their way past the end of the block, Wager lifted a hand in salute to the blue-and-white stationed discreetly on guard; a bored hand glimmered in return.

CHAPTER 10

Saturday, 14 June, 1142 Hours

The funeral, Mrs. Green had told them, was to be on Sunday at 2 P.M. That way a lot of people who wouldn't be able to take off work could come, and the expected long procession wouldn't disrupt the weekday traffic. Services would be in the Baptist Evangelical Free Church where Green had been a deacon, followed by interment in the Fairmount Cemetery. Wager and Stubbs marked their calendars with the date and time, though Wager suspected they would be reminded of the occasion by the bustle among city officials who would attend and require extra police details. But right now the department's problem was to get through the weekend with minimum damage to people or property from rioters. The best way to do that, Wolfard told Wager over the telephone, would be to catch the killer. But Wager's report was the same as when he talked to Wolfard two hours ago: nothing new yet.

"What's your next step?"

"I want to check out the furniture store manager." Even though they were using the telephone rather than radios whose transmissions were aired everywhere in the city, Wager was habitually cautious with names and specifics.

"Give me an afternoon report."

"Will do." He hung up and shook his head at Stubbs, who waited with a small batch of papers in hand. "I don't know why Wolfard just doesn't come on down to the office."

"He's afraid he'd have to give himself comp time," said Stubbs. "Here's what I've got." He had spent the last twenty minutes on the telephone verifying points of Sonja Andersen's story with local sources; Wager had spent the time trying first to reach, and then persuade the sheriff of Dawes County, Nebraska, that he wasn't trying to railroad one of the daughters of a local taxpayer.

"She rents a condo off East Hampden. The owner said she's been there a little more than a year and hasn't caused any trouble at all. As far as she—the owner—knows, Andersen pays her rent promptly and is an upright citizen."

"She got horizontal a few times," said Wager.

"Yeah. Too damn bad it had to be Green."

"What?"

"Black cock. Once they have black cock, they don't want anything else." Stubbs's head wagged at the loss. "Anyway, the bank where she worked before going to Embassy Furniture tells the same story—a steady work record, no disciplinary or money problems while with them, a trustworthy employee, nobody special she dated that they knew of. They offered her a raise when she told them she was quitting, but she said she wanted to try another field and liked the chance to become a manager."

That description pretty much fit what Wager had learned from the sheriff's office, and he traded that information with Stubbs: the second daughter of a farmer with a big spread of land north of Chadron. Married at the end of her senior year in high school and divorced two years later. Wanted, apparently, to get away from farm life more than from her husband. Moved to Denver to get a job and pretty much lost touch with most of the people in Chadron. The sheriff would be mighty surprised to find that she was part of anything shady or suspicious—her family was a good Lutheran family and hardworking. If she was into anything, it was because she moved down to Denver and not because of anything she learned at home.

"He said that? The sheriff?"

"Yes."

"You tell him about Councilman Green?"

"No."

"Probably a good thing. Her family find out about him, they'd want to lynch somebody. Two somebodies."

"That's all we need," said Wager. "Another motive."

They filed the corroboration statements with those pieces of paper that pertained to Andersen. Probably nothing would come of it, but that was the way of much police work: Take a statement, check it out, and see if anything rang untrue; file away the answers against that time when they might be needed.

In the background, the telephone rang and Stubbs answered. Wager, his mind juggling bits and pieces of information into various patterns of meaning, paid no attention to the distant buzz until he heard his name. "It's for you, Gabe—a Councilman Albro."

"I've got a note here saying you wanted to talk with me."

"Yessir. It's in relation to Councilman Green's murder. When's a good time for you?"

A silence. "I don't know what I can do for you. We did council work together and that's about it. We weren't close personal friends or anything like that."

"It's part of the procedure, sir. We're trying to fill in as much as we can about the victim."

"You have any idea yet who did it?"

"Nothing definite."

"The papers this morning make things sound pretty bad over in Five Points."

"Yessir. That's another reason we're checking in every direction we can think of."

"I see. All right, I've got a half hour starting at twelve-thirty. Can you make it then, Detective—ah—Wager? Every day's a busy day for me, and Saturday's busiest of all."

"I'll be there."

Stubbs raised an eyebrow and started to ask something when a bleary-eyed Golding came through the door, awkwardly sipping a cup of coffee. "God, this stuff's awful. How can you people drink it?"

"What are you doing down here?"

"Double shift; I'm on eleven to seven, too, we're so goddamn shorthanded." He sipped and shuddered. "Anything new on Green?"

"Nothing."

"What a hassle. Next goddamn time a councilman wants to get killed, I hope I'm on leave."

"I thought you only drank barley juice or something like that."

"I never tried that. But I need caffeine. God only knows what this stuff's doing to my aura."

Wager squinted at him. "I think it's turning yellow."

"What?"

Stubbs peered, too. "I see what you mean, Gabe. He looks a little . . . pale. Pale yellow—kind of like a sick haze around him."

"Batshit—you guys wouldn't know an aura if it strangled you."

"Some people can see them, Maury. And I think Stubbs is right. It's not a haze, exactly, it looks more like steam. Yellow steam."

"You guys laugh—go ahead. Just keep laughing. But there's a lot of truth in it. What goes in your body, that's what makes up your body. You put crap like this in your body, pretty soon you got a crappy body." He gave the cup a sour look. "It'll probably take me a month to get it out of my system."

The telephone rang again, Stubbs answering "Homicide" as Wager drained his coffee cup and forced a loud belch. "But one thing about this stuff, Maury—it tastes good going down and coming back up, too."

"Jesus, you're gross, Wager."

Stubbs waved a hand at Wager to pick up the extension and mouthed silently, "Lieutenant Elkins." Wager picked up his telephone to hear the department's neighborhood liaison officer say "and let me know what's going on."

"Yessir," said Stubbs. "But we don't have anything to tell you yet. I wish we did."

"We've got to have something for the people, Lester. I met with the Five Points Leadership Committee this morning. They're uptight about what might happen tonight and tomorrow night. I haven't seen people stirred up like this since the seventies. All sorts of rumors are going around."

"Like what?" asked Wager.

"That you, Gabe? I've heard stories Mrs. Green's been threatened again, that the White Brotherhood's going to make a raid, and that the police are trying to protect a racist killer."

"Lieutenant, you know that's a pile of horseshit."

"I know it. You know it. But they don't, and that's where the trouble begins. And I'll tell you something else: Rumor has it the Doo-Rag Devils and the Uhuru Warriors are getting involved. Is there anything at all you can give me to pass on?"

"All I can tell you is we're working as hard as we can on it. But we still have no suspects." Wager asked sweetly, "Have you talked to Lieutenant Wolfard yet?"

"I tried to reach him. He's not on duty."

Wager gave the man Wolfard's home number. "He's monitoring the case very closely, Lieutenant. We report to him every three or four hours. I'm sure he'll have a statement for you."

"All right—but for God's sakes call me as soon as you come up with anything concrete, will you?"

"Yessir."

Wager hung up his extension and checked his watch. "I've had my lunch."

Stubbs emptied his cup with a weary puff of breath. "I'll see you back here."

1228 Hours

Stubbs was to survey the people who lived and worked in Sonja Andersen's neighborhood, show them a picture of Councilman Green, ask if they had ever seen the man, and if so, when, with whom, under what circumstances. He would gather up a record of the little things that people wanted to do without being noticed; but because someone was usually nosy enough to look and remember, people weren't as inconspicuous as they thought they were. And in that predominantly white neighborhood, Councilman Green would be a very visible man, indeed—especially with a blond woman.

Wager stood rapping on the office door of Councilman Albro—"Smiling Ray" his official letterhead named him—in the now-familiar curve of hallway that banked around the City Council rooms. He knocked once and waited, peering through the frosted glass for a shadowy movement.

"You want to see the councilman?"

Wager looked over his shoulder; the stumpy figure of Jeremy Fitch, with its comb of floppy white hair, leaned around the hallway's bend. "Is he in?"

"Ah—the policeman!" Fitch came forward, the crepe soles of his shoes making whispery squeaks on the fresh wax. "What have you found out?"

"Nothing yet, Mr. Fitch. We're still beating the bushes."

The man's eyes glanced at Albro's closed door. "You're talking to him about it?"

"Routine stuff: when he last saw the councilman, any worries the man might have had. The same things I asked you." Fitch was slightly shorter than Wager so that the wag of his hair bobbed up and down in front of Wager's eyes. "Have you remembered anything that might be important?"

"What's to remember? The man was alive, now he's dead. It's making one hell of a stir in the city, I'll tell you that. The mayor even held a Saturday session this morning with his cabinet. There's a lot of worry about Five Points."

That wasn't something Wager needed to hear again. "I understand the council president, Mrs. Voss, appointed Green to the Zoning and Land-Use Committee."

"That's what the president does—that's how she gets her power. That, and run the meetings."

"Was there any objection to Green chairing that committee?"

"Objections?" Fitch tugged an earlobe that had a web of gray hairs curling from it. "Some other people wanted it—

it's a good committee to chair. But I don't remember anybody making any kind of stink about it."

"No one thought it was unusual?"

"Why should they? Somebody had to chair it. Green was a good choice. As good as any, anyway."

"Has there ever been any kind of trouble on that committee?"

"I don't know what you're getting at."

"Kickbacks. Payoffs. Anything out of the ordinary."

Fitch took a step or two back, distancing himself from Wager and anything he was suggesting. "It's happened—it certainly has. But not with this council. I haven't heard anything like that lately, and if that's where your investigation is taking you, I think you'd better run, not walk, to the nearest district attorney, young man. You're getting in water that's not only deep but a hell of a lot hotter than you'll like it."

"I'm only looking at all possibilities, Mr. Fitch."

"That's the kind of possibility you want to look at with your mouth shut, then. Unless you've got evidence of something—and strong evidence at that—you don't even want to whisper that kind of thing." An age-spotted hand slapped the polished stone of the wall. "Ears. It looks like rock, but it's ears. You understand me?"

"What's 'ears,' Jeremy?"

Fitch looked past Wager and his face folded into a pattern of smiling lines that masked his eyes. "Hello, Ray. Ears in the walls—ears everywhere. This young man's waiting to see you."

Albro, a leaky hamburger clutched with a napkin in one hand and a *Rocky Mountain News* in the other, nodded curtly. "You're the one who called? Come on in." He juggled the paper with a door key. "Any messages, Jeremy?"

"Not so far."

"Interrupt us as soon as anything comes up."

"Will do, Mr. Councilman."

He led Wager into the room whose height seemed equal to its depth. Like Councilwoman Voss's office, this one had a window looking across an open airspace to another gray stone wall.

"Now, Detective—ah—"

"Wager."

"Wager. What is it you want?" He busily shuffled the papers on his desk as he talked, eating with one hand and reading through them while he turned one ear to Wager.

"Anything you can tell me about Councilman Green and his work. How he ran his committee."

"Councilman Green was a fine man and his death is a serious loss to the city and county of Denver." Two papers went from one pile to another.

"Yessir."

He turned from a memo, his mouth full. "I'll be the first to tell you that we didn't see eye to eye on a lot of issues, but I had nothing but the highest respect for the man."

Wager nodded. "Were there ever any problems on the Zoning Committee?"

Albro took another bite of hamburger and dabbed at the corner of his mouth while he chewed. "What do you mean, problems?"

"Any decision you might have questioned?"

"There were some of those, yes indeedy. I respected Green, like I told you. But just between us girls, I don't think he ran that committee the way it should have been run. A lot of times I don't think he ran it at all. It was that aide who did all the work—what's her name, Julia."

"He wasn't a good chairman?"

"Let's just say the committee went a hell of a lot smoother and a hell of a lot more effectively when I ran it."

"Are you the chair now?"

The man winced slightly, the loose skin under his neck quivering. "That depends on Voss. Normally, I would be, yes. In the absence of the chair, the vice chairman's supposed to take over. But the death of a councilman in office raises a lot of procedural questions, and we're debating now whether Voss has the right to reappoint committee assignments or whether the charter spells out succession." He finished the hamburger in a large bite and spoke through the wad in his cheek as he began re-reading one of the papers he'd just moved. "The Law Department's working on the question. God alone knows what those people will come up with. Depends on who the mayor appoints to fill Green's seat, too. His appointment could carry all existing committee assignments."

"Any idea who that might be?"

"Yeah, I got an idea—it'll probably be another of those pro-divestiture, left-wing, pansy pinkos that the mayor's been stuffing on his cabinet. By God, the charter should be amended to prevent just this kind of corruption of the council." He paused to make a note on a blank pad of paper. "That's an amendment I want the Legal Office to draw up, by God." That note went into a clear section of his desk.

Wager noticed that many of the papers were either blank or seemed to be routine notices and bulletins carefully organized into some pattern of importance. "Aside from differences of opinion, Councilman Albro, did you ever suspect any kind of questionable activity by the Zoning Committee chairman?"

Albro's blue eyes, pale and slightly bloodshot, studied Wager for a moment. "Do you know what the hell you're suggesting?"

"I'm not suggesting anything."

"You're suggesting, by God, some underhandedness on this committee—a committee that I am vice chairman of!"

"I'm asking questions about Councilman Green. About any possible motives for his death."

"Well, before you ask any more questions like that, let me remind you the City Council has the duty to review police department finances. You understand me?"

Wager could hear in his own words the slight Spanish lilt that came when he was angriest, and he tried to keep his voice level and reasonable. "You have your duty, Councilman, and I have mine. And mine involves a Class One felony."

"Your duty doesn't include making accusations against city councilmen!"

"I'm not accusing you or anybody else. I'm trying to get information."

"Well, you're getting beyond the scope of your investigation, mister. Way beyond it. And by God, I won't put up with it, understand me?" He gestured an angry finger at the door. "Now take off—I'm busy."

Wager paused before leaving and tried to govern his Spanish inflection. "It's a murder, Councilman. People have to put up with a lot in a homicide investigation." He clenched his cheeks in a wide smile. "Thank you for your help."

He closed the door on Albro's hot silence; from the quiet emptiness around the bend of the hallway came the faint whisper of crepe soles.

1256 Hours

The telephone was already ringing when Wager reached the Homicide section.

"Wager? This is Captain Van Velson. I just had a call from Councilman Albro."

Van Velson was one of the captains in the administrative division, another of the recent promotions that would add to the number of chiefs and reduce the number of Indians. As a junior captain, he pulled duty on Saturdays and Sundays, and some of the more cynical said that that was the reason for all the promotions: so senior officers could have weekends off. "I just had an interview with Albro."

"I know that. He said you were in his office trying to dig up some kind of dirt on the City Council. The man was so pissed I could hardly understand what he was saying."

"Dirt? I asked about Councilman Green and his activities as committee chairman."

"Asked what, for God's sake?"

"The usual routine questions any homicide raises—any enemies, any causes somebody might have for killing him, that kind of thing."

Van Velson mulled that over. "I still have to make a report on this, Wager."

"You do what you have to, Captain. Just like I do."

"Right. As long as you know what's coming down."

"Thanks for the warning."

Wager held down the telephone's off switch and then dialed a number and waited while the bartender called Fat Willy to the phone.

"You got this crap settled yet, Wager?"

"A long way from it, Willy. Come up with anything?"

"Yeah—you sit there drinking coffee and want me to do your work, that right?"

"You got it. What've you heard?"

"A lot of heat, my man. A lot of angry people out on those hot streets. And tonight they'll be even hotter." He added slyly, "I even hear somebody say they going to take down a pig."

"Who's saying that?"

"What's new on my two people?"

"Nothing. You haven't given me anything to work with."

"Well, goddamn, this ought to be worth something!"

"I'll call Papadopoulos. How's that?"

"Shitty. Just like you. What good's that do?"

"I'll talk to the man again, Willy. That's all I can do. Now what do you have?"

"One of these punk gangs come here from L.A. The Uhuru Warriors, they call themselves. Sort of advertising what badasses they be. They say they going to shut down the plantation."

"Time? Place?"

"Well, they didn't send invitations, Wager! They just put the word on the street. You starting to sweat a little?"

No cop took lightly a threat to kill policemen; cops lived on the edge of that threat every time they put on the uniform that made them both authorities and targets. "What about Green—anything on him?"

"Nothing more than I told you already. He's clean."

"Is he?"

"What's that mean? You say it that way, what you mean by it?"

"It means there's things I want you to look into, Willy. His car, for one. It's missing. A black Lincoln Continental, license—"

"I know what his car looks like, Wager. Everybody knows what that car looks like."

"Then somebody should be able to spot it, if it's still around. Alleys, driveways, parking lots, wherever. Second, see if you can find out where he ate supper last night. Sometime between six and ten at night."

"What the hell you supposed to be doing?"

"Third, find out if he had a girlfriend—a blond one."

"Blond!"

"And fourth, find out if there's anything at all about a payoff for voting the right way on a zoning deal."

"Say, what?"

"You heard me."

"What's this crap, Wager?"

"Keep it quiet, Willy. Just see what you can find out." He added, "I hear the woman worked for him at the furniture store."

"No shit?" The heavy breathing slowed before he spoke half to himself. "A man got the itch, I reckon he got to scratch. But it don't sound like no Horace Green."

"See what you can find out."

He would, Wager knew, as much from competitiveness as from nosiness; Willy didn't like the idea of a cop—and a spic, at that—knowing more about his territory than Willy himself. And when he discovered the truth about Sonja Andersen, he would start to dig into the payoff question with both hands.

Wager's next call was to the Intelligence Unit. Fullerton, his voice muffled around something in his mouth, answered.

"Norm, this is Wager. I just heard a rumor about a threat to kill a cop."

"What? Wait a minute." In the background, Wager heard the busy tweedle of other telephones. "OK—just trying to get a little goddamn lunch down. What rumor?"

"One of my C.I.'s. He says it's supposed to go down to-night."

"Reliability?"

Wager sighed. "He's reliable, Norm. A long-time C.I."

"All right. What exactly did he say?"

Wager told him.

"You're sure it's the Uhuru Warriors?"

"That's what he called them."

Fullerton mumbled something to himself as he apparently made notes. "We've got a couple of those groups starting to form—moving from collectivities to gangs, you know."

"I remember."

"If one of them pulled it off, it'd give them a real boost. OK, Gabe—we'll shake a few bushes and see what runs out. If you come up with any corroboration, get on the hook right away."

Wager said he would and agreed to follow up the phone call with a memo; Fullerton wanted to make sure he had a paper trail on this one. Wager quickly wrote it and slipped it into an interoffice mailer, and then pondered the next name and number on the page of his notebook. Glancing at the wall clock, he decided he had time to call before Stubbs came back. The woman answered after the third ring. "Miss Wilfong? This is Detective Wager. I wonder if I can come by and talk to you for a few minutes."

1321 Hours

Julia Wilfong's apartment was in a four-plex of glazed brown brick and marked with glass brick panels, the kind whose design spoke, in its rounded corners and horizontal lines, of a 1930s sense of modern. There used to be a lot of buildings like it in Denver, Wager remembered, but most had been torn down and now only a few remained here and there in older neighborhoods that had once been fashionable. The tree-shaded street held a few other small complexes between large homes, many of which had been cut up into apartments. The next stage would be to divide those large apartments into smaller cubicles for a population that wanted only to rest and not to stay. That had happened already, a block or two down the street.

Apartment Four—upstairs and to the right. After buzzing himself through the entry, he followed the sweep of curving stone steps lined with bright aluminum rails. Julia Wilfong waited at the doorway. The glare of light from the glass-brick panel that formed the end of the hallway brought out wrinkles under her eyes that he had not noticed yesterday morning.

She led him through the short entry into a large living room with curtained windows that formed one corner. "Would you like a glass of iced tea, Detective Wager?"

"No, ma'am." He sat on a flowered chair across the coffee table from a matching couch where she settled. The table's glass top was clean of marks and held a stack of thumbed magazines on one end and a small pile of refolded newspapers on the other. The rest of the room, too, had the orderly air of someone who had worked out a place for each item and wanted to keep it there. "Have you lived here long?"

"Four years. Almost five, now. Why?"

"Just making polite conversation." He smiled. "Is Denver your home?"

"It is now. Like everybody else, I came here from some other place. It's a city of immigrants."

Wager could have told her that it was the same for a lot of people who had been born and raised here, as well—that everybody comes from some other place, and, finally, that place is only a buried corner in a fading memory. "Where's your home?"

"Philadelphia. It used to be. Detective Wager, I really am relaxed. Can we get on to your questions, please?"

"All right. Can you tell me if Councilman Green seemed worried or under any kind of strain in the last couple days before his death?"

She thought for a few seconds. "Not worried, exactly, no. Excited, maybe."

"How do you mean?"

"Hyper—full of energy and jokes. The way he got when a lot was going on and he was barely managing to keep up with it. He liked that: being on top of a lot of fast-moving events."

"Any idea what caused it?"

"I don't think anything special. It's a busy time on the council, plus all the committee work. And he was considering a reelection strategy."

Wager remembered she had mentioned that. He also remembered her reaction when he'd wanted to know about the councilman's personal life. "Some of the questions I have to ask don't make much sense, Mrs. Wilfong. But they have to be asked."

"Please ask."

"Did you ever hear any rumors or hints that Councilman Green had a mistress?"

Her reaction this time surprised him; instead of getting angry, she laughed—a rare flash of white that emphasized the width of her face, and maybe that was why she laughed so seldom. "Of course—he was a handsome man. And a lot of women find politics to be an aphrodisiac. I can name you a dozen who tried everything they could think of to crawl in bed with him."

"Did any do it?"

"A few claimed they did." The Afro wagged from side to side. "But I think they lied. Councilman Green loved his wife and children, and as far as I know he was faithful."

"Would it surprise you to learn he did have a mistress?"

"If you already know, why are you asking me?"

"I'm asking if it would surprise you."

"Yes. Obviously." She frowned. "Is that what you're saying? That he did?"

"No. I'm just trying to see him in the same way as those who knew him."

"You want to see him that way? Well, here's how I saw him: He was a fine man, an outstanding councilman, and a credit to his race. Anybody who goes into politics is going to have mud slung at him, Mr. Detective, and a black man is going to get a little extra from racists and bigots. I don't know who you've been talking to, but I do know that whatever bad they said about him was a lie."

He watched the quick anger ebb to leave her face placid.

"How did he get along with the other members of the Zoning Committee?"

"Fine. He was a good chairman."

"No hassles with any of them?"

"Hassles?" She shrugged. "They had their share of disagreements—every committee does. That's what the system's about: You have your disagreements and then work out something that satisfies everybody. Or nobody."

"Can you give me an example?"

She thought back. "The convention center site—that was a major issue with the whole council. The mayor wanted it one place, the council wanted it another. Horace—Councilman Green—was on the mayor's side in that one because it would have put it closer to the black community."

"I thought he was against any redevelopment that cleared out homes."

"There's redevelopment and then there's redevelopment. The convention center would have been set where there weren't any homes to worry about, and it would have meant jobs for people who need them badly."

"So he and the other councilmen argued over that?"

"Pretty hard, sometimes. Especially with Albro."

"He's vice chairman of Zoning?"

"That's the one. And it turns out he has a cousin who owns a lot of land uptown where he wanted to put the center." She rubbed thumb and forefinger together.

"A payoff?"

"Nothing that obvious. But you can assume that Albro and his cousin have a little understanding. Just don't you dare say I told you that, you hear me?"

"I'm only interested in homicide, Mrs. Wilfong." Wager glanced at his notebook, but he didn't see anything because, now that the topic was raised, he was concentrating on steering the conversation and he didn't want his eagerness to show. "Have you ever heard of any rumors of payoffs or influence peddling on the committee?"

"With Albro, you mean?"

"Or anyone else."

She looked at Wager, her eyes flat and expressionless. "Who've you been talking to?"

"A lot of people, Mrs. Wilfong."

She straightened out the stack of magazines, her eyes shifting from them to the gauze curtains swaying slightly in a breeze, to the Black Forest clock ticking steadily on the wall between two large paintings of flowers. Everywhere, in fact, except at him.

He waited.

"Councilman Horace Green was an honest man!"

He waited.

"Why don't you say something? Why do you just keep sitting there?"

"I'm waiting for you to tell me what you've heard."

"You are? You're that sure I heard something?"

"What did you hear?"

"What I heard isn't proof of anything. There are people out there who would like to see Councilman Green's name dirtied."

"How?"

"By telling lies about him."

"What kind of lies?"

"You don't give up, do you?"

That didn't require an answer.

Julia Wilfong stood and walked across the room to tap one of the paintings straight and then to the window to stare though the gauze into trees whose branches spread just beyond the glass. "It's not proof of anything!"

"If you've heard something, Mrs. Wilfong, somebody else has probably heard it, too. Why don't you tell me what you think the truth is?"

Lips tight, she came back to the brightly flowered couch and sat again. "It's not so much anything that's been said. It's the way a few things were done."

"In the committee, you mean?"

"Yes. There's a certain builder—he needed a zoning change, and he got it on a routine vote sponsored by Horace."

"But it wasn't a routine change?"

She shook her head. "It meant an R-1 to R-2 change— residential family to residential multifamily—and no one in the neighborhood knew anything about it until after it was done."

"What kind of property was it?"

"A retirement complex. Nursing homes, retirement homes—they're big things now. It used to be schools and apartment complexes, now it's retirement facilities. Builders are getting ready for the aging population, you know."

"What happened?"

"This developer bought an old school building and converted it into a retirement complex. He got it cheap because it was in an R-1 neighborhood—the only use it was supposed to have was as a school, nothing else."

"So after he bought it, he had the zoning changed and that increased the property's value?"

"He remodeled it, then sold it for four, maybe five, times what the whole thing cost him. It was very good business."

"Didn't anybody in the neighborhood ask about the building while it was being remodeled?"

"The builder didn't draw attention to it—he didn't begin remodeling until after the zoning change was approved, of course. Moreover, it's right on the edge of the zone—there's an R-2 area a block away—and most people don't know the zoning boundaries of their neighborhoods. This one, for instance, is a mixed zone now."

"What about the sign-offs from city departments? The impact studies and the posted notices?"

"Building inspection's only one part of the licensing procedure. Zoning's another. Most of the inspectors don't know anything about the zoning—they merely look at what they know: electrical, plumbing, fire codes, that sort of thing. And remember, they weren't involved until after the change was effected." She added, "As for the posted signs notifying residents of a proposed zoning change, there was some question as to whether they were properly displayed for the required period. Whoever was supposed to check on it, didn't—the order was lost. The change did appear on the council's agenda for both hearings, but not many people routinely read that document."

"So the change was acted on. With Councilman Green's support."

"Yes. And since it was in his district and no one on the committee knew much about it—and there weren't any objections from the neighborhood—it passed. Then, with that record from the committee, it passed the council as a piece of routine business."

Wager, too, watched the curtains sway slightly, the black edge of the windowsill first a sharp line against the gauzy light, and then an obscured and rippling shadow as uneasy as his own thoughts. "Do you have a name for the builder?"

She nodded. "K and E Construction. Kaunitz and Ellis."

CHAPTER 11

The word in Headquarters, when Wager returned, was that District Two had asked for reinforcements from the Reserves as well as from the uniformed divisions in the three other police districts. Both the motorcycle patrol and the horse patrol had been placed on standby, and medical personnel at Denver General were also on alert—though to Wager that seemed unnecessary, since Saturday night was always busy at the hospital's Knife and Gun Club. The tingle of excitement managed to stir the stale air of the hallways, and Wager glimpsed an occasional hurrying face that looked naked and out of place without the usual weekday crowds around it. He guessed that up on the fourth floor the Intelligence Unit would be setting up a briefing for the various commands and later for the Metro SWAT teams, and this afternoon the armory would be a busy and quietly tense place sharpened by the clean smell of gun oil and the efficient rattle and click of breech mechanisms.

It wasn't a drill.

That was the refrain that stripped away the usual wisecracks and the show of careless familiarity with threat that a lot of cops liked to use to prove how salty they were.

It wasn't a drill.

The phrase brought a wide look to eyes that passed in the hallways, eyes—Wager knew—that were allowed to show only eagerness and no hint of fear. The phrase even gave a spring to his own walk as his quick stride carried him past the location board and into the Homicide office.

A note in his message box said "Call Lt. W. ASAP" and Wager, thinking "All right, he's a sap," set it aside. Two calls from a William Jones had come in and the number on each slip was Fat Willy's. He knew what the man wanted and it wasn't going to be Wager's favorite chore. But he promised he'd try. He dialed Papadopoulos's extension, not really surprised to find the man still on duty. "Nick? It's Gabe Wager."

"Something you want?"

The bastard would want something from Wager some day. As sure as the sun crossed the sky, Nick-the-Greek would want a favor some day. But right now Wager was the petitioner and he had very little leverage. "That informant I told you about, he's the one who tipped us to the cop-threat. I'd like to give him something back."

"Give him our thanks and the good citizenship award."

"Come on, Nick. What can I tell him about Franklin and Roberts?"

"Tell him they're still in a holding cell."

"You know what I mean."

"And you know what I mean, Wager. Those scumbags are up for their last fall and I'm going to be the one to tuck them away for twenty-five to fifty."

"From what I hear, the case against them isn't all that strong."

Papadopoulos chewed that over a moment. "I don't know what you've heard. And I don't much give a damn, because it's not your case. I'm the assigned officer, remember? Now if you want to be their defense attorney, I'll send a copy of the charge sheet to you. Otherwise, Wager, butt out."

"Gracias, amigo."

"Thein pirazi."

Wager's hand rested on the telephone and his fingers drummed a moment. As sure as the sun crossed the sky . . . But that didn't help Willy now. A lot would depend on what more he had to offer. He swallowed a mouthful of now-lukewarm coffee and turned to the next item from the message box. Another slip told him that Fullerton had telephoned at 1252. Wager punched the numbers for the extension in Intelligence.

"Thanks for calling back, Gabe. Have you come across anything more on that threat?"

"No."

"We're taking it seriously—we've got some corroboration from other informants. Just a minute—" A hand covered the mouthpiece and then the voice came back. "Any possibility of getting you or someone from Homicide to be on-call tonight? The chief wants me to ask volunteers to come in. You know what that means."

It meant no comp time—you volunteered. "You want me in uniform?"

"No—just show up if the call goes out. We're trying to get people from each plainclothes unit—people familiar with the street."

That made sense: Homicide, Burglary, Assault, Rape—all the plainclothes units had officers who spent years building up contacts on the street. If some son of a bitch pulled anything, they might be able to recognize him later in a lineup. At best, they might even be able to stop it before it got bad. "I'll see what Stubbs can do, too."

"Great." Then he added in a softer voice, "By the way, I also got a line on the White Brotherhood. They're supposed to be having a meeting up in Morrison sometime this weekend."

That was a small foothills town about ten miles west of Denver. "When and where?"

"Don't know. Won't, until the last minute. That's the way they work it for security."

"Have you heard of any possible links to Green?"

Fullerton's voice dropped even further. "Nothing. I asked—in a roundabout way, you understand—but nobody's bragging. I figure if one of those scumbags did it, we'd hear about it because he couldn't keep his mouth shut. But nothing doing."

"I'd appreciate you staying on that."

"As much as I can, Gabe. I've already told you I can't push it. I'm taking a big chance tipping you about the meeting."

"I understand, Norm." He also understood there were ways of doing it if Norm had really wanted to. Still, it was a hell of a lot more cooperation than he got from Papadopoulos, and he was grateful for that much. "Thanks."

Wager was staring into space thinking about K and E Construction when Stubbs walked in. "Place is like a circus around here." He sank into his chair and wiped a handkerchief across his forehead. "And hotter than hell's basement outside. What's new?"

"Damned little—what've you got?"

He flipped open his notebook to tell Wager what he'd learned about the evicted families. It wasn't much. "I got in touch with every name except one—Calvert. Nobody knows where they went—probably living under a bridge somewhere. Most of the people never heard of Councilman Horace Green, and those who did weren't blaming him for the eviction."

"Despite what Dengren told them?"

Stubbs snorted. "From what I could tell, the only one listening to Dengren is Dengren. Anybody who heard about Green thinks he was killed by a white supremacist. And I tell you, there were a few times today that my arsehole puckered when I turned my back on a doorway." He wiped again. "Tonight's going to be a bad one."

Wager told him about Fullerton's request for volunteers. "I said I'd ask you."

Stubbs gave his little off-key whistle and didn't look happy. "I was supposed to visit the in-laws tonight, in Colorado Springs." But he finally said the right thing. "Yeah, why the hell not. A riot couldn't be any worse than visiting them. I just hope we get some comp time for all this crap." He began dialing the phone and a few seconds later was apologizing to his wife, "I can't help it, honey, it's the job. You know that. Yeah. . . . Yes, I will. . . . As soon as I can. . . . Me, too."

Wager only half heard Stubbs's words; in his mind, he was still going over what Julia Wilfong had told him and the possibilities her information had raised. Green was possibly cutting deals on the Zoning Committee. Of course, he may not have been, but the rumor had come now from two directions, and one of them—his aide—was worried about it. That gave it some weight. Nothing definite, no solid evidence of any wrongdoing, yet she had been worried and didn't want to say much more about it, so you had to give weight to that. At least one zoning change had been just a little bit irregular. Which was like being just a little bit pregnant. And it made the contractor a hell of a lot of money, as well as raising a possible threat if Green had decided to tell anyone about it.

Which, of course, opened a door to more motives for the councilman's murder, and all of a sudden the guy that everybody loved was turning into a guy that anybody could be after. And that, he reminded himself, could happen to anybody walking down the street, as the growing number of stranger-to-stranger killings proved. Which was one more possibility: that the killer had no motive. You had to remember that—it was as dangerous for a detective to start narrowing down too soon as it was to leave holes in an investigation.

"Did you happen to find out who the contractor is who's building that parking garage?"

Stubbs looked up from whatever he was writing. "No. I didn't ask. Why?"

Wager found the number in his notebook and dialed. A broadly accented voice answered on the first ring. "This is Detective Wager. Is Mr. Dengren in?"

The voice lost its accent. "Just a minute. I'll call him."

"What can I do for you, Officer?"

"Do you know who the contractor is who's building that parking garage?"

There was a pause. "That's all you want to know? You don't want to know anything about what's going down tonight?"

"What do you want to tell me?"

"Great God Jesus, man, this place is getting ready to blow all to hell and you want to know the name of a damn contractor? Didn't last night teach you damn people anything at all?"

"I'm listening."

"All right, listen to this: You better find that honky son of a bitch who killed Councilman Green. You hear that?"

"That's what I'm trying to do, Mr. Dengren."

"Yeah! I bet you are—contractors!"

"Do you know or not?"

"Sure, I know. K and E. They already got their damn sign stuck up in front of the apartments and they're starting to put up a big wire fence. Come Monday, it'll be a hole in the ground. But you better not worry about that, Mr. Policeman—you better worry about tonight. In fact, you better worry about the whole weekend. A long, hot summer all in one weekend." The line clicked dead.

1539 Hours

K and E Construction was open on Saturday until five, the woman's voice told Wager over the telephone, and, yes, either Mr. Kaunitz or Mr. Ellis would be in. The firm's office looked like a rambling one-story home that had a faintly Japanese roof line and a lot of wood siding to block out the street sounds. It blended in well with the few other low-rise apartment houses in the same block and with the remaining private residences that helped soften the neighborhood. Wager wondered if the zoning had to be changed to allow a commercial building in the area.

The entry, shielded by high hedges and a paneled door that managed to look both modest and expensive, opened to a reception desk and a blonde who did not look modest but who did look expensive. Wager identified himself and asked for Mr. Kaunitz or Mr. Ellis. The woman said, "Just a moment, please, I'll see if they're in," and pressed an intercom button. The answer was that Mr. Ellis was out, but Mr. Kaunitz could see him. "Right through that door, please." She smiled and aimed a long, red nail past the paper-littered desks and men and women too busy to notice one more visitor. Through the large windows, Wager glimpsed a grassy courtyard with a couple of umbrellas tilted over lawn tables and a sprinkling of empty chairs that might have been used on the lunch break. The office had an air of easy-going efficiency, as if the draftsmen and designers spent enough evenings here to make the place seem like home.

Mr. Kaunitz met Wager at the open door, a tall man whose nose had a sharp angle at the bridge and was as thin and bony as the rest of him. "Come in—what can I do for you?" A long-fingered hand waved toward one of the dark, padded chairs set around a coffee table. Kaunitz closed the door behind Wager before folding himself like a jackknife into another one.

"City Councilman Green. I'm investigating his murder."

"I heard about that. A real tragedy. He's going to be sorely missed."

"I understand you knew the councilman?"

"Yes. Mostly business, of course. We weren't close personal friends."

"Did you see much of him?"

"At City Council meetings, zoning hearings, that sort of thing. An occasional lunch when we could get together."

Kaunitz was younger than Wager expected, somewhere in his thirties, though with a thin and athletic man it was hard to tell exact age. He had heavy eyebrows and thinning hair and sat back in the curves of the chair, with his long legs crossed at the knees and his fingers crossed at their tips. He had a habit of waiting for Wager to talk and not volunteering anything beyond what was asked for. "I understand you recently remodeled a school building into a nursing home over on Fourteenth Street."

The eyebrows pinched together in brief recollection. "Oh yes, the Montclair property. Yes, we did."

"You make a lot of money off that one?"

"We try to make money off all our projects. We wouldn't be in business long if we didn't."

"You had to get a zoning change, right?"

"That's right."

"Did Councilman Green help you out?"

Kaunitz settled a little deeper into his chair and one of his bony fingers began to tap. But his expression didn't change. "He certainly helped as much as his official capacity allowed. We convinced him, and quite rightly, of the need for housing for our senior citizens, as well as the practicality of converting an idle and expensive piece of city property into an active and taxpaying enterprise."

"Can you tell me what kind of help he gave?"

"The same kind that any other petitioner gets going to his committee—staff assistance in filling out and filing the paperwork, careful attention to our argument. The usual."

"Wasn't there some opposition to the zoning change?"

"Some, of course. There always is. People tend to resist change even when it benefits them. But—" He didn't get a chance to finish; the door popped open and a stocky man slightly older than Kaunitz bustled in. He had a sun-reddened face and cropped hair that could have been either light blond or white. A band of pale flesh above the temples showed where a cap habitually rode. "Aaron, we've got . . ." He saw Wager and paused.

"Detective Wager, John Ellis. The detective's here about Horace Green's death."

"Jesus, that was shitty. Who in hell would want to kill a nice guy like that? You got any leads on it?"

"We're still investigating."

"He's asking about the Montclair project, John."

"What for? What's that got to do with Horace?"

"We haven't gotten that far yet."

Ellis tugged a chair around from the low table so he could sit and face Wager. "Well, let's get there." His trousers lifted to show the pointed toes of snakeskin cowboy boots. "What's all this about, Officer?"

"I'm trying to get an idea of the councilman's routine. How he did business, that kind of thing."

"Yeah? Well, he did his job. He was a good man to work with."

Kaunitz cleared his throat, and Ellis glanced at him and fell silent. The younger man asked, "You're interested in the process, I take it?"

Wager nodded. "That and anything else I can find out."

"I see. The process is essentially simple, though there are a lot of steps. After we locate a project and do all the cost estimates, we decide whether or not we want to go after it. Usually, if it's a bid-job, the owner handles the permits and clearances and we just concentrate on the work. Most people aren't going to get as far as asking for bids if there's any real question about permits."

"We get some. We been stung a couple times by some of those sons of bitches."

"That happens, yes."

"But the school, that wasn't a bid. You bought that before you applied for the zoning change, right?"

Ellis's pale eyebrows lifted and he looked at Wager with sharper interest. Kaunitz, fingers still laced, nodded. "We bought the property from the city, yes. Then we developed it."

"So you had to get the permits on that one after you bought it."

"It's not unusual. We often buy up properties here and there if the price is right and if they have a possibility of new life. It's good business for us and it's good for the city. A decaying core city means a lot of problems for everyone. Let's face it"—the corners of his mouth lifted in what might have been a smile—"the salaries of city employees—like you—depend on the tax base."

"Your company's putting up a parking garage over on Tremont, right?"

Kaunitz went through the list of properties in his mind. "Yes. The nineteen-hundred block."

"Did Councilman Green help you with that one, too?"

"His committee recommended approval of the application. Like all other applications, the final approval came on a vote by City Council."

"But did he help you get that vote?"

"Say, now—"

"It's all right, John. I'm certain the officer doesn't mean that the way it sounds. Councilman Green did no more for us than for any other petitioner to his committee. He was a gracious and fair man who looked after the city's welfare loyally, and he was gentlemanly in the running of his committee. But he did not do us any 'special' favors, and as far as I know he did none for anyone else, either."

"Listen—Aaron here's got the law degree. Me, I'm just a ham-handed builder, so I don't use fancy words. But I tell you flat out, Green didn't do us any favors, because we didn't ask for none. Now, if you got something you want to bring down on us, you just go ahead and try. We don't have a goddamned thing to hide."

Wager smiled. "I'm not saying you do. I'm just getting information. Did you see Mr. Green any time on the eleventh?"

"Wednesday?" Kaunitz shook his head and then double-checked a page in his appointment book. "No."

"When did either of you see him last?"

"What in the hell—"

"It's all right, John. Really." Kaunitz leafed deliberately back through the appointment book. "We met for lunch on Friday, five June. The Rattlesnake Club." Again the corners of the mouth lifted slightly. "I'm sure the maitre'd's reservations book will verify that."

"There's no need to ask, as far as I know, Mr. Kaunitz. Can you both tell me where you were on the night of the eleventh?"

"The night he was killed? I think you're getting out of line with your insinuations, Officer."

"You're goddamned right, and I happen to be friends—"

"It's a routine question, Mr. Ellis. I'm asking everyone who knew him the same question." He smiled again. "So there's no insinuation."

Kaunitz studied Wager with a sleepy but unblinking gaze, then shrugged and turned back to his calendar. "I left the office after a four-thirty appointment that lasted about an hour. Drove home—another thirty minutes or so. Then supper. Then my wife and I went to the Denver Symphony"—the eyes lifted—"we have season tickets. You can verify our presence with the Morrises."

Even Wager had heard of the Morrises.

"After the symphony—around ten or so—the four of us went to The Chrysler for drinks, and my wife and I returned home at about twelve-thirty or one."

"Me, I went home. Watched the Cubs, went to bed. I had to be on a job at seven next morning."

"You're married?"

A red flush came up Ellis's neck and settled in his cheeks. "You mean I need a witness? Is that it? Well, mister, you can ask my wife; and if that's not good enough, you can go to hell."

Wager stood. "Thanks for the information."

1603 Hours

Stubbs was still shoving papers from one pile to another on his desk when Wager got back. "Did you find out anything?"

Wager shook his head. "Nothing to put in the file."

"Lieutenant Wolfard called. That's about what I told him—nothing yet."

That saved Wager from having to talk to the man again. He spread his notes across the glass surface of his desk and scanned them for any mention of K and E Construction.

"Gabe?" Stubbs, looking uncomfortable, swiveled his chair around to face Wager. "Can I ask you something?"

"Go ahead."

He gnawed on his lip for a moment. "I know I'm new in Homicide, but I've been a cop on the street for five years. And a good one."

"Fine. You made detective, right?"

"That's right—I did."

"So?"

"So I want to know why I have this feeling that you're keeping stuff back from me."

Wager studied the man's face, a mixture of embarrassment and anger at having to ask that kind of question. "Like what?"

"Like the questions you had about the contractor—calling up Dengren and asking him who it was. It sounded like you had a lead on something. Then you headed out somewhere." He jabbed a finger at Wager's notes. "Now you're back to check out something, and not a word to me about what it is."

"I went over to talk to the contractors, Stubbs."

"There, see? I didn't know where you were going. And I still don't know why you want to talk to them. That's what I mean: Are we in this together or not? People told me you were hard to get along with, but I figured if we're working together on a case, we work together. You know what I mean?"

"So people told you I was hard to get along with. You don't want to listen to people, Stubbs, you want to listen to me. I'm the nicest guy I know."

"Yeah? Ross tells me Axton's the only one who volunteered to work with you. That's why he was your partner for so long."

"Is that what Ross says? By God, you better believe what Ross says. Ross knows every goddamned thing there is to know." Wager turned back to his papers. "We work with the people we're assigned to work with. You're here because your name came up on the roster with mine."

"Wrong, Wager. Believe it or not, I requested it."

"What?"

"I asked to work with you. Despite what I heard."

Wager looked at the man anew. His jaw—receding like his forehead from a pointed nose—thrust forward a little to make his face seem not quite so round and malleable. "That's really daring, Stubbs. Why would you want to do a daring thing like that?"

"I heard you were good."

Well, yeah, Wager could agree with that; he was good. What he couldn't decipher was Stubbs's willingness to say so. In the first place, he didn't need Stubbs or anyone else to tell him what a good cop he was. He knew. In the second place, Wager wasn't comfortable with cops who sucked around for something. "That makes me feel warm and wiggly all over. What am I, your Boy Scout leader or something?"

"No, actually, Wager, I think you're kind of an asshole. I think Ross might be right. But so far you know a lot more about homicide than I do, and I want to learn. So I'm asking you: What's with the contractors? Is it a lead or isn't it? And what the hell have you turned up to make them important?" Stubbs added, "I'm your new partner in this, like it or not. You want me to tell you anything I turn up, and you'd be pissed if I held something back. But you think it's OK to hold something back on me. Is that it?"

There was some fairness in Stubbs's accusation, and beneath his suspicion and even that shade of contempt he had for the man, Wager felt a mild twinge for maybe not giving him a chance. Every man deserved the opportunity to screw up. Wager had taken advantage of his own chances a time or two. "I guess I can tell you. But you'd better keep it quiet because it could be your ass along with mine if something goes wrong."

"What do you mean, my ass?"

Wager smiled. "Remember Councilperson Voss? Well, now I'm out on that limb. But there's plenty of room for you, too. You want to hear? Yes or no."

The little jaw moved out a fraction more. "Yeah. Yeah, I want to hear. What fucking limb?"

"I heard Green might have been on the take. Now I've got a little corroboration—I think K and E Construction paid him for at least one zoning change."

Stubbs took a few seconds to think that over and then a few more to consider what it meant. "Jesus Christ, Wager. That's a real bag of worms."

"You asked. Now, you can forget what you heard if you want to. As long as you keep your mouth shut, nobody will know I told you a thing about it."

The younger man frowned at his desk and the pictures of wife and kids lined up beneath its glass top. "The D.A.'s office should be in on this, Gabe. Christ, even the FBI. What the hell are you sitting on it for?"

"You're sure you want to know?"

He ran the tip of his tongue across a dry lower lip. "Yeah. Sure. I'm in it with you."

Wager still wasn't certain he should tell him all of it, but what the hell, the man was drawing a detective's pay, too, and he was old enough to know what he was getting into. Or thought so, anyway. "I'm sitting on it because it's still just guesswork. If the information's wrong, I don't want Green's reputation smeared. Especially if the street thinks we're doing it to cover up a racist killer."

"Christ, I never thought of that angle."

"And if the information's right, it might have something to do with the murder."

"Voss told you about it? I mean, it had to be somebody on the City Council, right?"

Wager shook his head. "I promised I wouldn't say."

"You know why she made you promise that, Wager! If something goes wrong—if the information's no good— she'll deny she ever said a thing to you."

"That's about it."

Stubbs's little whistle emphasized one of those sudden lulls in the telephone and radio traffic that echoed down the hallway. "We are on a limb, aren't we?"

Stubbs hadn't made the initial decision to crawl out there—that had been Wager's alone, and it wouldn't be fair to pull him along blindly. "You can still forget you heard anything. You don't say anything about it; I don't say that I told you. If something goes wrong, you're in the clear."

"No, I reckon not. We're on this case together. That means together." Stubbs's words sounded good, but they didn't bury all his worry. "Bribery and extortion involving public officials—that's definitely FBI. I read up on it: all bribery and extortion investigations of public officials alive or dead are supposed to be approved at FBI headquarters in Washington."

"This is a homicide investigation. It's my jurisdiction— our jurisdiction—and our sworn duty." Besides, from what Wager had seen of the FBI, they would screw things up. They'd want to solve their case, and to hell with Wager's. They'd plea-bargain away any homicide charge to get a conviction in the bribery case, and Wager explained that to Stubbs.

"Yeah." Stubbs was still trying to convince himself. "That's true. The homicide's ours." And Wager could see the thought in the man's worried face: It's too late to fret about it now. "So all right, what do you have on it?"

Wager told him about the zoning change for the schoolhouse and about Ellis's touchiness.

"And the guy was wearing cowboy boots?"

Wager nodded.

"You want me to check out his story?"

"It'll have to be quiet."

"So I'll be quiet about it."

1755 Hours

Officially, he was off duty now, but the only difference was that Wager drove his own car instead of a police vehicle. Being on call meant no drinking or going beyond the dispatcher's range; it meant going about your life while trailing a leash to the office.

He swung through the evening traffic on East Colfax and spotted the familiar pink sign for the Satire Lounge and turned into the drive leading to the parking lot behind. The last hour or so had been spent going over and over the time sequences of Green's last day, and arranging and rearranging all the known information about the victim and everyone who had anything to do with him. Stubbs tried to dig into the paper background of K and E Construction, but there wasn't much that could be learned on a Saturday. Wager had tried to figure out what Green might have had going in the time gap of 6:30 to 8:45 on the evening of his death. He had left Sonie Andersen around 6:30 or even earlier, missed his appointment at the Prudential buffet, and shown up at Vitaco close to 9 P.M. And, Wager recalled from the autopsy report, he had chicken and peas for supper. Unless he ate right after he left the Vitaco reception— which had not served chicken and peas—he must have eaten dinner in that two-hour period. All Wager had to do was discover which of ten thousand restaurants he might have dined at. If he had eaten at a restaurant instead of another girlfriend's home.

The Satire Lounge was one of the survivors along the East Colfax strip, thriving when the street had been the major porno and nightlife center of Denver and still doing well, despite the clean-up spurred by local merchants and residents. The bar side was crowded as ever with a lot of people who seemed to know each other, shouting jokes back and forth along the fluorescent gleam of shiny wood. The restaurant side, with its half-dozen wooden booths looking toward the open kitchen door, was almost empty, as usual. Wager had been coming here since he was in uniform; cops got a good discount because they helped keep the place quiet, and it didn't hurt to have friends patroling the streets. Generations of cops kept coming back because it didn't hurt to save a few bucks on meals, and the green chili was good. A pair of uniformed officers sat at the booth by the window, where they could watch the street while they ate. Their radio on the table between them crackled with the dim traffic of the district. Wager didn't know either man, a sign of how long he had been away from Patrol Division, but one of them recognized him and nodded hello.

"You ready to rumble, Sarge?" he asked Wager.

Wager shared a bench with the one who slid over to make room. His name tag said "Bennett," and Wager introduced himself. The one who knew him was Martin. "I hear tonight's the night."

Bennett turned the radio's speaker down to a mutter. "You can feel it. The street's quiet, but you can feel it." He pulled at his Coke. "You're in Homicide, Sarge?"

Wager said yes, and Bennett asked how he liked Homicide and nodded approvingly when Wager lied and said how much he missed the excitement of Patrol. Wager asked them about names they shared, on both sides of the law, and caught up on the precinct's latest gossip. To a civilian, it looked like a bunch of fat-assed cops telling jokes and wasting the taxpayer's money when they should be out arresting muggers and rapists. But it was the grapevine in action. Street cops knew their own territory better than anyone else—the buildings, the twisting alleys and nameless slots between dark walls, the tangles of parking lots and fences and trash dumpsters behind the stores, the people who lurked in the shadowy corners and dim doorways and usually didn't want to be found. And the only way a plainclothes cop could keep up with that subsurface current of humanity was to talk with the uniformed cops who patroled it regularly.

"Your people got any word about Five Points tonight?" Martin mopped at his rice with a tattered tortilla and came back to the subject that was always there even when they talked of other things.

"I'm on call, along with almost everybody else. That's all I know." Wager ladled more chili across the roll of tortilla and meat on his plate. "You heard anything?"

"Only what the sergeant said at roll call."

They talked awhile about that and other threats that had been reported over past years and what had happened during those times. Wager got the talk around to the White Brotherhood and even touched on the cause of the unrest—Green's killing—probing for anything the officers might have picked up without knowing they'd found an item of interest.

"Is that what it's all about? The White Brotherhood's supposed to have offed that councilman?"

"It's a possibility. Have you seen any of them on Colfax lately?"

"Naw, the precinct's pretty quiet anymore. Shitheads like that, they go out north of the city limits now. That's where the skin joints are now."

Bennett added, "Northglen. They can have them. I like the street quiet."

As if in answer, the radio popped a call for patrolmen to respond to a robbery in progress; Martin grabbed it up and took the call, and the two men hustled out to their cruiser, leaving their food half-finished, with a shout to the stocky, sweating cook who came to the kitchen doorway, "Be back, Ernie—keep it hot for us."

Wager watched the flickering lights of the cruiser swing across the lanes of traffic and out of sight toward downtown. Then he finished his enchilada, wishing for the luxury of a beer to soften the bite of the chili. A soda pop just didn't do it. His own radio picked up the police response to the robbery and in a few minutes he heard Martin's voice call for assistance from the Assault section. If the victim had been dead or dying, the call would have been to Homicide, and Max or Devereaux—who had tonight's seven-to-three—would be on their way. Despite the threat of a riot, the steady parade of the city's violence had to be matched by the equally steady parade of duty watches.

"You finished? Can I get you some coffee?" The young waitress hurried in from the barroom, her pencil still busy with an order from that side.

Wager checked the time and shook his head; the girl scratched the total and said thanks and went quickly to the kitchen. He left the usual large tip and stopped off at the men's room before dropping a couple of dimes into the pay phone lit by a white glow from the cigarette machines. After the routine, he heard Fat Willy's heavy voice. "Where the hell you calling from, Wager? Sounds like you in the middle of a riot already."

"The Satire Lounge. You have anything for me?"

"If I did, you're not in no hurry to get it—I called you this afternoon, man."

"Where do you want to meet?"

"Not that place—it's got about as much class as you do."

"Try the green chili—it's good."

"Yeah, that's all I need: a belly full of spic sauce. I'll meet you over at City Park, the east side. That way won't nobody see us together."

It was a quiet area, ill-lit by a few streetlights that shone emptily through the park's trees and across the mown grass of the municipal golf course. A steady stream of traffic pulsed through the darkness on Twenty-third Avenue, but the narrow winding roads leading to the parking lots that served the natural history museum and the zoo were almost vacant. Wager turned off Colorado Boulevard, between the old brick pillars that marked the park entrance, and began cruising slowly around the winding service roads. His headlights finally picked up the gleam of Fat Willy's white Cadillac moored like an ocean liner beside the shaggy dark of a towering spruce. He pulled the Trans-Am beside it and got out. In the open window of the Cadillac glimmered the wide-brimmed white hat and Fat Willy's face masked by dark glasses.

"Why the hell do you wear sunglasses at night, Willy?"

"Privacy, my man. I like to travel incognito."

"Right—a white panama hat and matching Caddy. You're incognito, all right."

"Let's just say I don't want to be seen talking to the likes of you. And the glasses keep your ugly face from hurting my tender eyes. You talked to that Nick-the-Greek asshole yet?"

"No," he lied. "I want to hear what you have, first."

Willy's breath panted slightly against the weight of his own flesh and he listened a moment to the distant night sounds of the city. "All right, I'll tell you. But by God I want something for it."

Wager turned his back to the faint gleam of a pair of headlights swinging around on the parkway across the wide lawns. "Let's hear it."

"I found the blonde he was planking—that store manager of his. Name of Sonie Andersen."

"That's not news anymore. Who'd you talk to?"

"My sources. That's all you got to know." The sunglasses turned to gaze through the screen of spruce limbs at the flicker of passing lights on Colorado Boulevard. "I suppose I can't blame him for dipping into that little honeypot." The glasses turned back, their lenses dotted with the glow of street lamps. "But don't get me wrong, my man—I got no itch to screw white or do white. I don't need one damn thing from whitey."

Wager didn't care about that. "Who else knows about it?"

"Enough so it ain't no big secret. But it wasn't all over the street, neither. The people, they didn't talk about it all that much. They was sort of protecting him against himself, you know what I mean?"

Wager got the idea. "What about payoffs? You hear anything on that?"

"Now that's a hard one. I caught some whispers, but that's all. That's not something a lot of the people would know about."

"What whispers, Willy?"

"That maybe he did do some favors for some big contractors. That maybe he was pulling in some extra cash because he could do favors for people."

And if he had to launder the money, the furniture store would be the place to do it. Wager made a mental note to ask for a subpoena for the store's books. "Any names?"

"Naw. It's not like him getting a little jellyroll on the side, you know? The people just ain't all that excited about no payoffs. That kind of shit happens all the time."

"Who told you?"

"That's my business."

"It's a murder, Willy. That makes it my business, too. I'd like to talk to your informant."

"No way, Wager! My people talk to me only. No way am I going to up and say, 'Hey, tell this policeman what you told me.' You think I want people to know what kind of company I been keeping?"

"So don't tell him I'm a cop."

"Shit, you got cop sticking out all over you."

"It could be important, Willy. I'd like to ask him some questions."

"What you like and what you get's two different things. I don't go handing my people over to the police, Wager. That I do not do."

"So far you haven't given me a damn thing I don't already know. I can't use any of that for leverage on Papadopoulos."

"The hell you can't—you better!"

"Then give me something I can use. What about Green's car? Any of your people find it?"

"No. That White Brotherhood's probably got it chopped up and sold in little bitty pieces by now."

"Did you find out where he ate supper?"

"No."

"Did you find somebody who saw him after nine o'-clock?"

"No, I didn't!"

"Then what the hell have you brought me? Franklin and Roberts have got your ass in a sling and Papadopoulos has theirs, and all you give me is crap I already know!"

"Yeah? How the hell did I know you already knew it? And I ain't telling you where I get my information, Wager. I goddamn know what will happen to my people if I lead you to them—they end up just like Franklin and Roberts!"

If a man has no honey in his jar, he'd better have some in his mouth. It was a saying he remembered from Grandma Villanueva, and Wager smiled and said quietly, "OK, Willy. I'll do what I can with what you've told me. I'll sure try. But since I didn't hear much, don't be surprised if I can't do much."

"Shit!" The wide-brimmed hat dipped to shadow the man's wide face and Wager saw the heavy shoulders clench angrily.

"Monday's day after tomorrow," he reminded Willy. "About thirty hours away."

The brim lifted. "I ain't telling, Wager! I'll tell you something else, though—Sister Green, the councilman's widow, going to be on the street tonight. Trying to cool things down."

"Who's idea was that?"

"Church people. Preachers and all. They got them some basketball player or something, and Mrs. Green said she be there, too. Talk to the people, you know; tell them ain't no sense tearing things up." Fat Willy grunted. "I hope to hell they listening. This here crap costing me money."

"How's that?"

"Business, my man. Deals in the air, deals on the ground, deals all around, and deals going down—business. Which, of course, I ain't telling no cop about, either."

"I'm only interested in Green's killer."

"Shit you are. You be out busting them White Brother-fuckers, you interested in his killer."

"That's what you think?"

"That's what I know. And I ain't the only one—the word's

all over: You cops ain't doing shit because it's the White Brotherhood killed Green."

"Get me something on them, Willy. If you have something, give it to me and I'll haul them in."

The sunglasses stared through the dark at Wager. "I believe you might. You just dumb enough to try something like that all by yourself, ain't you? I'd like to see that—I wish to hell I had something so's you would do it. But all I got is what's on the street."

CHAPTER 12

Saturday, 14 June, 1944 Hours

That was all anyone had: street rumors about the White Brotherhood, rumors about threats to his wife and to other prominent blacks, rumors about what was going to happen tonight and who was threatening to do it. Wager tried sitting in his apartment with the TV low enough so he could monitor the police traffic on his radio, but the air felt stuffy and the walls—bare except for a couple of pictures and his NCO's sword—seemed to swell inward from the pressures building up outside.

There were familiar pressures from inside, too: stray echoes of the visits Jo had made to this apartment, and he could even hear her laughter at his few wall decorations— "Uh, oh. I stepped on his macho"—which brought the ghost of a smile to his mind even now. That had been one of those times when they were hunting for some subject to talk about that didn't have anything to do with the job. It had been difficult, more so for him than for her, because until she forced him to, he hadn't considered anything beyond the job to be worth talking about. But slowly and with a lot of retreats back to police work, they had found other things, usually following her lead—photography, fishing, horses. They even had a ski trip vaguely planned. And the changes in his life wrought by her hadn't been so bad. Sitting in his apartment, the police traffic a steady buzz at the edge of silence, he could still see that little gleam of triumphant laughter in those golden eyes when she'd tricked or teased him into trying something new. It hadn't been so bad at all. Then, of course, he had talked her into that raft trip. That had been bad.

He stood and, with an effort, forced his mind away from that theme. It was one thing at night when the loss and sense of failure came on him in his sleep. But he didn't need to surrender to it now. He was awake. He could control his own mind. He didn't have to sit here and be drawn into a dead past like a cockroach down a swirling toilet.

The television show was lousy, anyway. Something about some old lady solving a homicide because the killer drank a certain brand of herb tea. Wager didn't think even Golding could do it that way. Better to ride around in the Trans-Am, where he could feel the wind across his face and see motion and lights; better than sitting here with the television on and not watching it, with the radio on and not listening. Better to be out close to whatever might happen than trying to keep his mind free of those other thoughts.

He drove slowly along Downing to Colfax, the street scene gliding past the window to bring its familiar narcotic for the images that troubled him in his apartment. The glitter of a cluster of emergency lights a block or two west caught his eye, and, swinging toward them, he pulled into the parking lot of an Arbie's. Hanging his badge on his jacket pocket, he strolled over to the teams of policemen standing beside a handful of civilians.

"Hello, Blainey. What's going on?"

"Gabe!" The black officer grinned hello and pointed his Bic pen at a figure sitting in the back seat of the cruiser. "We got us a social reformer." He lifted a butcher knife from the hood of the cruiser. The long, narrow triangle of steel flashed icily in the blink of the emergency lights. "He's trying to get rid of sin."

"Aren't we all. What's his gimmick?"

Near the second police car, a stout black woman shook her head angrily at something an officer said, and pointed indignantly toward Blainey's cruiser. "Him!"

"He's going after the ladies with this pig-sticker. Says he wants to get rid of abonibations in the sight of the Lord."

"Get rid of what?"

"Aboniba—whatever the hell he calls it. Tattoos. Tattoos are sinful, he says. They're not from God."

"So he's going to cut them off people?"

"You got it." Blainey set the long knife down and began writing again. "But I guess he couldn't find anybody to volunteer, so he had to go out looking for customers. I hope the good Lord can save me from people who want to save the world."

Wager peered into the cruiser's back seat, where a slender figure hunched forward against the pull of his arms handcuffed behind him. The pale face glared back at Wager, his eyes wide with silent, wild rage and a smear of grime and blood streaking one side of his face. Under the dirt and tangle of hair, he seemed somewhere in his twenties, skinny with an insane tautness, and shorter, perhaps, than Wager. He was another of those released from a mental hospital because the courts said they had a civil right to be free. And because there wasn't enough money to house and feed them.

"He from around here?"

"Won't say. No name, no address. Nothing but that there butcher knife and a thing for tattoos."

"First bust?"

"First time I seen him, anyway."

The victim was the woman talking to the other pair of officers. She was still shaking her head rapidly, her spray of stiff hair wagging in the haze of passing car lights, and Wager recognized her as one of the street's regulars. "Hello, Butterball. What kind of trouble are you into this time?"

"Officer Wager! I ain't in no trouble—it's him." She again pointed a long red fingernail at the police car where Blainey leaned over the hood to write. "He's the one got trouble. Coming at me with that knife like that."

"He just wanted your tattoos, Butterball."

"He ain't getting them! That man is crazy and he ought to be locked up!"

One of the uniformed officers looked up from taking her statement. "Is your name really Butterball?"

"Naw, it's Mary Murphy. Don't I look Irish? I been on this street ten years; I got rights! I ain't going to let him or nobody start chasing me around with no knife."

Wager caught a glimpse of a familiar Honda Civic turn into the parking lot and watched Gargan—pulled, like Wager, onto the streets by the uneasiness spreading from Five Points—walk toward him.

"I thought I recognized your smiling face, Wager. What's going on?"

"Officer Blainey's in charge. He can tell you."

"It's a real pleasure seeing you, too." The reporter glanced at the woman still talking loudly to the officers, and then bent to study the face of the man in the car. "Assault?"

"That's right."

Gargan snorted something from his sinuses and spit it out. "First call tonight. Saturday night, too. Colfax isn't the circus it used to be."

"Things change, Gargan. Most things."

"Ha. If I could get any better, I would change, Wager. And you're sure as hell not changing—you can't get any worse." He listened for a moment to a call for police to respond to a fight in progress a dozen blocks away. A voice answered the dispatcher and a moment later they heard the distant wail of a siren. "What have you heard about Five Points?"

"The same thing you have."

Gargan glanced at him. "You think the White Brotherhood did it?"

"That's the rumor."

"I'm asking what you think."

Wager smiled. "We've known each other for years, Gargan. And you know I don't think."

The reporter spat again. "Yeah. I keep forgetting." But he didn't walk away in anger as he usually did. Instead, he idly watched Blainey pause in his writing to ask the suspect a question before laboriously filling in another section of the report. The suspect only shook his head, eyes fixing hotly on Blainey as the officer wagged his head and went back to his paperwork. "I never got a chance to tell you this, Wager: I was sorry to hear what happened to Josephine Fabrizio. She was good people."

He didn't reply with the first thing that came to his mind. Instead, he answered stiffly, "That's right. She was."

"I met her a few times in the Records office. I just wanted to say I'm sorry."

Again, he forced himself to be polite. He didn't like Gargan—never had, never would. And he really didn't give one tiny damn what Gargan felt or thought. But the man was showing respect for Jo, and that demanded manners. "Thanks."

Gargan nodded shortly as if finishing an unpleasant chore he'd promised himself. "Just wanted to tell you." He wandered toward Butterball and the pair of uniforms finishing up their part of the complaint.

Wager had a twinge of something unfamiliar as he watched the narrow back swagger toward the police car. It wasn't remorse—he didn't feel remorse about anything he said to Gargan. It was more a recognition of having shared something valuable but fleeting: the sudden and ill-defined awareness that Gargan had a part in Wager's own life—that he was in the picture that had included Jo. After all these months, her name was still alive in somebody else's mind, and it turned out to be Gargan's. Of all people, Gargan had become some kind of reference point for Wager's memories of Jo. If he let it, the recognition might even generate a little warmth for the man—despite the defensiveness Wager felt about her memory. But he wouldn't let it, because he knew Gargan. The moment would pass, and Gargan would do something, say something, in some way show that he was the same anus he always was despite his appreciation of Jo. Which, when Wager thought about it, was a comforting idea; dislike of the man was more familiar than this uneasy and new feeling that one of Wager's most vital and important memories was shared with Gargan.

The calls began to come in just after 9:00, half-a-dozen alerts and requests for officers to respond to disturbances and crimes in progress in District Two. It had the marks of a coordinated plan—H-hour at 9 P.M.—and in his mind's eye, Wager spotted the locations on the city map. They formed a wide circle around the Five Points neighborhood, probably an attempt to spread out the police so the main disturbance could get well-started before enough cops could gather to squelch it. But the SWAT teams were already deployed and they would not be committed for such routine calls, Wager knew. Their vans would be in reserve at some quiet corner close by, and near them the K-9 trucks with their slotted air vents would be waiting, too, the tense night punctuated by the eager whines of the dogs.

He pulled his Trans-Am against a shady curb on Columbine Street and followed the reports as they came over the police band. Burglar alarms had been set off by broken windows in the fronts of two stores, and looters had been reported running from the scenes; responding officers were looking for suspects or witnesses and guarding the premises until the owners could come down. A car had been set afire at Twenty-eighth and Curtis and firefighters reported hearing gunshots as they responded. They wanted police protection immediately. A patrol car was fired on by a sniper in the vicinity of Twenty-seventh and High—half a dozen blocks from Wager—and backup units were responding to cordon off the area and begin a systematic sweep.

So far, the dispatcher had not put out the call for officers on standby to report, but Wager had the familiar feeling it would be soon. The watch was stretching thinner as more requests for backup came in, and call numbers for units from the adjoining districts began to be heard on the local frequency. He guessed that recruits from the Police Academy had been turned out to relieve those veterans for duty in this district.

A brightly painted Channel 9 television van, with a cherry picker folded against its roof, lumbered past Wager.

A pair of motorcycle officers followed, emergency lights dark as they slowed a bit for stop signs and then darted across in front of oncoming cars. The traffic sections would set up vehicle control points at the intersections surrounding the most volatile action, while Patrol would move in to determine whether or not a SWAT team should be called to the scene. That was often a tricky question; once SWAT was called, command of the scene shifted to the team commander. And despite a lot of schooling, many of the officers in Patrol did not like to give up their responsibility, because that meant they weren't cop enough to control their own territory.

Through his partly open window, he heard the drawn-out wails of sirens and, for a moment, the wind-tossed shouts of voices. He thought briefly about driving in for a closer look and decided against it; there was no sense adding to the confusion of traffic, and besides, he didn't want his Trans-Am trashed. A fancy car driven by a Chicano through the middle of a Five Points riot. All he'd need to attract more friendly notice would be a Confederate flag on the antenna.

Settling against the seat back, he listened to the muted sounds of the radio and waited for the alert that would call him and other standbys in. Initial queries and requests had slacked off and now situation reports were starting to come back. Wager recognized a few of the voices, and his imagination filled in the pictures that the words only hinted at. DiFeo, the born-again detective in Burglary who always said "God bless you" instead of "Thanks," called for an ambulance in the 3200 block of Marion, where a looter had been injured by a shattering plate-glass window. Ryan, the alcoholic sergeant from the district's fourth precinct, called for support in pursuit of a fleeing vehicle. Another voice that Wager did not know needed help to head off trouble: "We're going to need some backup. We got a bunch of juveniles down on the corner of Thirty-third look like they're trying to organize themselves into something."

"Yessir. We'll get it to you."

"Ten-four."

Wager started the Trans-Am and swung it around toward downtown and the Headquarters Building. It wouldn't be long now before they called in the standbys.

The personal car lot was almost full, the yellow-orange glow of tall lamps bouncing back from metal roofs to illuminate the occasional figure hurrying like Wager toward the entry. Above, in the bands of dark windows that striped the stone façade, lights from various offices dotted the building. Wager let himself through the security gate and nodded to the uniformed sergeant behind the long shelf of desk. Upstairs, the civilian on duty in Crimes Against Persons lifted a hand when she saw him come in.

"I was just going to call you, Detective Wager. Lieutenant Wolfard just sent out a call for all standbys."

"I'll tell him I'm here."

Despite all the activity in the halls, the offices were almost empty; most of the duty-roster were on the streets, and the off-duty personnel stayed only long enough to be told where to report. At his desk in the corner, beneath the silently flickering television set, Devereaux talked to someone on the telephone about a new development in one of his dozen open cases. "Four years ago—yeah—two kids burned to death in a dumpster. No, this kid comes in a couple hours ago to say his father set it on fire and burned them up. No, he's a screwball—the kid. He's such a flake—hates his father so much that he'd turn off a jury. No, I've got it down to where the old man did start a fire in somebody's backyard, but that's all I've got. Yeah. Yeah. He's got a brother knows something about it, too, but he's in jail for butt-fucking his brother, so what good's he in court?"

Despite the riot, routine work had to go on, too.

Wager stuck his head into Wolfard's office and the lieutenant, on the telephone, beckoned him to sit down. "Yeah, that's right." He covered the mouthpiece to tell Wager, "Kansas City."

Out-of-state units always wanted to talk to a detective, and at night C.A.P. got all the calls whether it was their work or not. Wager settled into the plastic chair and glanced through his mail while Wolfard kept saying "Yeah, yeah, that's right." Nothing from outside had been delivered in the last few hours, and none of the memos said anything that was important. But one did catch his eye, a warning from the chief against taking liberties with bodies of the deceased. Wager had heard the story: a decapitation victim found where he had committed suicide by hanging himself with a piece of thin wire; when the body was placed on the stretcher for conveyance to Denver General, the investigating officer tucked the man's head under his arm like a football. The memo said that when the sheet was pulled off, a nurse fainted and chipped her tooth and now was suing the city. All personnel were reminded of the appropriate section in the Operations Manual that prohibited unprofessional conduct, and of Section 18-13-101 of the Colorado Criminal Code, which classified abuse of a corpse as a Class Two misdemeanor.

"Do you have anything yet, Wager? Anything at all?" Wolfard was finally through with Kansas City and, rubbing at the dark flesh under his eyes, sipped at a steaming cup and stared at Wager like he was a stranger.

Wager shook his head. "Nothing more than I had at the end of the shift."

"That wasn't too damned much."

Wager stared back at the man's hostility. "That's right."

Wolfard rubbed his eyes again. "You remember what the chief said about keeping me informed so I could keep him informed?"

Wager remembered.

Wolfard slid a memo from under a blank sheet of paper and pretended to read it closely. "I thought you might have forgot. I goddamned thought you might have forgot, since you forgot to tell me about the possibility that Green was involved in malfeasance."

"I don't have any evidence of that."

"But you goddamned well had information about it. You had it and you didn't tell me, by God—what you did was go over to Councilman Albro's office and accuse him of taking bribes, too!"

"I went over to Councilman Albro's office to check out the rumor. If he thinks I accused him, let him file a formal complaint."

Wolfard snapped the memo at Wager. "What the fuck do you think this is? Van Velson sent it down. Councilman Albro states you were insulting and insubordinate to him in his office."

"If that's an official complaint, I want to see my copy of it. If that's an official complaint, I want my hearing properly constituted and the complainant present."

The lieutenant's mouth pressed into a dark, lipless line. "This may not be official, but by God it is a complaint—and it's from a city councilman."

"You know what the manual says about complaint procedure, Lieutenant."

"All right, Wager. Let's forget about this for a minute. Just what the hell have you learned about Councilman Green and possible influence peddling?"

"I never said anything to Albro about that rumor." Wager nodded at the memo pinned under Wolfard's forefinger. "There's not one thing about Green in that memo."

"I don't give a damn what's in the memo or not. I'm asking you what you've found out about Green!"

"I haven't found out anything about him. I heard a rumor he was peddling votes on the zoning board and I've been checking it out. So far, no evidence."

"Where'd you hear that rumor?"

Wager felt his head lower stubbornly; it was the habit of a lifetime, and his mother when she saw it used to say, "There he goes again—*un torito testarudo,* 'stubborn little bull.' " And he heard the angry Spanish inflection in his own words, "I promised I would not say."

Wolfard sagged back in his chair. "You promised." He leaned forward again. "I don't give a shit who you promised. You tell me."

"No."

"What?"

The word had been clear. Wager didn't need to repeat it.

"Detective Sergeant Wager, that's an order. I want to

know who gave you the information that Councilman Horace Green may have been selling votes."

"It's a politically sensitive source, Wolfard. I promised I would keep it confidential. I'm going to keep it confidential."

"I can suspend you, Wager. You were ordered by the chief to keep me informed. You've disobeyed that order and mine as well. I can have your goddamned badge, Wager!"

Not without a long series of hearings and a hell of a lot of due process and paperwork. Wolfard should have thought of that before he started threatening. "I'm the assigned detective on this case, Wolfard. It's my case and my judgment how I get information about it."

"I can by God reassign the case."

"You by God better have good reason to. Or I'll file my own complaint."

"You haven't kept me informed!"

"There's nothing to inform you about. Nothing but rumors. Unsubstantiated rumors. No goddamned cop is going to run in and out of here with every rumor he hears on the street, and no administrator worth a damn is going to want him to."

"This isn't an ordinary case—we've got a fucking riot about to happen out there!"

"So you want to go out and cool it by telling them Green was crooked? Is that what you want to do, Wolfard?"

The lieutenant sagged back again, a deep breath puffing his lips wearily.

Wager jabbed him once more. "That would really quiet things down, wouldn't it? Those people already think we're covering up for the White Brotherhood. Now you go on out there and tell them Green was crooked. See what that gets you, Wolfard."

"Jesus."

Wager stood up. The lieutenant's face didn't follow him but kept staring at the now-empty chair. "I'm the assigned detective, Wolfard. It's my case. Any facts I get—facts!—I'll inform you. But by God I'll run my cases the way I think right."

"Wager—" Wolfard sighed again and rubbed his eyes. "Ah, shit."

Stubbs was busy at his desk and didn't look up when Wager came in.

"I want to ask you something."

"Hi, Gabe! Seems like we were here only a couple hours ago."

"Why did you tell Wolfard about those rumors on Green?"

"Hey, I—" He studied Wager's eyes and then shrugged. "He cornered me. He had a complaint from Councilman Albro on you and wanted to know what it was all about."

"I told you to keep your mouth shut about it."

"Listen, Wager, I did it for your own good. He wanted to know why you went over to see Albro in the first place, and I told him it was nothing heavy—you went over to check out information."

"So you told him what information?"

"Well, yeah. He wanted to know all about it, so I had to tell him."

"No, Stubbs. You didn't have to tell him. All you had to do was tell him to talk to me." Devereaux came quickly into the office to grab his radio and hustle back out with a quick "See you on the street." Wager dropped his voice as the man disappeared around the door. "When I tell you to keep quiet about something, Stubbs, you do it. Now that rumor's going to run all through this goddamned building like Epsom salts, and you can bet your pimply butt we're going to hear from the goddamned FBI or somebody about why we didn't bring them in sooner."

"Gabe, the lieutenant said—"

"To hell with what he said. This is my case."

Stubbs, his face a shade of red, repeated, "I did it for your own good, Wager. I wanted him to know you weren't screwing around with a city councilman for no good reason. And by God it's our case, not just yours."

Somebody else's good is nobody else's business no matter whose case it was. "You let me worry about my own good."

"Wager—Lester. I want to see you two a minute." Wolfard's voice came around the door frame and cut into the tense silence between the men. They masked their feelings as they went into the lieutenant's office. He glanced at them and seemed about to ask something, then thought better of it. "I just got word from Intelligence that the White Brotherhood's meeting up in Morrison at a place called the Four Aces. I think you'd better talk to them."

Nothing would come of it, Wager knew. What were they going to do, throw up their hands and surrender when he asked them if they killed Green? "You really think it's worth the time to interview those people?"

Wolfard's voice was almost a whisper. "Yes, Wager. That's just what I do think. Rumor has them connected to your case. Your case. I want you to find out what they know about your case."

Wager shrugged and started to leave.

"And one more thing—maybe just as important." Wolfard almost smiled as his eyes held Wager's. "Intelligence says the Uhuru Warriors put out the word to the White Brotherhood—dared them to be on the streets tonight."

"They'll get their little black asses kicked," said Stubbs.

"Any ass-kicking goes on, we'll do it. You tell them that, Wager. You tell them to stay the hell out of Five Points this whole weekend."

Wager nodded. Wolfard was right about that item, anyway: It was at least as important as the lead on the killing. And knowing they were already under police surveillance might keep the White Brotherhood from answering the Warriors' challenge. For a while, anyway.

2157 Hours

Morrison was one of those mountain towns molded by the shape of creek beds that carved their way down the face of the Rockies to spew into the cottonwood tangles of prairie. Tucked between the Hogback and the foothills, it was surprisingly close to Denver, yet kept its feel of isolation because it was still too expensive to develop the steep slopes and rocky cliffs that surrounded it. The main street—almost the only street—twisted along the foaming waters of Bear

Creek and was lined by stone-faced shops and small frame houses turned into stores and boutiques. Nearby and out of sight behind outcroppings of weathered cliffs, was the Red Rocks amphitheatre whose weekend crowds pumped money into the small town. Even now, they could hear the thud of heavy electronic instruments and an occasional roar like distant surf as the crowd cheered whatever rock group was filling the open night with noise. Wager swung into a gravel lot crowded with four-wheel vehicles, pickup trucks carrying camper shells, and an assortment of city cars bearing Denver plates. In the twilight that gathered like thin smoke among the folds and valleys of the mountains, he saw a couple standing on a large boulder washed by the creek and half-hidden by the screen of willow and wild plum that lined the stream. Isolated by the sound of water, they slowly turned to kiss, their bodies pressed tightly against each other from lips to knees.

"By God, if I ever have any time off, I'd like to come up here with Nancy," said Stubbs.

It was something Wager and Jo had planned to do, too, but they never got around to it. He found a space at the end of a straggling line of cars near the creek and pulled in. "Let's get this over with."

"You've got no romance in your soul, do you, Gabe?" Stubbs said it in a joking tone, willing to forgive and forget the argument over Wolfard.

Wager glanced at him and then nodded at the door that gaped in a plain stucco wall and had two steps that led down to the slanting sidewalk. "That's the bar." In one of the two cramped windows, pink neon spelled BUDWEISER, and unlit above the door a faded tin sign displayed four aces fanned out just under the dark second-floor windows. Lined up at the high curb in front of the bar, rear wheels nudging the worn concrete, a row of gleaming choppers waited.

Stubbs gave up trying to be Mr. Congeniality. "Fine. Let's do it." He got out and eyed the motorcycles. "Looks like about twenty of them." Then, "And two of us."

Wager nodded. They paused to let a string of cars wind down-canyon toward Denver, then crossed the street.

The two or three small houses turned into shops, to the right of the tavern, were dark except for one that had its display window lit to show awkwardly crafted coffee cups. They looked as if they would slosh over their rims when you tried to drink from them, but that just seemed to make the price higher. To the left, across the town's other street that led up toward Red Rocks, a Mexican restaurant glowed under a battery of outside floodlights, and its large plate-glass windows were filled with silhouettes moving back and forth in front of white neon bar lights. Another distant roar echoed from the canyon walls and they heard a series of climactic chords and an amplified voice shout something unintelligible.

A pair of young tourists came quickly out of the tavern, their half-frightened expressions changing to awareness as they noticed the line of motorcycles. The boy looked back over his shoulder once and then, trying to hide his fear and embarrassment, spat at the building's blank wall.

Stubbs hesitated, to check his holster, then fell in step behind Wager. Even in the twilight, the doorway seemed dark, and it took a moment or two for Wager's eyes to adjust to the faint light from the bar. The only other light seemed to be a dull moonglow from overhead bulbs turned low on a rheostat, and from the red of cigarettes at the tables. In the back, partitioned off from the barroom by a plywood wall, the smoky glare of a pool table spilled into the hallway, and he could hear the crack of a cue ball break rack, followed by a laughing voice, "Shit, look at that fucker drop!"

There was no sense pretending they weren't cops; already the low talk had faded until the only noise was the pool game and a hoarse voice that sang happily from a speaker about the joys of eating crawdads and making love to Cajun women. His vision clearing against the dim light, Wager strolled past the tables of silent, bearded faces that looked back with surprise and suspicion. The record ended in a clatter of guitars and drums and sudden blankness.

"They don't have their women with them." Stubbs's voice muttered at Wager's shoulder.

"How can you tell?"

"Well, the women have bigger mustaches."

The absence of women meant a business meeting or possibly a war council, possibly something in response to the challenge from the Uhuru Warriors. At a table near the door to the poolroom, Wager saw a swelling mound of hairy darkness that looked familiar, and he headed that way, his back feeling the silent interest from the other tables. "Hello, Sonny."

The large man grunted something, his breath a cadenced, pumping sound in the silence. From the corner of his eye, Wager saw the bartender nervously work his way to the nearest end of the counter, his bar apron a wad of cloth in his hands. Stubbs turned to keep casual watch on the rest of the room.

"Is Big Nose around?"

"You're out of your jurisdiction, Wager."

"Who said anything about a bust? What about Leon? Or Two Fingers?"

"What you want with them?"

Wager smiled. "Friendly conversation. Nothing heavy."

Sonny, his neckless head turning on his shoulders like an owl's, bobbed his chin at the man sitting beside him. That one stood to stare at Wager and tug the fringe on the leather vest that rode over his T-shirt. Then he strolled toward the sound of the pool game. The clatter of the balls fell silent and the vest came back and sat down without a word.

Sonny said, "In back."

Wager and Stubbs were greeted with the same silence from a row of bodies lounging beyond the glow of the pool table. Their legs and feet caught the light, frayed and dirt-stained jeans that showed the heavy soles of boots, some with thick metal toe-guards, others narrower like snubbed cowboy boots and with raked heels.

"Hello, Big Nose." Wager made out the familiar face in the lineup. "It's been a while."

"Could have been longer, Wager. What's that following you?"

"Detective Stubbs, meet Jerome Davis, a.k.a. Big Nose Smith. I'm sure you've seen his publicity photos."

Neither man offered to shake hands.

Big Nose's beard showed streaks of gray at the chin, and his long hair, pulled back into a ponytail, was also streaked. Beside him, Leon Oakland showed his years in the deep lines that creased his cheeks above the clipped beard. "Leon, I believe you're getting bald."

"What the fuck you want here, Wager?"

"I want you to tell me you didn't have anything to do with the murder of Councilman Green."

"Oh yeah? We offed him. We did it and we're glad." Laughter ran like a mutter along the row of watching men.

"Want to say that after I read you Miranda?"

"Fuck you. I wish we had killed the nigger." The voice from a seated figure drew another laugh. "Maybe we'll go after the next one."

"What's your name?" asked Stubbs.

"What's it to you?"

"His name's Two Fingers Marshall. That's because the rest of them are shoved up his ass," said Wager. He turned to Big Nose. "The word on the street's that you people killed Green."

Smith shrugged, the gesture making the chrome badges on his denim jacket catch the light. "Maybe we did, maybe we didn't. That's your problem, ain't it?"

Wager shook his head. "No, amigo, it's yours. We'll be all over you like stink on shit until we find out one way or the other. You won't be able to peddle an ounce of pot without somebody busting you."

"Fucking chili bean talks big, don't he?"

"Does your p.o. know you're consorting with known criminals, Two Fingers? You just sit quiet and maybe I won't jerk your chain."

Smith scratched thoughtfully somewhere up under the ragged hair that came down to his collarbone. "If you had something on us, Wager—if you even thought we did it— you wouldn't be here talking about it. Just what the hell do you want?"

"Green's killer."

"You think we'll help you? You think that?" asked Smith.

"That or take the heat." He added, "A lot of it, because

somebody keeps pointing the finger at you. As long as they do, we'll keep looking."

"Yeah? We'll give them the finger back—and you, too: Here's the finger."

"Marshall, you better keep what fingers you've got."

"Shut up," said Smith over his shoulder to the seated figure. "I'm thinking."

Wager let Big Nose scratch in meditative silence. Somewhere in the back of his mind, he remembered the man when he had been some fifteen years younger. Smith, then known by his real name of Jerome Davis, had stomped and permanently crippled a teenager who accidentally backed his car into one of the gang's motorcycles. Wager, then in uniform, had busted him and watched as the man, grinning, was set free by a court that thought Wager's justification for arresting the scumbag wasn't sufficient; the charges were never even heard. That he got away with it was a boost to Big Nose's rise in the gang. Ironically, the case had been a help to Wager, too: It brought home the awareness that a good cop didn't just get arrests, he got convictions—no matter how silly the court made the rules of the game. Since then, Wager had followed Big Nose's rise in the gang and his occasional falls in court as he'd made his way from the early juvenile arrests to involvement in murder. In a way, they were matching each other's careers.

Smith finally looked up, his stomach bulging softly against the stained T-shirt that shone under the open denim jacket. "We didn't do it, Wager. I don't know who did, but it wasn't none of our people." He added, "I'd of heard about it and I ain't."

"You want me to take your word for that?"

A note of anger tinged his voice. "What the hell else you got? I can't fucking prove we didn't do something we didn't do."

"Cops and dumb—they go together like niggers and tennis shoes," said Marshall.

"Have you heard anything about who did do it?"

"No." Smith shook his head slowly. "Not a word anywhere." He looked up, his blue eyes catching the dim light from under heavy eyebrows. "But we been asking around;

I want to know who the hell's fingering us for it. Nothing. Nobody's come up with nothing."

"Have you heard from the Uhuru Warriors?"

"Shit—those faggoty punks! They want stomping, by God they'll get what they want!"

"Not this weekend they won't—any of your people come near Five Points, and they're going to eat county food for a long time. That's from the chief."

Smith said nothing.

The main business over, Wager turned to go.

"Wager?"

He looked back.

"How'd you know where to find us?"

"You people are popular, Big Nose. And hard to miss on those crummy machines. We asked Smokey; they told us."

"Yeah?" A tinge of smugness at having their trips monitored by the Highway Patrol. "We got you cocksuckers worried, huh?"

"Not worried. We just like to know where the sewage is."

CHAPTER 13

The dispatcher told them that Lieutenant Wolfard was at the temporary command center which had been set up on Thirty-second Street. It was near enough to the troubled area for accurate information and quick response, but far enough away for security purposes.

"You think Big Nose was telling the truth?"

"I wouldn't bet the house and farm on it," said Wager. "But I think he was." He steered the car down the long, sloping stretch of I-70 that led toward Denver, with its lights that spread as far as the horizon and clotted here and there into white glow. In the far distance, it was hard to tell where the ground lights ended and the stars began, not only because they looked about the same, but also because the glare from the freeway lights smothered the sky to make a tunnel floored by the strip of concrete with its dark patches of oil stain and the jostling traffic outside the windows. It was as if the city were built to force the eyes to the ground, to close off the heavens and shorten the reach of one's yearning to objects advertised for sale in neon or in the white glare of billboards. It was a feeling of loss—of rediscovering the burden of his city—that Wager had not had since he and Jo would come back from one of their trips to the mountains. The brief escape from the city's presence that had been hinted by the small town with its quiet twilight and the soothing sound of rushing water had stirred up those memories again, and with them the matching memories of returning. Only, at the time with Jo, he had not felt the smothering grip of the city as sharply as he felt it now. With her, the knowledge of what was waiting had been softened by a comfortable feeling of sharing it with someone. Now, there was no comfort, just the awareness of what was ahead.

"Yeah, I thought so, too." Stubbs peered out the window at passing houses and shopping centers. "Wolfard won't be happy about it."

Wager cared less what made Wolfard happy.

2243 Hours

A cordon of police vehicles blocked access to the command center, and in the shadows, Wager made out a picket line of dark uniforms at strategic points, covering other avenues of approach. In the pulsing flicker of red-white-blue emergency lights, figures clustered in little groups listening to radios and waiting for the call that would set off whatever response they specialized in. Further down the street, a pair of ambulances sat in silence, an occasional cigarette glowing behind one of the dark windshields; across from them, a crew busily set up antenna and ran wire from a blank-walled communications van. Wager and Stubbs dangled their identification badges from their lapel pockets and nodded to those faces they knew as they made their way through groups of waiting police. Here and there, a low rumble of nervous laughter or a mutter of conversation, but most of the men were silent, watching, listening to the pop of radio transmissions. It was the same feeling of muted expectancy, of well-rehearsed alertness that preceded raids on dope factories or hideouts. But the magnitude of support forces and the distances to be scouted and defended reminded Wager of sorties in Korea, patrols that moved out from the line of departure when it was fully dark, to probe into no-man's-land for the enemy patrols that groped toward them. It was a fragment of memory that made the familiar streets and brick buildings, the clusters of trees, and the front yards of hushed and curtained homes seem suddenly alien; it was an echo of feeling that pressed on the mind with the same gray weight as the routine wail of defense sirens, and as with that reminder, he felt a pang of new distance between him and the small houses huddled against the cold flicker of emergency lights. The empty litter of children's toys on a worn front lawn—a rusty wagon tilted on its side, a tricycle, the fragile pattern of Popsicle sticks and scraps of wood built into a world for tiny cars and trucks to dig between—and the silent, waiting homes brought the sting of mutability.

"By God, we're ready for 'em." Stubbs gave a quick count to the units spread over the empty lot and surrounding streets. "I think every SWAT team in the metro area's here."

Wager thought so, too. He followed the black line of comwire toward the command post, estimating, like Stubbs, the firepower poised to react.

"Detective Wager—wait a moment, please."

The woman's voice sounded odd among the pinched crackle of radios and the low mutter of male sounds. He saw the figure in high heels pick its way toward him across the uneven and weedy ground.

"Councilwoman Voss."

"Yes. They told me you were coming down. This is terrible—it's truly terrible."

"Yes, ma'am."

"These people don't want violence, Detective Wager. The great majority of them are peaceful, law-abiding citizens. Church people. They don't want to see their neighborhood go up in flames."

"No, ma'am." It was a speech that should not have been aimed at him but at the chief. Or at those in the neighborhood who didn't fit Voss's description and who saw violence as a strike against the white society that had killed Green.

Or at the group of rioters whose sudden appearance in the radio reports caused a flurry of traffic and an expectant stir among the groups listening in the half-dark.

"Have you found out anything at all about the murder?"

"There might be some truth in that rumor you told me about. But I don't know how it fits with his death."

"You've talked to someone about it? Who?"

"Kaunitz and Ellis. They didn't admit anything, but they got quiet pretty fast."

"Would they—?"

"There's no evidence of a thing. And I won't be able to work on it until Monday."

It took her a few seconds. "You mean because their offices are closed over the weekend?"

"Theirs and everybody else's. Can you think of any reason Kaunitz and Ellis might want Green dead?"

She shook her head, her dark hair looking wind-tossed. "No—and that sounds so . . . cold and terrible." She considered it again. "If Horace was taking bribes, they wouldn't want him dead at all. He'd be too valuable to them. Unless"—the thought brought a frown—"he'd threatened to tell someone." She looked at Wager. "Suborning an elected official is a federal crime. Conviction could cancel any city and federal contracts they were developing."

Wager liked the way Councilperson Voss thought, because that was the way he figured it, too. The problem, of course, was lack of evidence to show either bribery or Green's intention to talk to someone about it. "Do you know his aide—Julia Wilfong?"

"Yes, of course."

"She's heard the rumors, too."

"You asked her about them?"

He nodded. "She told me about a zoning change that stunk, one for K and E Construction. But she doesn't believe Green was mixed up in it."

Voss asked, "She came to you with it?"

"No. I told her I was chasing down the rumor. She didn't want to talk about it."

"I see."

"Who did you hear it from, Mrs. Voss?"

She hesitated. "I promised I wouldn't reveal that."

Wager wagged a hand at the surrounding weapons and vehicles. "It could be important. If we can find the killer in time, this might be stopped."

She tugged nervously at a tendril of ill-governed hair that curled down behind her ear. "I'll have to ask if I can tell you."

Her tone told Wager that was about as good as he was going to do. "I'd appreciate it."

"Did you talk with any of the White Brotherhood? Are they involved in any way?"

"They say no. And we don't have anything that says yes."

"The people I talk to think they are—people in the neighborhood here. That's what's causing so much of the hostility. They think the police are unwilling to do anything to them."

Wager tried to keep the Spanish lilt from his voice. "The police are unwilling to do anything to them because the law says the police can't do anything to them, Councilwoman Voss. Scumbags have their rights, too."

"I understand that, Officer Wager. I just wondered—I hoped—I could have something to tell these people. Something that would show them we are trying to find Green's killer."

"If I had cooperation from everybody, I might have something to tell you."

The shadow of her mouth twisted into a wry smile. "Touché—I understand. I'll ask the person who told me— that's all I can say. You've kept your promise not to say anything about the rumor; I want to keep my promise, too."

Wager glanced at Stubbs, who stood just out of earshot, staring their way anxiously. "Yes, ma'am."

2251 Hours

Lieutenant Elkins was at the command center—a police cruiser with all four doors flung open and a technician running another telephone wire to it from the communications van. In a larger city—New York, Los Angeles—the riot drill

would call for a local business or home to be comman-
deered and it would be marked with radio antenna, a portable switchboard, and even a police department flag so
officers unfamiliar with the precinct could spot it. But in
Denver, property owners didn't accept the police taking
over their buildings, and there was no money to pay for
police damage to the property, anyway. So here, the command post was simply a vehicle that could be moved as the
situation demanded.

But even if it lacked the dignity of a flag, it was marked
by the glitter of uniforms standing around in tight clusters
and talking quietly, by the splatter of radio transmissions
from all four districts, by technicians still puttering with the
telephone hookups, by newspaper and television crews
who kept wandering away from the space that had been
provided for press vehicles.

"Wager—anything new on Green's killing?" Gargan's
voice came from a blurry face hovering over a black tur-
tleneck sweater. A television announcer, following Gargan's question, began yanking her cameraman's wire to
lead him toward Wager.

"Ask the Public Information Officer, Gargan."

"Wager, God damn it—"

Elkins, wearing his uniform, pulled away from a group of
men in civilian clothes, and Wager recognized the chief's
profile as he leaned forward to listen to something said by
a very tall silhouette—probably the basketball player Fat
Willy had mentioned.

"Over here, Wager." Elkins gestured. "I hear Mrs.
Green's coming down, too."

"You hear more than I do. What the hell's she think she
can do?"

"She thinks she can help calm things down. Maybe she's
right. The chief said it's worth a try, anyway." He added,
"A group of ministers are already telephoning people in the
district."

"Crap, Lieutenant," said Stubbs. "They're not rioting
over Green—he's just an excuse for a couple gangs to pump
themselves up and do a little looting. That's not the kind of
people who'll listen to her."

Elkins stared down at them for a long moment, the gleaming bill of his cap hiding his eyes. "That's a part of it, it sure is. But if you think the people aren't upset over Green's death, you've got another think coming. They are upset—damned upset—and that's the people we don't want joining those gangs in the street." He lifted his cap and swabbed at the sweat band with a handkerchief before settling it back evenly over his eyes. "The chief figures— and I happen to agree with him—that if we can keep the gangs from getting citizen support, we can minimize the damage."

"The fewer the better, that's true," said Wager. "Is Wolfard around? He wanted us to report to him."

"Yeah—he's over—"

Elkins's words were cut off by the sudden thud of an explosion that slapped against Wager's shirt like a gust of wind from the darkness. Eyes around them lifted as if they could see something in the night, and the silence was like a pent breath. Beside him, Stubbs whispered, "Jesus, that was a big one." Then the radios began to pop with taut voices, and a murmur from one of the shadows said, "Fucking bomb!"

"What was it? What's the report?" A voice that sounded like Gargan's came from somewhere, and a mutter of inquiry and guesses stirred the restless shadows. A dozen blocks away, the wail of a fire siren began at a neighborhood station.

"It's a car's gas tank. A car's gas tank went off." The answer started from the command center and went from shadow to shadow, and the shapes settled back into clusters that shifted from foot to foot, and began talking again in muted voices.

"Lieutenant Wolfard? Detective Wager's here. Him and Detective Stubbs."

A figure detached itself from the small crowd around the chief. "This way, Wager." He gestured toward an empty space on the other side of the police car. "Did you see them? Were they up there?"

"They were."

"Well?"

"They say they don't know who did it."

"You didn't expect them to tell you the truth, did you?"

"I didn't expect them to tell me anything, Lieutenant. But what they did say and the way they said it makes me believe they didn't do it. If you want to believe something else, that's up to you."

"Lester? What about you? Did you hear what they said?"

"Yessir." He added, "I go along with Gabe."

Wolfard looked at Stubbs for a long minute, studying his face in the half-light. "You're sure?" Wager waited to hear if Stubbs said the right thing.

After a moment, Stubbs's head nodded.

"Very well." He turned back to Wager. "Did you tell them to keep their butts out of here?"

"Yes."

"And?"

"I think they will. For this weekend, anyway. But they're not going to let it slide. They can't."

"That's all we need is a goddamned gang war." Wolfard paused to listen to a radio transmission call for an ambulance. Behind them, one of the dark vehicles started its motor and flipped on its emergency lights as it pulled away. "But as long as it's not this weekend . . ."

Wager turned to go.

"Where are you going?"

"I'm still working a homicide."

"You got a new lead?"

"No, Lieutenant. What I've got is a few strings I want to pull."

"And what I've got right now, Wager, is a riot. And an assignment for you."

He waited.

"You're to drive Mrs. Green around the neighborhood while she makes her appeal."

"What?"

"You heard me. The chief wants her in an unmarked police car—he's afraid of that sniper rumor. But he's not letting her go in uncovered."

"But why the hell—"

"Because she doesn't want any uniformed cops with her. She'll take the plainclothes, but no uniforms."

"There's a hell of a lot of plainclothes around here—look at them: standing with their thumbs up their asses!"

"But she knows you, Wager. She even seems to like you." In the dim light, Wager could see the glint of Wolfard's grinning teeth. "She asked for you personally—'those two officers I talked with yesterday,' she said. The chief said yes."

"God damn."

"I guess you made an impression on her. Anyway, the man wants to talk with you before you take them for a spin."

The chief saw Wolfard lead them over and stepped away from the cluster of listening ears. "Wager—Stubbs. Anything new on the murderer?"

"No, sir. Not yet. There won't be, either, if I'm going to be driving people around here."

The chief's eyes got the sleepy look that showed he was trying to hide his thoughts from someone. "I understand how you feel, Wager. But this is an emergency situation and it takes precedence. A lot of people have set a lot of things aside for a few hours, understand?"

"I understand, Chief. What I don't understand is why somebody else can't drive her. I'm not the only plainclothesman here."

"She asked for you and Stubbs." He added, "And I wanted some people I could trust to look after her—some people who would do a good job."

"Well . . ."

"Besides, I'm ordering you to. Any questions about that?"

"No, sir."

"Fine." The chief's pause held them a moment longer. "Lieutenant Wolfard told me about that rumor on Green, Wager—the one that has him taking bribes."

He glanced past the chief to see Councilwoman Voss talking with someone near the reporters' vehicles. "That's only a rumor, Chief. And I'd like to keep it quiet until I find out a little more on it."

"That's exactly what I told the lieutenant. For two reasons: We don't want these people to think we're trying to smear Green, and I damned well don't want the FBI sticking its nose into my jurisdiction. Certainly not while all this crap is going on." The chief let that sink in. "You dig into it as part of your investigation of the homicide. If something about a bribe turns up—anything concrete—you get word to me in writing through channels. Otherwise, I didn't hear that rumor, Wager; and I told Wolfard he didn't, either. And if anybody asks us, that's what we're going to say. You understand what that means?"

It meant the chief sure as hell didn't want to share the same limb Wager perched on. "That's all right by me." Wager glanced at the man beside him. "What about you, Stubbs?"

"Ah—yessir, Chief. I understand."

"Fine. Now Mrs. Green will be here in just a few minutes. Drive her around the neighborhood but steer clear of any hot spots. I'll have a car about a block behind you in case you need help. If something does happen, get out fast—I don't care what she wants to do, your first responsibility is to look after her welfare. Understand?"

"Yes, sir."

"You have an unmarked car, right?"

"Yes, sir."

"Fine. The bullhorn works?"

Wager never had to use it. "I'll check it out."

"Fine. She should be here in a few minutes."

2308 Hours

The car's bullhorn, mounted under the hood, worked; Wager gave a quick test—one through five—that bounced his metallic voice off the neighboring houses and brought a momentary hush to the command center as faces turned toward him. In that brief silence following the echo, he heard the end of a radio transmission: ". . . at St. Charles's Park. God bless you."

"I guess you were right about not telling Wolfard, Gabe. I'm sorry."

Beside him, Stubbs looked out the window toward the lot and its vehicles sitting in the dimness. Stubbs's apology wasn't needed or wanted, and in fact it embarrassed Wager. "Remember it next time."

The man's profile nodded.

Wager, restless with the sense of time wasted, switched to the quiet frequency of the Fourth District and queried MVD for any report on Green's missing automobile. He was spelling the man's name and explaining once more that the automobile was material evidence in a homicide when Stubbs said, "Here they come."

"They?"

"That councilwoman's with her—Mrs. Voss."

"Crap." The MVD said they had nothing; Wager flipped back to District Two channel and got out to greet the two women and the chief, who led them over.

"Detective Wager, you remember Mrs. Green and Councilwoman Voss."

"Yessir." He nodded hello and opened the rear door. "I'd like you to sit in back, please."

"That's a good idea, ladies. It'll be a little more secure." The chief leaned to the window to say a few more things to the women, then he stepped away. "All right, Detective Wager. Keep your eyes open."

"Yessir."

He pulled slowly across the sidewalk and curb and onto the street while Stubbs showed Mrs. Green how to work the microphone. She looked tired in the gliding light of street lamps, and large circles of dark flesh hung beneath her eyes. But her voice was strong and unwavering, as if hers was a duty that only she could do, and she'd made up her mind to do it.

"Should I start?"

"Yes, ma'am. Any time." Wager added, "Roll up your windows, please; and sit more toward the middle of the seat." He explained, "It's harder to see who's in the car that way."

"But I want them to see me."

"Mrs. Green, you're doing a brave thing coming down here. But your life's already been threatened." He didn't have to add that her husband's killer was still free—it was a thought he felt go through all their minds like a chill breeze.

"He's right, Hannah." Councilwoman Voss gripped a dark hand in both her pale ones, but Wager couldn't tell who was giving strength; Voss, too, looked worried and worn, and the taut curve of her body on the seat showed the nervousness she felt.

"We'll make a run through the Points," said Wager. "And then circle around the neighborhood. Take your time talking, Mrs. Green—if you go too fast, the words get all tangled up in that thing."

"I understand."

The street ahead was empty under the pink glow of sodium lights, and the cars that normally would line curbs in front of rows of vacant yards and silent houses had been moved away from harm. A cat trotted across the pavement—its legs a quick blur—and then broke into a frightened, low run as the headlights glinted in its eyes.

"This is . . . Everybody, this is Hannah Green. Horace Green's wife."

The voice echoed back from the closed doors and the brick walls of stores and seemed to make the street even emptier.

"Horace would not want this violence. Please don't do something we will all be sorry for. We're hurting only ourselves this way. . . ."

The coiled wire of the microphone trembled past Wager's right shoulder to the figure leaning forward over the seat back, linking the tense, high voice with the metallic words that bounced around them a split-second later. But though Wager heard the voice, he did not really hear the words. His attention was focused on the street. There, shadows pooled at the foot of walls and the light broke into shapes under tree limbs and behind fences. He looked carefully as the cruiser glided past gaping darknesses between buildings, and when Mrs. Green paused for a moment to rest her voice, he heard the distant pop of weapons and the thin buzz of faraway sirens. "You don't have to shout, Mrs. Green. That's what the bullhorn's for."

"I understand. Thank you."

As they neared the business district of the Points, many of the windows in the fronts of houses were dark, but glows of muted light down narrow alleys showed that life had drawn back away from the street and was waiting. A flickering glow of scattered fire and embers smoldered on the sidewalk in front of a darkened appliance store: The remains of a trash barrel that had been fired and rolled toward the doorway. But no one hovered near, and through the taped glass of the emptied display window, Wager caught a glimpse of a man's silhouette peering out at the passing voice and holding the rigid blackness of a weapon.

Ahead, a police car—lights flashing erratically—bounced quickly across an intersection and disappeared, and farther down they saw the flicker of fire-truck lights and the smoky orange of a large flame.

"That must be another car they set on fire," said Stubbs. "You see anything on your side?"

"No."

He held the speed at about ten miles an hour, the car's worn and ill-tuned engine beginning to heat up and lurch slightly. Behind them, he saw the headlights of the backup vehicle pace itself to their speed and relaxed a trifle. Mrs. Green was saying something about her husband again, and that she had faith the police were doing all they could to find the killer. Beneath that, the flurry of messages on the radio called for support on the corner of Marion and Thirty-third, where looters were reported breaking into a liquor store. Wager turned away from that area and they cruised a darker street that ran parallel to the business strip.

"Please don't choose violence—I'm begging you, in Horace Green's name, not to do this to our people. . . ."

"Union six-nine."

Wager had to take the microphone to answer the radio's

call, switching from "Announce" to "Radio." "Six-nine. Go ahead."

"How's it going, Wager? Any trouble?"

He recognized the chief's voice. "No, sir. Everything's calm so far."

"Ten-four."

He handed it back to Mrs. Green and switched the control back to the bullhorn.

Stubbs muttered something and pointed toward a narrow driveway that led behind the whitewashed walls of an old wooden church. Christ the Redeemer African Methodist Church. It looked deserted and run-down, but Wager had seen services there last Sunday. "What'd you see?"

"Looked like five or six people moving around back there."

He pressed down a bit on the gas.

"This is Hannah Green, Horace Green's wife. Please listen to me. . . ."

The sentences had started repeating. Her voice lost the high-pitched urgency and now had a clearer note of appeal as if the woman had begun to listen to herself and changed her tone for better effect. In the rearview mirror, he could see her eyes stare ahead, but they weren't looking down the street; rather, she gazed at some vision of her own, maybe some picture of her husband's response to the streets around them and, from that, gathered the conviction that strengthened her voice.

"Smell that?" Stubbs asked Wager. "Smells like a body been lying around awhile. It always smells like that around here."

He caught the familiar odor, a kind of musty sweetness on the edge of being rotten, a smell that was sensed by the skin and tongue as much as by the nose. Stubbs was right: This part of the neighborhood—with its sagging houses and frazzled patches of lawn, its dented cars with flat tires, and the scatter of bottles and litter on curb and sidewalk—always smelled like that when the night air cooled and gathered over the pavement to draw warm odors through leaky walls. "It's dirt. Unclean houses, unwashed skin."

"It's the smell of poverty," said Councilwoman Voss. "It's why these people are so angry."

"Yes'm. Maybe so," said Stubbs. "But when I first smelled it, I looked around for a body."

The radio called again for backup on Marion Street, and Mrs. Green turned from the microphone to Wager. "I want to go there—Marion Street."

"No, ma'am. We're doing fine here."

"But there's where I'm needed, Officer. These people are in their houses—they're not out on the street."

"And you're helping to keep them there."

"I insist!"

Stubbs tried to explain. "We've got orders from the chief to avoid hot spots, Mrs. Green."

"But I can be of some use there. More than I am here. I insist you drive me there!"

Wager shook his head. "Not without the chief's OK."

"She has mine." Councilwoman Voss leaned over the seat back, too, a curling tendril of her long hair brushing Wager's neck. "Hannah's right—we can do more good where we're really needed."

"It's too dangerous."

"Officer, people are being hurt there! Didn't you hear them call for an ambulance?"

"That's exactly what I heard."

"Ma'am—Mrs. Green . . ."

"Horace would want me to go. He would go himself."

Horace wouldn't have to explain to the chief how she got injured. "I've got orders, ma'am."

"He would not surrender to fear. Neither will I!"

"Get the chief on the radio," said Councilwoman Voss. "Let me talk to him."

A city councilperson had the right to talk to the chief of police. Wager took the microphone from Mrs. Green and switched to "Radio." A moment later the chief answered his call number. "Go to channel seven," said Wager; there was no sense clogging up the district's busy frequency with an argument between Voss and the chief. When the chief's voice came up on seven with Wager's call number, he showed the councilwoman how to use the mike.

"This is Councilwoman Voss, Chief. Mrs. Green wants to go to the trouble on Marion Street. She can be of help there."

"I'd rather you and Mrs. Green avoid that area, Council-woman. Detective Wager's been told where to drive."

"I'm aware that the detective has his orders—he's told us. But we're doing no good at all here. There's where we're needed."

"It's too dangerous, Councilwoman. There's shooting over there."

"They can hear Mrs. Green's voice from a block away. You know that."

"I have to tell you no, Councilwoman. In my judgment, it's too dangerous."

"It's either that or we get out and walk over there and talk to them up close."

"You can't do that—you stay in that car!"

"The only way to hold us against our wills is to arrest us, Chief. Are you willing to have Detective Wager arrest a councilwoman and Horace Green's widow?"

The chief's microphone clicked off as he started to say "Damn—"

Voss asked Wager, "What happened?"

He stifled a grin. "Radio procedure. He'll be back."

He was, this time talking to Wager. "What do you think, Detective Wager?"

"Mrs. Green has the door open," he lied.

". . . All right. But by God you don't get any nearer than you have to. Understand? I don't want those two endan-gered in any way. Understand? They are not to be left alone and they are to stay inside that vehicle. Understand?"

"Ten-four."

"Thank you," said Councilwoman Voss to Wager.

"We'll see about that."

2329 Hours

On the way over, Wager asked Mrs. Green about one of the loose threads he had been mentally tugging. "Do you know where your husband ate supper the night he was killed?"

She thought back as if there were so many things to get past before that day was reached. "I can't say—I don't remember him saying anything about it."

"The medical evidence says he had chicken, peas, and rice two to four hours before he died. But he didn't make the buffet at the Brown Palace Hotel and the Vitaco reception, where he was last seen, only served these little meatballs and wieners and things." He explained, "It could be important, Mrs. Green. We need to account for all his time on that last day."

"I understand, Officer." She tried again, the effort to recall bringing lines between her brows. "I really can't remember. He told me he would be eating at a function and not to save anything for him. That was probably the Brown Palace. But if he said so, I didn't pay much attention." It was her turn to explain. "It wasn't unusual, so we didn't make much of it when he missed supper." She added softly, "It's the little things like that: the last time we ate together . . . the last, quick kiss good-bye . . . the last bedtime story for our son . . ."

"Yes, ma'am." Wager nudged her back on track. "Can you think of any place he might have gone to eat? Any favorite restaurants?"

"He had several." She named them and Wager, steering with one hand, noted them in his little book.

"Did you have anything to do with the furniture store's bookkeeping?"

"No. That was—" She caught herself before she mentioned Sonie Andersen's name. "No."

"So you don't have any idea how big a profit the store was making?"

"It was doing well. Horace was very satisfied with it. But he ran the business. He and . . ."

"But you're not aware of the profit margin?"

"No. Why?"

"Just trying different possibilities." And having equal luck with all of them.

A patrol car blocked the street ahead and, Mrs. Green giving the bullhorn a rest, Wager coasted silently toward it.

The two officers standing behind the car's opened doors looked back at them with brief curiosity and then turned again to stare intently at the empty intersection.

Blainey, called up from Colfax, leaned a heavy arm on the cruiser's roof and squinted against the flash of its emergency lights. Wager stopped in the middle of the street, short of the blockade, and got out. "What's going on, John?"

"Heyo, Gabe—there's a bunch just down there behind that shoe store on the corner. We think it's the same ones that trashed out the liquor store."

"Waiting for them to come out?"

"Sure as hell don't want to go in after them. They back there getting liquored up."

The other officer, whose uniform still had the stiff, new look of recent issue, shook his head. "We ought to go in there and pop heads. That's what the sons of bitches are asking for."

Blainey's eyes caught Wager's and he lifted his eyebrows slightly. "What you doing here, Gabe? Moonlighting?"

"Green's widow's in the car—she came down to try and keep things calm."

"Mrs. Green?" Blainey turned to stare a moment at the car and then walked over to it and tapped on the rear glass. It rolled down and he leaned, hatless, to say something. A minute later he returned, settling his cap back on his round head. "He was a good man, Horace Green. It don't do anybody good to lose somebody like that."

"You knew him?"

"I met him a couple times, is all. It's a shame. A real shame."

"Can we drive ahead? Mrs. Green thinks she can talk people off the streets."

"I wouldn't. SWAT team's patroling down there somewhere. Over in them houses on that side." He shook his head. "I wouldn't do it, Gabe. All shit could break loose."

He explained it to Mrs. Green.

"Do you think they can hear me from here?"

"That thing carries a half mile against the wind. They'll hear you."

"All right." She keyed the microphone and started again, "This is Hannah Green, Horace Green's widow. . . ."

The first sign of life at the intersection was a loud pop that cut through the echoes of Mrs. Green's voice: the hollow shotgun sound of a gas grenade fired somewhere out of sight. A moment later, they saw a steamy cloud spread past the brick corner, and another pop sent a second grenade into the night. Then they saw a blur of figures dart through the gas—rags tied over their faces and heads low as they ran—scattering like blown leaves through the foggy street and darting for cracks between silent buildings. Then emptiness. A distant wail of shouting voices bounced up the pavement, and, first a pair, then a half-dozen, shapes followed by dark-uniformed figures in gas masks and baseball caps, sprinting through the thinning fumes. Blainey and his partner loosened their sticks and closed the doors to the police cruiser, and Wager started his car's motor. "They're coming this way."

"Wait—don't go—wait!"

"No, ma'am. We've got—" He didn't get a chance to finish. A howl of shouts and curses exploded from a narrow driveway between two houses beside them. The yells overwhelmed Mrs. Green's amplified plea and were followed by the clatter of stones and bottles thudding loudly on the car.

"My God!" Councilwoman Voss stared wide-eyed at the charging wall of screaming faces.

"You two get down—get down below the windows!" Wager backed the car like a weapon at the running figures and swung close to Blainey to offer what shelter he could. A club smashed the rear window, shattering flakes of glass into the car like a spray of ice chips, and one white-eyed, snarling youth swung a brick on the end of a rope to smash against the windshield. Wager stepped on the gas, swinging the fenders at the dodging shapes that danced wildly around the car in a storm of shouts and curses and rocks, then he lurched forward again as he saw Blainey and his partner swept over by arms that rose and fell with bats and chains, lashing at the two officers.

"They're killing them! My God, they're killing them!"

He thudded the bumper against something soft and then

the swarm of arms and legs and hunched, jerking shoulders scattered into fleeing fragments as Blainey, his uniform ripped open above the badge to show his white T-shirt, rose above a tangle of writhing figures. His baton swung hard and repeatedly against jabbing clubs and flesh. Wager backed up and rammed forward again. His wheel lurched over something that howled, and he backed hard again and swung his bumper to snag what it could.

The masked face of a SWAT officer loomed against the splintered windshield, bloodshot eyes wide behind the goggle lenses, and then a dozen blue shapes ran past the car toward the two policemen as the rioters fled. Blaine's partner—stunned, hatless, blood smearing his face—staggered to his knees to look after the disappearing shapes as Wager's backup car squealed to a smoking halt beside them and its two officers tumbled out of the vehicle and ran toward Mrs. Green and the councilwoman. Stubbs spilled out of the car and sprinted for Blainey and a SWAT member who struggled to hold a flailing rioter.

"Cuff that fucker! Get the fucking cuffs on him!"

"Goddamn motherfucking—"

"Get the cuffs on him!"

"Stay down, both of you!" Wager, out of the car, shouted at the two huddled women and rested his pistol on the roof as he searched the dark emptiness of housetops and driveways for the flash of a weapon or the spurt of fire in a Molotov cocktail. "Stay in the car—stay down!"

"My God," the councilwoman's voice was muffled by her hands. "It happened so fast!"

"Cuff his goddamn feet."

Hannah Green, the silent microphone still gripped in her fist, stared through the broken windows streaked with spittle, her own cheeks streaked with tears.

CHAPTER 14

Sunday, 15 June, 0916 Hours

The clock radio woke him with the cadenced earnestness of a sermon, and he lay under the sheet, half listening to the voice but not hearing all the words. It was something to do with God's forgiveness, and that was fine with Wager—he couldn't think of anyone who didn't need forgiving for something, himself and God included; and the urgent voice, full of pauses and emphases, seemed certain that God would welcome all sinners. Why not? He put them here in the first place. Yawning with a weariness that lingered in his burning eyes and in the cottony feeling surrounding his thoughts, Wager stumbled into the kitchen to start water for coffee and to slice into one of the Rocky Ford cantaloupes he'd found last night at a twenty-four-hour supermarket. He could still remember the strange dislocation of the early morning quiet, wandering along the neatly ordered rows of food while twenty minutes across town the sirens, the tear gas, the batons were cleaning up the last of the rioters.

After the mob swept across the car, Councilwoman Voss agreed with Wager that Mrs. Green should quit, but the woman held on long enough to make one more tour around the edges of the neighborhood. Her voice was hard to understand because she kept catching the words in tears and gasps. Neither woman urged Wager to drive into the neighborhood's center, where more reports of quick strikes by gangs kept erupting on the radio. Finally, they convinced Mrs. Green she had done enough.

The papers said YOUTH KILLED IN FIVE POINTS RIOTS and named a fourteen-year-old boy who had been shot, although it wasn't clear whether the bullet had come from rioters or from the police. Some civilians in the neighborhood blamed the police for the death, while others said the youth was shot when two gangs tangled over a looted store. The chief said the matter was under intense investigation and he expected to have a formal statement within twenty-four hours. Wager figured Max and Devereaux were still at work taking statements and collating the physical evidence on that one. Eighteen other civilians had been arrested allegedly for rioting and looting, and, far down the front-page story, a brief paragraph noted that an officer had suffered a heart attack while chasing a group of fugitives down an alley. Damage estimates were mounting—added to, Wager reckoned, by more than one shop owner who saw a chance to clear out his inventory for the insurance. The *Post* editorial lamented the death and destruction and called for calm; the *News* ran a story on the bottom of the front page headlined GANG LEADERS PROMISE WORSE TO COME. A spokesman for the Uhuru Warriors, photographed in his dashiki, warned that last night was only a warm-up and that tonight there would be massive riots to protest the murder of a brother by the police.

Wager sipped his coffee and folded the newspapers onto the stack saved up for the apartment's recycling drive. One of the tenants had organized the Saturday collection to earn money for handicapped children, and it was as good a cause as any. The world was full of causes—good, bad, all kinds. And Wager was faced with his own: Councilman Horace Green's death. He refilled his cup and cleared the breakfast table to spread the papers and notes he'd accumulated in the last three days. One sheet listed the times and events of Green's final day—Wednesday, the eleventh—and a little star was penciled by time periods that had not yet been accounted for. A separate sheet listed the restaurants Mrs. Green had given him last night, and he would start that round of the investigation when they began to open today.

Another sheet held a series of questions, some crossed off now and a lot added. A few of them had little stars, too: "Killed nearby? Killer would have looked for a safer dump but was in a hurry?" The answer for Wager was that Green had probably been killed in his car—another starred question—and then dumped. Which brought a new question to Wager's mind and he glanced through a Xerox copy of the wound chart. One close-range shot to the back of the head—entering just to the right of centerline. That was consistent with Green sitting in the driver's seat, turning his head to the left, being shot by someone in the rider's seat. Then they would have to slide the body across the seat and walk around to drive the car. If that's what happened, there would be plenty of evidence in that vehicle. All they had to do was find it—which, another phone call told him, MVD had not yet been able to do.

But, and this managed to work its way through the slowly ebbing fog of a lack of sleep, that car could help explain the killer's haste: As Fat Willy said, everybody knew that vehicle. A car that big with Green's vanity plates. Parked where it could easily be seen. Driven through familiar streets. Half the people in the district recognized it. And, quite possibly, the killer believed that those who knew the car would also remember who was driving it and where. Someone driving that car who could be recognized. Or who shouldn't be behind that wheel—a white man, perhaps. . . . Cowboy boots. Vote buying. An urgency in getting rid of the body in order to get rid of that car. Why not leave the body in the car . . . ? Simply shoot him and walk away? Same reason: The killer might be noticed walking in that neighborhood. The car was needed for escape. To get back to wherever the alibi was, or to the killer's own car or motorcycle. Shoot Green quickly before he could become suspicious or could call for help, dump the body as soon as possible so the killer or killers wouldn't be seen driving that car, use it to get back to cover. Why not just drive to the other car or alibi with the body still in the Lincoln? Why stop to dump it? Perhaps—and here Wager's pencil started another little star—because the body might have been seen in the car? Or because the killer had been seen recently in the car with Green? Where would the car be driven that Green's body might have been seen? Who might have seen Green and his killer in the car? A parking attendant . . . a security gate with a guard . . . a ticket booth . . . A lot of possibilities but fewer than before. He made a note to himself and turned to his section of notes on K and E Construction and began going once more over those items. The construction firm's name had come up with persistency—enough to make Wager want to dig for more. But proving any link between Green and K and E would be tough.

He glanced at the clock and decided to take a chance on calling this early. After four or five rings, the woman's sleepy voice mumbled hello. "Miss Andersen? This is Detective Wager. I wonder if I could come over and talk with you for a few minutes?"

"It's . . . it's Sunday morning."

"Yes, ma'am. I'll be there in about a half hour."

"But . . ."

He hung up before she could think of some objection; in less than half an hour he nosed the Trans-Am slowly past groups of condominiums, built to look like mansions that spread over the dark green of lushly watered lawns and thin new trees. Tasteful wooden signs listed the house numbers for each cluster, and he finally found the one he looked for. It was a middle unit, two buildings away from the street, and as Wager walked down the gently arcing sidewalk he could hear carried from the distance the amplified chime of a church carillon ringing a half-familiar hymn. At the far end of the trimmed green, he saw the white frame of a lifeguard tower and a young couple, towels slung around their necks, walking toward the pool, holding hands. Miss Andersen answered the door in jeans and a sweatshirt; the lined paleness of her face was accentuated by the lack of makeup, and she was awake now but said nothing.

Wager smiled. "Can I come in?"

Still silent, she stepped back, turning to lead him into a living room that was designed to make up in height and openness what it lost in narrowness and a lack of windows in two walls. "Would you like some coffee?" A pot steamed on a divider between the kitchen and dining area. "I just made some."

He watched her fill the blue cup, a slight tremor in her hands. This morning her hair was pulled back into a loose ponytail that made her seem less enameled and more vulnerable. "Are you going to the funeral?"

"I don't know. I want to. He was my employer and, if I don't, it'll look . . ." She gestured at the cream pitcher and sugar bowl; Wager shook his head. "But I don't know if I ought to."

"His wife knows about you. She's known for a long time."

"Oh."

He sipped, studying the woman's face. It was good coffee—freshly ground and made with some kind of filter machine. Wager had been thinking of trying one, but it might spoil his ability to stomach the coffee at the office.

"I suppose I'd better not, then." The gray eyes looked up. "Perhaps the interment. I can stay at the edge of the crowd." Her voice broke slightly as she explained. "I just want to say good-bye!"

"Yes, ma'am." He watched her walk slowly past the fireplace and settle on the tan rug to lean back against a raised hearth. "There'll be a big crowd."

"I know."

"You are the only one who handles the books for the store?"

"What? Oh—I'm sorry. I was thinking of something else. The books? Yes—I do the books."

"You're the only one?"

"Yes. Horace would look them over once a week, but I make all the entries."

"Was the store profitable?"

"Yes." She looked puzzled. "You've asked me that before. Why?"

Wager smiled. "Sometimes I forget what I've asked. Furniture sales—that's the store's total source of income?"

"Sales and leasing. We lease some items but we don't really advertise that side of the business; it's more of a service for certain clients. I don't understand the question—what else would a furniture store do?"

"Some business owners run their personal income through corporations so they can get a better tax break."

She shook her head. "No—not Horace. His councilman's salary was taxed before he got it."

"Investments?"

"A few. Real estate, mostly. But I don't know much about that side of his finances." He had all her attention now. "Why are you asking me these things?"

"There's a rumor," Wager emphasized the word, "that he might have been involved in selling votes on his zoning committee. If so, he might have run the money through the furniture company so he could account for it."

"No—not Horace."

"It's just a rumor, Miss Andersen. Something I have to check out."

"He wouldn't do that. He didn't!"

"You saw nothing like that in the company books?"

"No. And it would be hard to do—the books are a simple credit and debit system. Income in one column, expenses in the other, and each item noted. I set it up that way when I came in so we could tell what pieces were selling well and which ones weren't. It's as much a running inventory as an accounting sheet." She shook her head again. "There's no way to bring in any extra money without selling an item."

"What about false sales?"

She thought a moment, diverted from the idea of Green as a crooked politician by the challenge of an accounting problem. "It would be too easy to spot—the invoices: stock numbers and delivery sheets. Just cross-check the invoices with the income record."

"Can you tell me anything at all about his real estate investments?"

"Not much, no. He mentioned them a time or two—he had a lot in Arvada he was going to sell, but it fell through, I think." She remembered something and it pushed her chin out a bit: "He did tell me once he was worried about being an investor in a group that intended to apply to his committee for a zoning variance, so he bought out of it. He didn't want any hint of conflict of interest. Does that sound like a man who would sell votes, Officer? I don't think it does. I know Horace would not do something like that."

"Did he need money?"

"No. I don't think so. He never said so."

And nothing Wager had seen so far indicated the man was living beyond his means, but that was a step that would have to come later: subpoenas for bank records, financial statements, property records—all the documents of one's financial life that needed probable cause to be opened to investigation. And it was a step he couldn't take by himself. "Miss Andersen, you say you and Green made love regularly in the afternoons between five and six."

". . . Yes."

"Where did you go?"

"What?"

"Where did you go to make love, Miss Andersen? It's too far to drive down here. Did you stay at the store?"

"No. The first time . . . No."

"Where did you go?"

"He had an apartment." Even in the room's silence, it was hard to hear her answers.

"Address?"

"Centennial Towers. Number ten-fifty-one."

That was a large residential complex in lower downtown, one of those clusters of high rises that formed its own court-yard and had commercial space on the first two floors and apartments with individual balconies all the way up to the thirtieth. "Did he rent it for you and him?"

"No. He had it before we met. He said he used it to get away from the telephones—it was his refuge, he said." She added, "He needed someplace like that, some place where

he could just lie down and listen to nothing but quietness."
Her eyes met Wager's. "A lot of times we didn't make love.
He just slept. We held each other, we talked, he would rest
for a little while."

"But not on Wednesday?"

"No."

"Tell me what happened."

"We . . ." She hesitated, then lifted one shoulder in a half
shrug. "We made love. I'm not sure what you're asking
me."

Wager wasn't, either, but he knew he wanted to understand this man who was a mixture of saint and sinner as well
as a victim of someone's hatred or fear. "Was it like the
other times? Was there anything different about him?"

She watched the light hairs on her arm flip in a gold blur
as her fingers ran slowly up her flesh. "He seemed . . .
wounded."

"Wounded? Where?"

"Not that way—physically. Mentally. It was as if I reas-
sured him in some way. As if I returned something to him.
He was very yearning and . . . tender. . . ." A small sound
of irritation. "I don't know exactly—he didn't say anything
was bothering him. But when we left, he seemed more at
peace."

"He was worried?"

"He didn't tell me what it was; he never liked to bring
his troubles there, he said. But something was bothering
him. I didn't want to ask what it was."

Wager gave her a few moments, but she said nothing
more. "Did you eat supper there?"

Sonja Andersen was reliving that last day. Wager could
see it in the wetness that hovered at the edge of her eyelids.
"No."

"Did he ever go there with anyone else?"

"He gave parties there two or three times a year for
jobbers or big buyers—he could write most of it off as a
business expense that way."

Tax-supported fun and games. Why not? That was the
meaning of free enterprise. "Did he ever take other
women there?"

The blond ponytail wagged no. "He told me I was the only one who knew about it. It was our space. Only the two of us."

Wager wanted to be certain. "His wife didn't know about it? Or his aide, Julia Wilfong?"

"They never telephoned him there. No one did." She added, more to herself than to him, "I should cancel the lease, shouldn't I? There's no reason for her to find out about it now."

"It's in the account books?"

"Under fixed expenses. Rent."

Wager rose and paused to look at the scarlet dots of color tumbling down among the greenness of a plant hanging in the sunlight of a shallow bay window. It was the same kind of plant that his mother used to have in her kitchen window and for some reason he remembered its name: bleeding heart. "Thank you, Miss Andersen. We may have to take a look at the books later. They may be subpoenaed." He explained, "You won't want to remove them or alter them in any way."

She didn't answer or stand. On his back, as he closed the door behind him, he could feel her large gray eyes, empty of everything except sadness.

1004 Hours

He radioed for a telephone warrant, hoping that a bailiff could find a judge on duty, and get it signed before he reached Centennial Towers. It should be routine, but a lot depended on which judge and what he'd had for breakfast. That was the way of the court many times: Judges expected the police to obey every rule of evidence courts invented, but when it came to providing their help in obeying, a lot of judges were a lot less dedicated. Some cops saw that hypocrisy as anti-police feeling, but Wager didn't think that was it. To him, it came from arrogance; a judge had the power to tell the law "Do as I say" and that made most of them resent being told the same thing, such as "Sign a warrant." If they were subject to orders, then they weren't any better than the people they ordered, and once they got on the bench, damned few of them could stomach that idea.

The apartment hideaway was something he should have discovered earlier, and he felt a little self-contempt for not thinking of it sooner. What he was thinking of now, of course, was Green's missing dinner: It could explain the gap between taking Sonie Andersen back to the furniture store and showing up at the Vitaco reception. It could also be the place he went after he left the reception—he, and whoever went there to meet him.

Parking downtown on a Sunday morning was no problem, and he pulled into the last of an empty row of parking meters that picketed Larimer Street in front of the yellow brick of the apartment towers. A large brass sign said Centennial Square and led under a bricked archway toward the splash of a fountain and a scattering of concrete benches and large planters holding young trees. The inside door to the apartment lobby was locked, but the column of names and buzzers listed apartment 5 as the manager's. Wager pressed the button, and a few seconds later a voice said, "Can I help you?"

"Police. Would you come to the front entry, please."

"Just a minute."

While he waited Wager ran his finger down the names behind the slotted windows. Apartment 1051 was blank.

The manager, a short man with stiff, iron-gray hair and a mustache that struggled to look impressive, peered at Wager's identification through the inner doors. Then he unlocked them. "What's the problem, Officer?"

"I need to look at apartment ten-fifty-one. A warrant's on the way."

"An arrest?"

"No. It belongs to a homicide victim. Horace Green. You know him?"

"Ten-fifty-one . . . Ten-fifty—" The manager blinked. "Black fellow? Tall?"

Wager nodded. "You didn't know him by name?"

The man held the elevator door for Wager and then followed him in and pushed number 10. "No—that's a corporate rental. We have a lot of those," he explained. "Business rents an apartment instead of using hotel rooms, to put up visiting firemen. Better tax break. Had a lot of oil companies did it, but that fell off. Now they're coming back, though." He added, "Thank God."

"Embassy Furniture."

"That's right—it sure is! Embassy Furniture. And he used it for a few parties, I remember, because sometimes I'd let people in." The elevator stopped and he held the doors again for Wager. "It gets pretty busy around here some evenings—if there's a lot of parties, I watch the door to keep things from jamming up there, you understand."

"Did you ever see him use it at other times?"

"I'd see him around now and then. But it's hard to say—the residents have underground parking and their own elevator up from the garage. They don't have to come through the lobby."

The hallway was a short one in both directions, quiet, with the feel of thick walls and softened only a little by a couple of small pictures and an end table holding paper flowers. He followed the manager around the corner to the door of the apartment. The man pressed a security code into a panel and then opened the lock with a passkey. "You sure you have a warrant for this?"

"I phoned it in."

"OK—I want to cooperate with the police, of course. But I got to be sure, you understand."

"Did you ever see Green with anyone?"

"The black man?" He nodded. "Came here sometimes with a blond woman. Saw them in the elevator once or twice. Before that, a black woman." He pushed the door open and stood aside for Wager. "It's not my business what people do in the privacy of their own homes, you understand."

"Did he bring many women here?"

"I don't think so. Three, maybe four, I guess. I guess whoever he was going with at the time. What I mean is, he didn't mix them up, you understand—he'd have one for a while and then some time would pass and I might see him with another."

"The blonde was the last one?"

"As far as I know."

The room had the musty odor of unopened windows and trapped summer heat, despite the air conditioning. A half-bath to the left of the entry, a closet to the right, and then widening into a living room that, had the blinds been opened, would have been full of light from the two corner windows and the patio doors that led to a balcony. Dining area with the kitchen beyond, also opening to the patio; two bedrooms linked by the master bath.

"Don't look like he used it much," said the manager. "Nice furniture, though."

A show room. That's what struck Wager when he glanced over the apartment—each piece of furniture seemed to have its own location, as if Green had carefully selected the best from his store to display in the apartment. Wager started going through the drawers. "What's the rent on a unit like this?"

"Eleven hundred. That includes water and heat, parking, recreation and health facilities. It's one of the less-expensive units. Phone's extra, of course, and electricity."

Good thing most of the cost went to the taxpayers, Wager thought; even a successful furniture dealer felt eleven hundred a month. "Do you have any list of people who visited?"

"No, sir. When residents have guests, generally they buzz themselves through. Unless, like I say, there's a lot of parties and it gets real crowded. Then I help out at the door. Usually, people buzz themselves through."

The drawers in the living room furniture were empty except for an unused telephone book; the closets held a few shirts, an extra suit and shoes, a raincoat. Nothing in the pockets. The dresser drawers had a few pairs of shorts and another shirt still in its laundry wrapper; the bathroom had shaving gear, toothbrush—two of those—a bottle of aspirin, shampoo, a shower cap, a set of towels on the racks and one in the closet, with some extra sheets. Some cleaning items. The refrigerator was empty of everything except a couple of bottles of mix for drinks, a few beers, a partly used quart of milk. No frozen dinners, nothing to cook. The garbage pail was almost empty, too: a paper-bag liner held a wad of cellophane from something, a bottle top that matched the beer bottle lying beside it, and a cash-register receipt from a liquor store for $4.73 and dated 9 June—three days before Green's death. Both beds were neatly made; the dishwasher contained some glasses, no plates, and a few pieces of silverware waiting to be washed.

"See what you're looking for?"

"No." Perhaps forensics would find something of interest, but Wager didn't think so.

He slid back the patio doors and went out on the balcony. Ten floors below, the vacant streets of downtown held an occasional pedestrian or car; the Sunday tide of diners and boutique haunters had not yet begun. This apartment faced east, into the morning sun, and across the roofs of neighboring low rises he could see the steady glide of a distant jet sinking across Green's district toward Stapleton. A set of plastic patio furniture and a small table were pulled back against the wall; a portable barbecue sat dusty in a corner.

"Did you ever hear Green and the blonde argue?"

"No. Just saw them going up or down in the elevator."

"The woman Green went with before the blonde—how long ago was that?"

The mustache bristled out as the man puffed his lips in thought. "Long time. Two Christmases ago, maybe. It was a Christmastime, I remember. But two or three, I couldn't say. After a while they all run together, you understand."

"Not this last Christmas?"

"No—two, maybe three, Christmases ago."

"Let's go down to the garage and look around. Do you know what his car looks like?"

The manager didn't, and Wager wasn't able to show him because the car wasn't there. The slot for 1051 was vacant and a slow tour in the chill air past the other stalls turned up nothing. Wager handed a business card to the manager. "Lock up the apartment and don't let anyone else in unless it's a policeman. If someone wants in, give me a call right away—any time."

The remnants of last night's activity still marked the littered ashtrays and trash baskets of the C.A.P. offices, and an occasional desk held a weary cup of cold coffee, left behind when its owner was pulled away in a rush. The weekend had only a skeleton crew of janitors and they hadn't worked their way up to the third floor yet. Wager nodded to Theresa, the civilian who sat at the reception desk, thumbing through the Sunday comics.

"Morning, Sergeant Wager. Were you in on that riot last night?"

"Yes."

The woman's straight, short hair wagged with sympathy. "Papers make it sound pretty bad. Have you heard about Officer Wunderlicht?"

That was the cop who had the heart attack. "How's he doing?"

"Intensive care, still. But they think he'll make it."

"I hope so." Wager didn't know Wunderlicht, but he was a cop, and he was suffering one of a cop's favorite diseases. When any cop went down, it was like someone in the family: sometimes a distant cousin who was only a name, sometimes a brother. Wager flipped his name to the IN column and glanced at Stubbs's tag. It still said OFF-DUTY, and Wager, thinking of Wunderlicht, felt a twist of irritation and wondered if the man would bother to come in today.

"Paper says it's supposed to be worse tonight. That kid getting shot and all."

"We'll find out."

Theresa called down the hall after him, "You have a message from Councilwoman Voss—it's in your box."

He lifted a hand thanks and paused to take a small stack of papers from the pigeonhole above his name. The while-you-were-out note simply said, "Councilwoman Voss," followed by a telephone number and an *X* in the box for "Call Back." Other papers were the routine notices and queries that steadily accumulated like dust and were just about as important. Wager dialed the number and listened to the rings while he glanced over the page of his notebook that listed words and phrases cueing possibilities in the case. There were still too many of them for any pattern, and they still led in no special direction.

"Mrs. Voss?"

"This is Elizabeth Voss."

"Detective Wager. I have a note to call you."

"Oh, yes!" Her voice warmed with recognition. "Thank you for returning my call. I wanted to say how grateful I am for your protection last night. I'm afraid I didn't realize what you and the chief were warning us against until that gang came out of the alley. It was so sudden—so . . . ferocious and mindless. . . ."

"Yes, ma'am. I hope you're not planning on being down there tonight."

"Well, yes, I am. But not to drive into the neighborhood. I want to be there, but I'll stay at the command center."

"Your husband doesn't care if you go there again?"

The question made her pause. "My husband's dead, Officer Wager. And even if he weren't, I would not need his permission to go anywhere."

She didn't sound as if she would. "Have you talked to Mrs. Green this morning?" The councilwoman and Lieutenant Elkins had taken the shivering woman home last night.

"I called earlier. Her mother told me she was still sleeping. It's the best thing for her."

Wager thought so, too, especially with the funeral this afternoon, which would be another drain on emotions. "When you talk to her, tell her we're doing the best we can."

"I know you are, Officer, and that's a second reason I wanted to talk with you."

He waited.

"Are you there?"

"Yes, ma'am."

"You were so quiet I wasn't sure." The momentary lightness left her voice. "Have you learned anything more about the possibility of Horace selling votes?"

"No, ma'am. That's one of the things we're working on. Are you ready to tell me who your informant was?"

"I haven't had a chance to talk to the person, Officer. I probably will this afternoon." She added, "I understand you asked Councilman Albro about it."

"That's right."

"He called me this morning. He was quite upset."

"That's what I hear."

"I understand he complained to the chief."

"That he did."

"Please know, Officer Wager, that I intend to make the chief fully aware of the professionalism and cooperation you've shown in your investigation of the case."

"Thank you."

She wanted him to know that, she said once more before hanging up; and Wager, gazing at the telephone his hand rested on, wondered why.

"Hi, Gabe." Stubbs, a fresh scratch of blood under his chin from a shaky morning shave, came in holding a cup of coffee. "I thought I'd find you down here. What's new?"

Wager told him about Green's love nest and his real estate venture.

"But Sonie Andersen didn't find any money laundered through the company?"

"That's what she says. I don't want to subpoena the books yet. That'll bring in the D.A. and open up the malfeasance crap."

Stubbs nodded and tried not to look uncomfortable about that issue. "What about forensics going through his apartment?"

"Give them a call. I don't think they'll get much, but it has to be done."

The younger detective paused, his finger on the telephone's cradle. "I found out where that receptionist for K and E Construction lives. I thought she might have some idea of her bosses' whereabouts on the eleventh."

"Did you talk to her?"

"Not yet. I figured I'd ask you first."

Wager nodded and glanced at the wall clock. "Let's check out the restaurants first, then we'll talk to her."

The glossy coating on the reprint of Green's photograph was beginning to show the mark of Wager's sweaty thumb. Mrs. Green had given him the names of a dozen restaurants where her husband liked to eat—"He tried to go to a lot of different ones; he didn't want to favor any particular one"—and they were spread all over Denver's north side. Most were in his district and many were close to his headquarters. But a few were nearer his furniture store, and they started with those. Wager showed the photograph to yet another manager who recognized the man and said what a tragic thing his death was.

"Do you remember if he ate here on the afternoon or evening of the eleventh?"

"That would be Wednesday?" Again the shake of a head. "I'll ask, but I don't think so. He came in, what, two weeks ago. I remember seeing him around then. But not last Wednesday."

Back in the car, Stubbs sighed. "That's five?"

"Yeah." Wager crossed off that name and looked at the next address. It was a small place that served only barbecued ribs, beef and pork, and Wager drew a line through it, too. No chicken and vegetables there.

"We're pretty near Gail Haney's place," said Stubbs.

"Who?"

"The secretary for K and E. Gail Haney." He told Wager the address.

"Might as well break the monotony." He glanced at his watch as he swung onto Colorado Boulevard and headed south. The funeral was at two, and the chief had called a staff meeting at four to prepare for tonight's festivities. Turning onto Seventeenth Avenue Parkway, he followed it to Jersey and then turned and slowed to look for the number. If Wager wanted to make the funeral, he'd have to move a little faster.

"That's it—the four-plex."

Wager pulled the car to the curb of the quiet street. It was one of those settled neighborhoods whose trees and hedges seemed to keep the rest of the city at a distance.

The young woman who answered their ring wasn't the long-haired blonde, but she nodded when Wager identified himself and asked if Miss Haney lived here.

"Can we talk to her, please?"

"Just a minute, I'll call her."

"Must be a roommate," Stubbs murmured, watching the glimmer of the girl's legs beneath the rise and fall of her shorts. "She's not bad, either."

Gail Haney, minus the bright makeup that she wore at work, seemed much younger and the straight blond hair that came down each side of her face and dangled over the tips of her breasts emphasized her girlishness. "You want to see me?" Her blue eyes were round with surprise and innocence.

"We'd like to ask you a few questions. Can we come in?"

"Sure." She wore a thin cotton shirt with tiny blue checks, sleeves rolled up and tail out, and a pair of yellow shorts creased tightly where creases should be. The roommate disappeared to leave the small living room to them. Miss Haney gathered up the scattered Sunday paper and carried empty coffee cups into the kitchen. "I've never talked to a detective. It's kind of exciting."

Stubbs smiled. "It can get real exciting—depending on what we talk about."

She giggled, pulling her chin nervously against her neck. "I'll bet!"

Wager showed her Green's photograph. "Have you ever seen this man around the K and E offices?"

She looked at the picture. "Councilman Green? The one who got shot?"

"Yes."

"No. I've heard Mr. Kaunitz talk about him, but as far as I know he never came to the office."

"What did Mr. Kaunitz say?"

"I'm not sure. That he had a meeting with him. That he needed the councilman's OK for a project. Things like that."

"Did he meet often with the councilman?"

"It varied. When a zoning request was going up for a vote, they'd meet and either Mr. Kaunitz or Mr. Ellis would present it to the councilman or his committee. Otherwise, I don't think they saw much of him."

"Did you ever hear either Kaunitz or Ellis mention any private business with Green?"

"Private business?"

Wager nodded. "Dinner meetings, accounts, personal messages, that kind of thing."

"Not that I know of. When they needed to meet with him, I'd call his office and make an appointment. Sometimes they did meet for lunch, though. I guess that's kind of private."

"You called the furniture store?"

"No. His council office—I figured it was council business so it seemed right to call him there. It just seemed more businesslike, don't you think?"

Wager did. "The request for zoning changes—do you keep a record of those?"

"Sure. I keep a record of all correspondence—it's on the computer. We have a main disk and a backup that we run off at the end of each day."

Stubbs asked, "Do you keep both of their appointment books?"

"For company business, sure. Their private appointments, they keep themselves." A worried look came into her eyes. "You're asking an awful lot of questions about the firm. Is there some kind of trouble?"

"No." Stubbs smiled. "The law wouldn't let us ask questions like this if we were looking for evidence. We're just trying to get a sense of Councilman Green's activities. It helps to see him through the eyes of people he did business with."

"Oh." She smiled brightly back at Stubbs. "I guess that makes sense."

Wager asked, "Do you know if either Kaunitz or Ellis had a meeting with Green last Wednesday?"

She thought back, the white of her teeth nipping at a full lower lip. "I don't think so. I'd have to look at the appointments, though, to be sure."

"Do you know what Mr. Kaunitz or Mr. Ellis did on Wednesday evening?"

Eyebrows lifted, she stared at a corner of the room; a long inhale tightened the checkered cloth. "I think Mr. Kaunitz went to the symphony. That would have been the second Wednesday—he has season tickets, so I can't book any meetings on the evenings of the second Wednesday of each month. I don't know about Mr. Ellis." She went on, "I've never been to the symphony, have you?"

"Not yet," said Stubbs.

"Maybe your wife'll let you go someday," said Wager. Then to the girl, "You don't know what time Ellis quit work?"

She stopped smiling. "It was late, I know that. He came in close to five and was pretty upset about something." Then she smiled again, this time only at Wager, a dimple in each cheek. "He gets upset a lot, but he doesn't really mean it. Mr. Kaunitz is the calm one." The blue eyes blinked as they remembered something. "It was Councilman Green! I mean, not him exactly—not by name. But Mr. Ellis was upset over something to do with the zoning for the Tremont project."

"The parking garage being put up over on Tremont Street?"

"Yes. Mr. Ellis said something about it being too late to do anything about it now and that if the Zoning Committee tried, he—Mr. Ellis—would pull the whole thing down."

"Pull down what?" Wager asked. "The parking garage?"

"I guess so. Mr. Kaunitz shut the door. I didn't think much about it at the time—Mr. Ellis always goes off like that and gets all excited." She smiled widely at Wager. "Is it something important?"

That was the question Stubbs finally asked in the car, and Wager could only shrug. The importance was there—he felt the weight of it. But exactly why it was important, he had not yet figured out. There were pieces—fragments—that wanted to fit together, and he didn't know yet what pieces they were or even how many.

CHAPTER 15

"**Y**ou sure you want to do this, Gabe?"

They sat outside the large home in the Country Club neighborhood. Its wings were hidden behind thickly growing spruce that filtered out the last of the faint traffic noise from busy First Avenue, a block away. A brick walk curved up to a front door recessed into the stone façade like the gate to a castle. Only a few cars were parked, like theirs, along the curbs beneath the tree-shaded street; cars belonging to the sprawling homes went through alleys to parking space on their own grounds. "We may not have enough for an arrest," said Wager, "but we sure as hell have probable cause for a talk."

"On just what Gail Haney said?"

"That and the rumors of payoff. And that boot heel." He opened the car door. "Let's find out what he says."

They had to wait a few minutes in the entryway while a blond youth—apparently Ellis's son—called the man to the door. Stubbs's feet nervously scraped the gray slate as he craned his neck around at the wood and mirrors and lamps of the hall.

"Looks like a goddamned hotel lobby."

Wager was listening to the distant murmur of voices from somewhere beyond the large living room that he glimpsed through an archway. Then heels thudded on the carpeting and Ellis came through the arch to ask, "What can I help you people with?"

"We need some more information on Councilman Green, Mr. Ellis."

"All right—what about him?"

"Why don't you start by telling us what the trouble was last Wednesday with the zoning permit for the Tremont project."

Ellis's eyes beneath the almost transparent paleness of their eyebrows and lashes blinked as he stared at Wager. "How'd you hear about that?"

"We hear about a lot of things. That's our job. What's your version of the zoning problem?"

The man looked from Wager to Stubbs and then jerked his head. "Let's go into the study."

He led them through the living room, with its towering fireplace whose moss-rock dwarfed the furniture, and into a smaller room. Lined with bookshelves, it held a desk with a gilded leather top placed to catch the window light. Ellis sat there, motioning abruptly for Stubbs and Wager to take the leather reading chairs that faced it. Stubbs did; Wager didn't.

"Damn it, I want to know who's been telling you stories. I've got a right to know my accuser!"

"We're not accusing anybody, Mr. Ellis. We're just trying to find out the truth." Wager's voice was mild, almost friendly. "Then we'll make the accusations."

"I thought you were working on Green's murder."

Wager nodded.

"Then I don't see what the zoning issue has to do with it. I damn well didn't kill him."

"Why don't you just tell us what happened? Maybe it'll turn out there's no connection at all with Green's death."

"Damn right there's not!" Ellis looked from Wager to Stubbs. "I heard the Zoning Committee was under pressure to reconsider the Tremont project. Some bunch of neighborhood do-gooders or something wanted to keep that stinking slum over there."

"The Northeast Denver Action Committee?"

"Yeah—that bunch. Listen: They're nothing but a bunch of goddamn rabble rousers, and I wouldn't be surprised if they're behind these damned riots. God damned bunch of animals—live like pigs and fight each other like rats."

"The Action Committee protested the evictions?"

"Hell, they protest anything a white man does! It wasn't our damned fault the owner wanted to sell his property— we didn't have a damn thing to do with evicting anybody; the owners did. But we're sure as hell getting the blame. That project, it gives work to Negroes—if that project wasn't going up, there'd be fifteen, twenty Negroes back on welfare. Goddamn it, K and E Construction has a good record of minority hiring! We're not the ones causing all the trouble!"

"Who changed the zoning from residential to business? You or the previous owner?"

The sun-reddened face darkened a bit and Ellis ran his hand through the pale hair on the side of his head. "That parking garage is an improvement for that whole neighborhood."

"You bought the property because you had a prior guarantee of approval on the zoning change, right?"

"It wasn't Aaron. Aaron wouldn't have told you that."

"I'm not allowed to say who we've talked to, Mr. Ellis. It's a question of immunity from prosecution."

"Immunity?"

"From prosecution. But I can tell you the person who spoke with us knows the company inside out."

"I can't believe it!"

"Mr. Kaunitz had lunch with Green on five June at the Rattlesnake Club. To your knowledge, is that when they arranged for the zoning change on the Tremont property?"

"Aaron—Jesus God. Aaron!"

"Mr. Ellis, do you agree that is when they made the deal?"

"Is that what Aaron told you?"

"I haven't said that we've spoken with Mr. Kaunitz."

Wager smiled. "But you can't blame a man for looking out for himself first."

"That son of a bitch!"

"Is that what the deal was? Green guaranteed the zoning change?"

"I don't know!" Ellis lunged out of his chair and gazed stiffly at something beyond the walls of the study. His lips clenched as he tried for control. "I don't know what they talked about. I wasn't there. Aaron takes care of that end of it. He's supposed to, anyway. I'm just the goddamned builder—he takes care of that end of it and half the time I don't know what the hell's going on." He turned to Wager, hands open and lifted for help. "I'm just the goddamned builder!"

"Tell us what you do know."

The man sagged into his chair and stared at the leather inlay of his desk. "There were some deals," he admitted wearily. Then he glanced at Wager. "It's nothing new—it happens all the time. We didn't do one damn thing every other builder in the city doesn't do."

"Did you give Green money to pass the zoning changes?"

Ellis shrugged. "It's business. Never have any goddamned progress if you let the goddamned neighborhood people run things—not a damn one of them wants to see anything new at all happen in their precious neighborhood. You try to bring in quality projects, new jobs, build a goddamned city to be proud of, and there's not a goddamned neighborhood you can name that wants the growth."

"How much did Green get?"

"Enough. I don't know exactly—Aaron, that son of a bitch, he took care of it. But it was enough."

"Cash?"

"Hell yes! You don't think you write a check for something like that, do you?"

"Who delivered it to Green?"

"You have to ask Aaron—" Ellis looked up suddenly. "Who delivered? Aaron didn't tell you?" He leaned slowly back in his chair, thick arms straight out to the desk. "Answer me yes or no: Did you talk to Aaron? Yes or no, God damn it!"

"I'm asking the questions, Mr. Ellis."

"Get out!" He stood and aimed a rigid finger at the door. "I don't have to talk to you—get the hell out of my house!"

"It'll help if you cooperate with us."

"Out!"

"If we hadn't left, you think he would have called a cop?" Stubbs rolled his head back against the taut muscles of his neck and tried to stifle a yawn as the car's air-conditioner struggled against the trapped heat.

Wager headed south on University toward I-25; Kaunitz's address was just across the city-county line in one of those exclusive residential areas labeled a "village." Without a warrant, without probable cause for arrest, there were no grounds to sit there and argue with Ellis, and the man had begun making noises about his lawyers before Wager and Stubbs had reached the front door. "He's probably calling Aaron right now. And then his lawyer."

"Yeah." Stubbs shifted on the seat. "But you were good, Gabe—you didn't say a thing that could be used in court against us."

"I know that."

"That bastard really fell for it."

Wager's mind was no longer on Ellis. "If Green was on the take for zoning changes, why would he get religion on this one?"

"I don't know. I hadn't thought of that."

Green was killed because someone was jealous or because he was a threat to someone: Those were the most likely motives, now. At least two people could have been jealous, but neither Sonja Andersen nor Green's wife seemed to fit. They both had a kind of resignation that didn't mark them as murderers of passion, and neither woman was very big. According to forensics, Green, a big man himself, had been half carried rather than dragged to where he was found. Ellis was big enough. And Ellis had something to lose. But why would Green suddenly decide to turn against them? They all had a good thing going.

"Kaunitz ain't hurting for money, either." Stubbs gazed at the approaching house. Backed against an abrupt rise in what had been prairie, its flat roofs staggered at different heights and lengths to join a rock outcropping, so that the whole thing looked as if it grew out of the heat-shimmering earth. Here, all the utilities were underground, and despite being within twenty minutes of downtown, the widely spaced houses gave a feeling of the countryside. As they parked and walked up the broad redstone flags the front door opened and Kaunitz stood squinting in the sun, waiting.

"It's Detective Wager, isn't it?" He held out a bony hand for Wager to squeeze and raised his eyebrows at Stubbs.

"Detective Stubbs," said Wager. "You've talked to Ellis?"

"He called, of course. Quite upset. Come in."

Kaunitz's study, just off the entryway, was a long, low room with a wall of glass overlooking a raised flower bed, and beyond that the distant Rampart Range. To Wager, Ellis would have seemed more at home here, and Kaunitz in the old-fashioned room that Ellis used. But sometimes houses were less expressions of what people were than of what they would like to be, and the modern architecture along with a series of paintings on the wall opposite the window hinted that Kaunitz thought of himself as a discoverer of the latest thing. Wager eyed the paintings; one was a flat-looking picture of mountains, rows of dimly colored peaks set one behind the other and fading into a pale-green sky. He had seen the mountains look like that on certain summer evenings, and he kind of liked that one. The others were wide scrolls of paint like Japanese writing, or blocks of color that looked more like a design for curtains than something to put in a frame and hang on your wall. Wager didn't like those.

"I understand you did not read the *Miranda* warning to John."

"That's right."

"Then of course anything he told you is inadmissible in

court." Kaunitz folded himself into a chair made up of cloth and angled wire and nodded to a pair of similar chairs. "Your methods were very harsh—they upset John quite a bit."

"I'm sorry to hear that."

"Yes, of course you are. They did make John say things he perhaps should not have without legal advice."

"That's right."

Kaunitz waited for something else, perhaps a *Miranda* warning of his own. "You can't expect me to incriminate myself."

"Any investigation of bribery won't come from me, Mr. Kaunitz. That's a federal crime—the FBI will handle it." He added, "If it comes to that."

The man's long fingers made a little tent under his narrow nose and he rested his lips against them a moment. "If?"

"What Green did while he was alive is important only for what it tells me about his murder."

"And you think his death might be related to . . ." A graceful flap of his fingers finished the sentence.

"Maybe. I don't have enough information yet to say either way."

Again, the prayerlike gesture. "That means you suspect me or John. That's ludicrous."

"Maybe it is. But then maybe it went something like this: You got the Tremont property cheap the same way you got the Montclair school building—because the owners had been told by Green that they couldn't get a zoning change. Then once they sold to you, he put the change through and the property doubled or tripled in value. But then Green wanted more. Especially after the Northeast Denver Action Committee started the fuss about the evictions on Tremont. A fuss that could cost Green his reelection. And you didn't want to give him more."

Kaunitz's crossed leg swung steadily in slow rhythm as Wager spoke. Then the leg stopped. "You're very good at your work, aren't you? Certainly, that makes a good hypothesis. It does indeed. But it's not what actually happened."

Wager didn't need Kaunitz's approval for the job he did. "A hypothesis is all I've got until you tell me what did happen. Why was Ellis upset about the Tremont property on the day Green was killed?"

"I have not been warned of my rights, I am not admitting to any wrongdoing in my dealings with Green or anyone else, and I will not talk to two of you together."

Wager glanced at Stubbs, who looked surprised and stood quickly. "You want me out?"

"You may use this door." Kaunitz pointed to the one in the glass wall. "The path leads around to the front."

They waited until Stubbs was out of sight beyond the hot tumult of reds and blues.

"John told me what you said to him—obviously, you've been talking to someone in the office."

Wager ignored the hint. "Was it at that lunch on the fifth? Is that when you arranged things with Green?"

"No. As a matter of fact, I never did 'arrange things' with the man. He was very particular about denying any hint of impropriety. Not, of course, that I or the corporation would be involved in improprieties."

"Right. What was that meeting about?"

"Zoning questions, yes. But routine and perfectly honest issues that had nothing to do at all with either the Tremont or Montclair projects. The corporation's thinking of developing land in the Montbello neighborhood for the expansion of Stapleton Airport. There's a strong sentiment among the City Council members to restrict commercial development when the airport expands—they don't want it to become entirely commercial, as the area is now around the existing airport."

And zoning restrictions would keep that from happening. "So you made an offer?"

"Not at all. I explained the increased tax advantage to the city of allowing limited development. It's my hope that a compromise can be reached between those who want absolutely no development and those who want absolutely no restrictions." A long finger tapped emphasis. "Believe it or not, many developers do understand and are sensitive to neighborhood wishes—we realize that as a very practical matter. That vague thing called 'quality of life' is a valuable commodity. But growth will come; that's a given. The question is, What kind of growth?"

"That's what you were telling Green?"

"Essentially, yes. That, and getting an idea of the committee's schedule for the next few months." He explained, "We need a calendar to prepare proposals and present them; a well-thought-out plan doesn't just appear overnight."

"And you mentioned nothing to Green about what his cut would be?"

"Never. We never spoke of that in any way at all."

"You just gave him what you thought his help was worth? A little present between friends?"

Kaunitz's crossed legs tightened slightly and for the first time he shifted his eyes away from Wager's. "I am admitting nothing, you understand." He looked up. "I will deny we ever spoke of this if I must."

"Mr. Kaunitz, if I want your ass, I can use the Grand Jury to nail it—either you'd testify with immunity or go to jail for contempt. So why don't you just cut the crap and tell me the truth."

"I am not a felon, Detective Wager!"

"And Richard Nixon wasn't a crook. How did you pay off Green?"

The man's lips became a line that puckered little bunches of white flesh at each corner. "Cash."

"How was it done?"

"We mailed it to a box number."

"Where?"

"The Park Hill station—80207."

"Number?"

"Seventy-five, ninety-five."

"Addressed to Green?"

"Yes."

"How much?"

Kaunitz's long fingers laced together and pressed tightly against his chest as if to hold in the admission. "Twenty-five thousand."

"How many times?"

"Twice."

An extra fifty thousand would make Green's furniture store very profitable indeed. "You bought just two votes?"

The man blinked at Wager's words, but grudgingly accepted them. "Three. The Montclair school, the Tremont garage, and an earlier one, about three years ago: a motel that needed a variance for its liquor license."

"Just after he was elected?"

"It was a piece of business that began with his predecessor."

That would be Thaddeus Blackman—whose original name had been McBain, but who changed it when he decided to go into politics: "Vote Blackman." And whom Green had defeated on rumors of dishonesty. "Green came to you?"

"No. We had the usual cocktail party to honor the victor. I mentioned we had some business coming before the Zoning Committee. I told him it might be controversial—some neighbors were objecting to the liquor license that the motel would need, and they had a strong argument because it was within an elementary school's protected zone." He explained, "The motel was in a commercial zone on a main street, but the school's zone overlapped it at this point. The committee had to decide which zone had precedent."

"And he said he'd take care of it?"

"No. He only said he would look it over carefully. But his aide came up later and hinted that a contribution to the election fund would be appreciated. And rewarded."

Elections were expensive. And created a lot of debts. "Julia Wilfong?"

"Yes."

"How much did that cost?"

"Five thousand."

"Is that how the other two worked? You told Green you needed help and then mailed an envelope?"

"Nothing so overt. We drew up our proposals and presented them just like all the others. But a few weeks before the hearing, we'd send an envelope with a note. Just the name of the project we needed help with, and the cash."

"Twenty-five thousand."

"They were bigger projects. Much bigger."

"Where did you get the box number?"

"I told Green we'd like to contribute to his reelection fund. He said fine, he'd have his aide get in touch. She called and gave me that box number."

"So Green never had to see the money or hear of a bribe?"

"That's what he wanted. He never once referred to any of it. Nor, of course, did we." Kaunitz reminded Wager, "And what I've told you I will deny."

"Why was Ellis upset last Wednesday?"

"He heard from someone in City Hall that the Zoning Committee was going to reopen the Tremont application— that someone had called up the file for study."

"Who?"

"John's source didn't know. But we assumed it was Green because of pressures from the Northeast Denver Action Committee." Kaunitz shrugged. "I explained to John that it was too late. The variance had been approved by Council on second reading, the residents already relocated, and notice of demolition posted. It's due to start tomorrow."

"You move fast."

"It's a plan we've been working on for almost two years— nineteen months, to be exact." And planning was something he was proud of. "The preparation for a project that size is considerable—site studies, marketing research, property acquisition. Most people don't realize what has to take place before construction can even begin."

"The Montclair school conversion was in the works a long time, too?"

"Of course. We started planning that as soon—"

He hesitated and Wager finished it for him. "As soon as you made payment on the motel zoning variance?"

Kaunitz's head tilted agreement and he said quietly, "The opportunity was there."

"Where was Ellis Wednesday night?"

"You're not serious."

"You have an alibi. What about Ellis?"

"He told you he was at home. I have no reason to doubt him."

"You both had a lot to lose if Green rescinded the variance."

"Neither John nor I are murderers, Wager. I swear to you—we may have stretched the law in a very few business ventures, but neither of us would kill anyone. The Tremont property would be a loss, but not one we couldn't weather, and certainly not one worth killing anyone over. I've been very honest with you about what happened; I want Green's murderer caught just as much as you do."

"You both had a lot to lose," Wager said again.

"Green could not have rescinded the council's vote, not without exposing himself."

"It's not just the loss on that property. It's the city and state contracts. You people would never get another contract; you'd lose a hell of a lot of business."

"Not that much. Believe it or not, it would not be nearly so costly." A twitch of his eyebrows dismissed the threat. "It would be in the newspapers for a brief while, but not many people would condemn us for doing business that way— they couldn't afford to, because they do it themselves. It's a way of life. A brief embarrassment, which is all it would be, simply is not worth killing anyone. Such an act would entail far more risk than profit."

"That's what you told Ellis last Wednesday?"

"I didn't have to, because the issue never came up. John is excitable, but he is not the kind to murder someone. You have my word on that."

Wager stood and opened the door in the glass wall and eyed the large gardens with their planting areas divided into masses of color by rows of stone. "We'll see what the evidence says, Mr. Kaunitz. That carries a hell of a lot more weight than your word."

1455 Hours

He gave Stubbs the highlights of it and the round-faced man started to worry again. "You sure we shouldn't go to the chief now, Gabe? I mean it's a fucking confession!"

"Kaunitz will deny everything. And he'll ask for a jury trial—you know what that means."

It meant that juries tended to believe respectable, wealthy businessmen rather than cops. And since Green, the other major figure, couldn't testify the D.A. would think the expense of an investigation and trial wouldn't be worth the gamble. Stubbs understood that, but still he fretted. "It would cover us, that's all. Just in case."

"Let's stick to Green's killer, Stubbs. The chief's got another riot scheduled for tonight, and that's what he's worried about most." And besides, Wager was beginning to see a few things now—things that fit most of the facts and, perhaps equally important, most of what he felt about the case.

"Yeah. I suppose so." The man sank against the seat. "You want to try the post office?"

"It's Sunday. They're closed until tomorrow."

"Yeah. Crap. I forgot." The head wagged once. "The way we've been going lately, I don't even know which day it is."

The only reason Wager knew was because he kept thinking of places he wanted to check and kept reminding himself they were closed: the Park Hill postal station, Green's bank accounts, Zoning Committee records. The only places open were restaurants, and he headed up I-25 to swing back toward downtown and the next name on the list of Green's favorites.

But they didn't get there. The radio called his number and the dispatcher told him he had an urgent call. The telephone number was a familiar one, and Wager pulled off the freeway at Sixth Avenue to spot a blue telephone hood at a gas station.

After the usual exchange with the bartender, Fat Willy's voice panted against his ear. "I got something for you, Wager."

"What is it?"

"We got a deal, remember?"

"I remember, Willy. But you've got to give me something to work with."

"Try this: I found somebody who saw Green Wednesday night."

"Where?"

"The deal, Wager."

"What time? We've got most of his time accounted for, Willy. If you're telling me what we already know, you've got nothing to bargain with."

Two or three lurching breaths. "About seven at night."

That was one of the gaps—the time between Green's going back to the furniture store with Sonie Andersen and his showing up at the Vitaco reception at eight forty-five. The time when he should have been at the Prudential buffet. "I'll get back to you."

"You get back to me soon. Before tomorrow—that's when Franklin and Roberts got their hearing: tomorrow."

"As soon as I can."

Stubbs asked Wager what it was all about.

"A tip. It may be something; I hope so." He watched the traffic for a gap to pull into. "But it's up to the chief to get it."

1521 Hours

They had to wait until the chief returned from Green's funeral before he answered Wager's call. He was still in his dress uniform, a tailored glitter of dark blue and silver, when he asked Wager up to his office.

"Well?"

"I have an informant who can fill in one of the time-gaps on Green's last night."

The chief stared at Wager for a moment. "But he wants something for it?"

"A pair of meatheads Papadopoulos picked up for assault and arson. He wants the charges dropped."

"Maybe you'd better explain this to me. All of it."

Wager did, pointing out that the case against Franklin and Roberts was weak.

"Have you talked to Papadopoulos about this?"

"I did. He wants to pin them."

"It's not my policy to deal with criminals."

Wager looked to see if the man was serious and decided

he was. "It's a trade-off. It happens a lot, Chief. You know that." Before filing, it was called "reduced charges"; after filing, it was called "plea bargaining."

The man said nothing; he stared at the desk top and thought. "You believe the information's important?"

"It could be. It's the first lead on that time gap. But the informant's holding it until he finds out what it's worth."

"Franklin and Roberts are convicted felons. And now they're up for two more serious charges."

"The case is a weak one. The complainant was violating the law, too."

"That's for a jury to decide, Wager. I don't like pulling the rug from under one of my detectives."

"You don't like having a riot, either."

A slight lift at one corner of the man's thin lips. "Right: I don't like having a riot." He leaned forward. "Find out some more about what the informant has to trade. If it truly sounds important—if it defuses the problem—I'll do what I can for his two friends. If it's nothing, I'm not going to cross any lines."

CHAPTER 16

Sunday, 15 June, 1604 Hours

"**H**e ain't going to cross no lines?" Fat Willy leaned through the window of his white Cadillac and spat on the grit that streaked the alley's worn asphalt.

"If the information's important, he'll help. That's the best he can do."

"Shit. Best he can do ain't much at all." Willy wiped his glistening face with a handkerchief; a heavy cologne radiated from the man's sweating body. "If it's important, he'll 'see what he can do'! That ain't no kind of promise, Wager. That ain't a damn thing!"

"We're wasting time, Willy. And I don't see what choice you have."

"I could let you goddamned cops hang by your balls."

"And I could help Papadopoulos make a stronger case against Franklin and Roberts."

"You would, too, wouldn't you?"

Wager shrugged. "We're wasting time."

Willy made up his mind with another puff of Sen-Sen. "One of my people seen Green at this Korean restaurant over on East Colfax, long about seven-thirty."

"In Aurora?" That was where the Koreans had built up their businesses side by side, just beyond the Denver city-county line. "By himself?"

"With his assistant, that what's-her-name."

"Julia Wilfong?"

"Yeah. That's the one."

Wager thought about that a moment. "What were they doing?"

"How in hell do I know, Wager? They was there. That's all he told me."

"I want to talk to him."

"You what?"

"Don't waste time, Willy. I want to talk to him."

The big man studied Wager. "All right. I got to find him."

From his car, Wager watched the white Cadillac turn out of sight down the alley. A few more of the bits and pieces were starting to fit together now; and Wager could sense a motive. Dimly, incomplete, but motive nonetheless. Means, motive, opportunity: A pistol was the means, now motive was coming clear, and that left opportunity. And the evidence to prove it.

He backed his car down the alley and pulled into the wide area beside a trash dumpster. The rear of the buildings, closed against burglary, formed an uneven wall of blank doors and occasional barred windows between the alley and Colfax. But the corner Laundromat was open today as it was every day of the year, and in the back, near the manager's office for its protection, Wager found the telephone booth.

"Mrs. Voss?"

"Yes?" The voice was faint and slightly impatient as if she had traveled a long way on an unpleasant road and now was prevented from resting. It was the voice of someone just back from a funeral.

"It's Detective Wager. Was your informant Julia Wilfong?"

The voice hesitated. "Is it vitally important to know who it was?"

"It's important to know right now if it was Julia Wilfong."

"You mean she's a suspect?"

"She told you about the bribery on Thursday, is that right?"

" . . . Yes. I suppose I can honestly say I didn't tell you—that you found out on your own." Voss added, "I saw her at the funeral, but I didn't ask her if I could tell you. It didn't seem the place for that."

"What time on Thursday did she talk to you?"

"I'm not positive. It was early. Nine or nine-thirty. She was waiting for me when I got to the office. Why?"

Because it was something someone might do to turn suspicion away. But that's not what Wager told Councilwoman Voss. "Please don't say anything about this yet to anyone."

"Is she really a suspect? Do you really think Julia did it?"

"I'm not sure. That's why I don't want you to say anything."

"Of course—yes. . . ."

1630 Hours

He wasn't certain that Julia Wilfong would be home after the funeral, but she answered his knock, her brown eyes widening slightly with surprise. She still wore the dark funeral dress, and a black hat rested on the table near the hall closet.

"Can I talk with you?"

"Of course. Come in." She led Wager across the freshly vacuumed carpet to the chairs near the windows. Her low-heeled shoes, like the heels of cowboy boots, drove muffled dents into the nap. "The funeral was a long one; there were many people paying their respects to Horace. I just now got home."

"Yes, ma'am."

The woman settled in one of the upholstered chairs and Wager sat in another as he studied her immobile face.

"Have you found out something, Detective Wager?"

"I think so. I think I found out why he was killed."

Wilfong's eyes were heavy-lidded, almost sleepy, as she watched him. "Tell me."

"He was killed because he discovered something. He threatened to expose somebody."

A cord jumped out in her neck, but she remained motionless. "Who?"

"He discovered that somebody had made a deal with Kaunitz and Ellis Construction to approve some zoning requests. That somebody was paid twenty-five thousand dollars each time. And that somebody made it look like Green was taking the bribes."

Her voice was still calm. "And you of course know who that somebody is."

"Only one person fits: somebody who could speak for Green, somebody who could intercept the payments so he never knew of them. Somebody who could manipulate him. Somebody like you."

The woman stared back at him. "Nobody manipulated Horace Green, Detective."

"You did the research on zoning requests—including the Montclair school and the Tremont property. He took your word for it; he supported the requests when you suggested it." Wager added, "We'll find the paperwork tomorrow in the committee records."

A slight smile. "If I did what you say, I'd be a fool to leave any papers anywhere. I'm no fool."

So much for that bluff. Wager, too, smiled. "Three years ago, you accepted five thousand dollars from Aaron Kaunitz for the right vote on a zoning conflict."

"That was a campaign donation. And it had no impact on that vote."

Wager nodded. "Then I'm sure you kept a record of the money. As well as how you spent it." She didn't answer and he went on. "Then you found out Kaunitz wanted to make another contribution. You rented a box in Green's name and told them to mail the money. You took it, and Green never even knew about it. Park Hill station, seven-three-nine-five."

"That, too, was for campaign contributions."

"Then, like that first five thousand, the fifty thousand will be logged in and accounted for in the campaign records.

And we'll find out tomorrow from the postmaster just how much mail went to that box."

"None of this means anything—you can't prove anything. It's circumstantial, that's all."

Wager went on as if she had not spoken. "Last Wednesday night you were seen at a restaurant with Green. He skipped the Prudential buffet for a more important meeting—to talk with you about the Tremont zoning study." Wager was going completely on guesses, now, but it still made sense and the stiffening of Julia Wilfong's expression told him he was right. "He wanted to know why you hadn't told him about the residents who would be evicted—the ones the Northeast Denver Action Committee raised such a stink over that afternoon. And he began to suspect a payoff: He remembered a few puzzling things Aaron Kaunitz hinted at now and then."

"You weren't there. You don't know what he thought—you don't know what he said. You're just guessing!"

"We have other evidence, Miss Wilfong. From the crime scene."

"What kind?"

Wager smiled again. "Serious evidence. The kind that links you to the murder."

"No, you don't. If you had something like that, you'd be handing me a warrant instead of all this bull. You're guessing—you don't have evidence; you don't have a thing but guesses!"

"Why don't you make a statement, Miss Wilfong. You know what's going to happen tonight—you know a lot of people might get hurt, a lot of property destroyed. Why not make a statement and keep all that from happening?"

"You want me to sacrifice myself for them? They don't care—they never did! Not a one of them knows how much work, how much sweat and tears, people like me give just so they can complain all the more. Most of them don't even vote because they just don't care! Sacrifice? For them?" She stood, a wide figure almost as tall as Wager and the Afro no longer dwarfed the breadth of her face but seemed to increase it like a warrior's headdress. "No—I'm admitting nothing, Detective Wager. If you have evidence, arrest me. If not, leave my home."

Wager, too, stood and gazed deep into the hot anger of eyes that dared him to prove what he suspected. "I'll be back, Miss Wilfong."

1712 Hours

He made the call from his car parked where he could see both the apartment's front walk and the row of closed garages behind. Stubbs soon pulled up to his rear bumper in a second unmarked automobile and wearily slid into the seat beside him.

"I should be used to this by now."

Wager ignored the hint about overtime. "Sit on Wilfong. Everything she does, everywhere she goes."

"You think she's the one?"

Wager sketched it for him.

"Jesus—all this time I was thinking a man wearing cowboy boots." Stubbs peered toward the curved thrust of the apartment's brick walls glowing in the afternoon sun. "All right, no problem. You want a phone tap, too?"

Wager shook his head. "Who's she going to call? She's in it alone."

"You think those heel prints are enough to tie her to the killing?"

"They'll help, anyway." He started the car and Stubbs got out. "I'll stop by Admin and arrange for your replacement."

The man's rounded face pushed toward the car window with a touch of aggressive determination and a taut smile. "Hey, no rush, Gabe—I want to be in this all the way."

"All right," said Wager. "That's fine."

1735 Hours

He was explaining his request for twenty-four-hour surveillance on Wilfong to the new shift-sergeant when Fat Willy's call came through.

"All right, Wager. I got him. Where you want to meet?"

"That little park behind St. Luke's Hospital." It was nearby and usually crowded with kids and strollers, so that a couple more cars wouldn't be noticed. And the area was open enough so no one could overhear.

"Ten minutes."

1753 Hours

Wager was there when Fat Willy's long, gleaming automobile pulled up the narrow lane to the turnaround and parked behind his car. Wager slid into the back seat behind Willy so he could see the face of the youth who looked back without smiling.

"Cop, this here's Rabbit. Rabbit, this here's a cop. Now, tell him what you seen."

The young man shrugged and scratched at the spotty curls of a light mustache that struggled beneath a narrow, hooked nose. "I seen Councilman Green and Julia Wilfong. They come out of the Gold Dawn restaurant last Wednesday—that Korean place out there on East Colfax."

"You're certain it was them?"

"Sure. I was surprised to see them, so I looked real close to make sure. It was them."

"About seven?"

"More like seven-thirty. I was waiting for my woman to come out of this beauty shop they got there." He added, "There's maybe twenty places closer, but she got to go to that one. Say nobody else knows her hair like they do. I told her I be glad to introduce her hair to somebody closer, but she don't want that."

"How were they behaving?"

"How you mean?"

"Were they talking to each other? Did they seem mad at each other? What?"

He raised his face to the car's upholstered ceiling and thought back. "Now you mention it, they was mad. Not talking-hard mad, but quiet mad. You know, walking kind of stiff and pretending that each of them wasn't there and then acting real polite when they got to the car."

"His car? The black Continental?"

"Yeah. HRG-1. I saw the plates—cool, you know? Here I am, Horace R. Green, number one!"

"How were they dressed?"

Another upward stare. "Regular, like."

"How, regular?"

"Regular—you know. He had on this suit and tie. Looking good, you know. She had on one of these dark dresses with a frilly white thing coming down between her tits. Looked like . . . I don't know, a bunch of wadded-up handkerchiefs."

"Did you notice her shoes? Did she have high heels on?"

"Naw. These stubby heels like big women wear. They was going *pow-pow* when she come marching out of that restaurant. That's one reason I figure she was mad: *pow-pow-pow.*"

They would check out the restaurant and somebody would remember the couple. Perhaps even note that they had an argument, but over what no one would know; Green and Wilfong would have kept their voices low and private. That was the reason she—or he—chose a restaurant away from his usual haunts: for the privacy. It wouldn't be much—one more item of circumstantial evidence. Enough to convince Wager. Maybe enough for a warrant. But not enough for a jury.

Fat Willy heaved around with a grunt to glance sideways at Wager. "Well?"

Wager shook his head. "It's not enough."

"Wager, damn you—"

"I need a witness from the murder site."

"God damn you, Wager, it's too bad what you need—what about what I need!"

"That big empty lot over there on Twenty-fifth Avenue. You know the place?"

"Yeah, I know it. But I ain't got—"

"That's where he was dumped. She drove his car there, hauled him out, and walked in with him propped over her shoulder like he was drunk. Then she came out alone and drove off."

"Wilfong? Julia Wilfong done that?"

"It probably happened around ten-thirty or eleven." It might have been earlier—forensics said it could be as early as nine. But the car had been seen around eleven, and Wilfong wouldn't have an alibi for that hour—eleven to midnight; she'd be too busy getting rid of that car somewhere, after dumping Green, and then trying to get home.

"Why would she leave him there?"

"In case someone remembered seeing them together at the restaurant. She could say Green took her home before he went to the Vitaco reception and that was the last she saw of him." She wouldn't say that she agreed to meet him somewhere after the reception to tell him what she decided about quitting or confessing to the police, or whatever scheme Green may have had in mind for setting things right and clearing his name at the same time. He might have come by her apartment later to find out her decision. She couldn't think—she wanted to go for a ride, anywhere, just around, because it was easier to tell him about it when he wasn't standing there looking at her. Easier to explain just how it all started and how sorry she was and how they would straighten things out. Easier to apologize for getting so mad at the restaurant earlier this evening. Easier to ask him to park for a minute so she could tell Green he was right and she'd do anything to make sure his name was clear. Easier to shoot him when his head was turned from her. Then dump him quickly and drive his car to hide it somewhere before returning to her apartment or to her own already-placed car. And the next day start her own disinformation campaign: a hint to Councilperson Voss, whispers about that crank call to Mrs. Green—the White Brotherhood.

"Why you telling me this, Wager?"

"I said I need a witness."

"I told you I ain't got one. This here's all I come up with."

"With the right kind of witness, I can help you out, Willy. Without him . . ." Wager shook his head.

"God damn—" Willy paused in midcurse, his eyes blinking twice as they looked at Rabbit. "A witness, huh?"

"Somebody who might have been visiting in the apartments across from the lot; somebody who was just walking down the street. A witness who saw a woman dressed like she was when she came out of that Korean restaurant."

"Hey, now—" Rabbit's face turned quickly from Wager to Fat Willy and back. "Hey, now."

"I think I got your witness, Wager. You go see what you can arrange."

"Hey, now!"

1834 Hours

The chief wore wrinkled civilian clothes and he didn't appreciate Wager asking for time when he was busy charting troop deployment for the coming riot. The napkins and crumbs from a boxed dinner had been shoved to one side of his desk, and the bags under the man's eyes told Wager he was another one who had not slept much this weekend.

"Do you have something?"

"Almost." He told him about Julia Wilfong.

"By God—it makes sense!" He drank something from a Styrofoam cup. "You talked to her, right? What do you think?"

"She's guilty."

The chief wiped his mouth with a paper napkin and wadded it into the trash basket. "We can match the heel prints, maybe. And if we ever find that car, we might find something there—prints, hair, something."

"Try the airport parking lots."

"What?"

"It's fifteen minutes from the murder site, and a car could sit there six months before it's noticed." And a person going in had to stop at a gate house to pick up the parking tag—a well-lit gate house that shone into each halted car. "From there, the shuttle to the airport and a cab back home." Nothing unusual about a person taking a cab from the busy airport at any time of night.

"We might get lucky with a cabbie remembering her. But she was in Green's car earlier—her prints there could be explained away."

"We have a witness who saw her at the murder site."

"You what?"

Wager said it again.

"Bring him in! We can get this on a television news flash and defuse the neighborhood!"

"Remember Franklin and Roberts? Those two dirt-balls Papadopoulos picked up?"

The chief leaned back. "You're telling me your witness wants a trade?"

"That's it."

"I don't like letting people off, Wager. Not even for this. There are other ways of making that witness come forward."

Wager had thought about that, too. "That'll take time. And might not work. What about suspending the charges for a year on Franklin and Roberts?"

"Suspending them?"

"That way, if they're convicted, they don't get sentenced as habitual criminals. A year puts them beyond the ten-year limit on their first conviction."

"And they'd still stand trial."

Wager agreed. "If they're convicted, it's their third felony. One more and it's life. Automatically."

"Would your informant go along with that?"

"I can make him see it."

"Very well. I'll talk to Papadopoulos. How soon can we move on Wilfong?"

2253 Hours

The riot standby had been cancelled by the time Wager reached his apartment. He had finished the last paperwork and had had a matron escort Julia Wilfong to the holding cells in the sheriff's building. The woman had been shaken when she learned of the witness who saw her at the scene, but she still admitted nothing, "I have a right to a lawyer."

She was probably talking to him now in one of the quiet cubicles whose only adornment was the fixed worktable and benches and the white paint on the walls, and whose only sound—other than the muted voices—was the steady buzz of fluorescent lights. A grinning Adamo had brought in a pair of shoes from the woman's closet and held them aloft like a prize-winning fish: "A match, Gabe—perfect match with the casts. And we found traces of soil from the crime scene in the cracks between the heel and the shoe. These are the heels that went in heavy and came out light." And with that evidence and the arrest, the chief had turned loose a detachment to look in every parking lot surrounding Stapleton Airport. The word had come in maybe ten minutes before Wager left: Green's Lincoln had been located.

Wager stretched back in his chair to reach the beer on the table behind him. He figured the weapon never would be found; Wilfong was too smart to keep it. But they would search all along the route from the murder site to the car for any place a person might lose a pistol. With luck, they'd find it; without luck, they still had a strong, logical case against her. Thanks to Rabbit, the witness, and to Willy, who only nodded and smiled when Wager asked if the youth would keep to his story on cross-examination.

It wasn't all that legal, but it was justice nevertheless. And it was the best Wager could do for Green. He felt satisfaction with it. Green had been a man with faults—a lot of faults, like a lot of people. But he still had virtues enough to be loved by his women and admired by most who knew him. Sufficient virtues, anyway, to soften those faults and to make his death a loss to others. So it felt especially good to find his murderer before even more harm was done under the excuse of avenging his death. It kept Green's name decent.

Yawning again, he looked without seeing the tail end of the late news on television where the featured story was an interview with the chief and Lieutenant Wolfard of Crimes Against Persons about an arrest in the Councilman Green homicide. A vague thought crossed Wager's mind as it slowly relaxed like the tight muscles of his back and neck:

Jo. He hadn't thought of her once in the last twenty-four hours. He had been too busy to surrender to the screaming nightmares, the swirl of guilt, the angry self-blame. It was as if the intense focus of the case had burned that away to leave him missing her, yes, but no longer cursing himself for her death. For some reason he felt that's what she would want, and as he accepted that idea, the more convinced he was of it. It's what she would want. Eyes heavy, the natter of television voices sliding away into the rush of sleep, Wager felt something inside gradually unfold like a fist easing into a hand, and his self-anger and guilt for her death began to sift away between the opening fingers like sand.